ASSUME
TREASON

PAUL LISNEK

"Paul Lisnek's analytical skills from his years of experience in the world of law and politics are evident as a compelling storyteller in *Assume Guilt*."

—Larry Potash Anchor, WGN-TV Morning News Chicago

"Paul Lisnek slowly peels the onion of his legal mystery, keeping his reader in suspense until the core is revealed. Jury Consultant Matt Barlow is a believable character, and Lisnek breathes life into all of the twists of *Assume Guilt*."

—Charles M. DuPuy, Author of the E.Z. Kelly Mystery Series

"Paul Lisnek seamlessly carries the reader from conference room to courtroom, while lending a keen and compassionate eye to the human efforts of self-examination and acknowledgement."

—Donna King-Nykolaycuyk, Author of *Stand Like A Man*

ASSUME
TREASON

A Matt Barlow Novel

PAUL LISNEK

Green Bay, WI 54311

Publishing Editor: Brittiany Koren
Cover Art Designer: Ed Vincent/ENC Graphics
Interior Layout Designer: Katy Brunette
Ebook Layout Designer: Maria Connor

Category: Political Thriller/Legal Mystery
Description: *With time running out to prove an assassination plot is in the works, jury consultant, Matt Barlow must dig deep to find answers.*
Hardcover ISBN: 978-1-951375-39-3
Paperback ISBN: 978-1-951375-40-9
Ebook ISBN: 978-1-951375-41-6
LOC Catalogue Data: Applied for.

First Edition published by Written Dreams Publishing in January 2021.

Green Bay, WI 54311

Dedication

In memory of my parents, Sandy and Seymour Lisnek, who I continue to miss every single day and with love for their bringing me into this world and guiding me to the adult I became.

In honor of my kids, Alexandra and Zachary, (and their mom, Janet Contursi) for the pride and joy they represent in my life as they forge their own paths to success and adulthood. What an amazing ride it has been and continues to be.

With love to my brother Rick, sister-in-law Judy, and my nieces and nephews for their faith in me throughout this process and always. None are bigger supporters of my dreams and goals.

Prologue

Chicago's United Center, known by sportscasters and fans as "The house that Jordan built," was alive with hats—top hats and visors, straw hats and bowlers. Streamers crisscrossed in intricate patterns above the center of the space and formed a false ceiling that did only a fair job of hiding thousands of balloons held back with mesh. The room was thick with signs bobbing up and down to the beat of Lady Gaga, John Legend, and many other artists I couldn't identify over the crowd noise.

None of this celebration had anything to do with basketball, not for these four sweltering, sticky days of July when a national political convention came to town. The Democratic Party's primary victor was accepting the nomination for President of the United States, and once the balloons dropped, the presidential hopeful and the winner of the VP stakes for running mate would have a little more than three months to make their case to the voters. This convention was the culmination of a dreary, awful primary season. I looked around and wondered if the electric excitement rippling through the crowd was maybe a little forced. If the past was prologue, we faced some hellish weeks ahead.

As for me, this was a first. I got tickets to this shindig, even VIP status, or so I was told, because Barlow & Associates—I'm the Barlow, Matt Barlow—my jury consulting firm, played a largely unknown, to the ever interesting worlds of politics and media, that is, role in

9

this political cycle. All well and good in normal times, but if I'd had my choice that night I'd have preferred watching the events of the last many months from my couch with a Lou Malnati's pepperoni pan pizza and a can of soda.

These weren't normal times, though. Despite the excitement ripping through the legendary arena, I didn't want any of the people in the crowd to be there, not me, not the thousands of strangers in the crowd. But here I was, along with the people who made up my staff—and my friends. The most important people in my life.

All five of us kept our eyes open, as we had for weeks and months now. No one knew we were watching, observing, not able to clearly define the signs of danger we were on alert to notice. Maybe we wouldn't know until they happened. Or maybe nothing would happen at all. A half-assed way to prevent a tragedy, if, and that was a big if, one was ready to unfold.

"Hey, Matt," Wendy said. "I don't see a thing out of the ordinary."

I shook my head and then glanced over Wendy's head to fix my gaze on Rick, our premiere data analyst and more. "Not yet, anyway."

Rick shook his head, and Bo, Wendy's boyfriend added, "Me, neither."

Janet, my firm's office manager, said, "Maybe we're sitting ducks. Lambs to the slaughter…"

If it were any other day, we'd have groaned—in a good-natured way—over Janet and her love of the well-timed cliché. Not today.

When the music got louder and confetti fell to the stage, we got to our feet with everyone else in the restless crowd. We clapped along with a crowd favorite, Springsteen belting out, "Working on a Dream" and joined in an uproarious cheering when Nancy Smith, the current Vice President crossed the stage. It would be her job to introduce the nominee, once the standing ovation for the VP finally came to an end. The crowd took their time showing appreciation for Nancy Smith.

As we'd planned, the five of us scanned the crowd unnoticed when everyone else was distracted by the action on the stage. We all knew what to look for. So far, after three nights, we'd come up empty.

Another ovation followed when the nominee crossed the stage. More confetti, more music, more bobbing campaign posters. Finally, the speech, a little disappointing, but then we weren't surprised. The nominee was many things, but he was no Obama, no Reagan. The happy talk speech more or less ignored the months of hardship and confusion—and tragedy— the country had endured. It was all about the future. Although to be honest, I was having a lot of trouble believing in a rosy scenario no matter who won, and the nominee, despite his boring speech, was my guy.

But, as always, in the spirit of the-show-must-go-on, the speech ended, the stage filled with family and the party poohbahs.

"Here come the balloons," Janet said, pointing to the mesh.

I took out my field glasses and pretended to get a closer look at the stage from the cheap seats. Probably another futile effort. The seats were good for observation, because they gave a view of the upper level railings and the convention floor and fewer balloons blocked my vision. Springsteen blared again, piercing my ears.

All five of us carefully scanned the crowd.

Suddenly, a face appeared. My stomach flipped. A face I'd been looking for, but hoped—and even prayed—not to see.

"Rick...look up and to your right," I said.

Before Rick could react, Janet nudged me. "I see him. I see the guy."

I used the glasses to follow her line of vision. My heart pounded in my chest. I could barely speak. Sure enough. It was the second face.

"They're fucking here!" Rick muttered, alarm taking over his face.

"Scatter," I said, "like we planned. Find security. Make them pay attention. Raise a ruckus." As if making noise could ever be heard over the roar of the convention crowd. That was probably the point. Make a move when everyone is completely focused on the high energy and distractions of the moment.

"Got it," Wendy said, pushing Bo to the end of the row. He finally caught on that what he'd feared was coming true.

No one paid any attention to us as we rushed up the stairs to the back doors. Then we scattered, with Wendy and Janet hanging a right, and Rick and Bo taking off to the left.

I rushed the uniformed guard and waved my arms in front of him. "Block the stairwell from the upper level."

That got his attention. Two secret service agents gave their identity away with their earpieces and suits, and they did exactly the right thing.

I pointed up, knowing the two women agents could barely hear me and did not know who I was. As they approached me, I was acutely conscious of the fact they considered me the immediate threat.

"Danger in the crowd—follow me."

Janet and Wendy were already going out a set of double doors behind a male agent.

I pointed ahead. "Follow them."

I pushed through the set of doors and out in the nearly empty hallway with the panoramic view of the city lights visible through the mostly glass walls. "Empty the arena. Possible shooter in the section above."

Was this really the best we could do? Rick and Bo had come out the doors farther around the curve of the arena, but three agents were roughly pushing them against the wall and putting their hands in cuffs. Fuck, we'd talked about this. But we didn't actually think it would happen.

"No, no," I shouted. "They're with me. You have to listen to me. Slow down."

The two women agents were holding on to my arms. I knew better than to try to shake myself free. I'll never know what made these two agents listen, but without the time to tell the whole sad tale, I spit out a quick version of the story. We'd just spotted two people we suspected of plotting against the nominee, and there could be more people involved and in the arena. I gave them a description and said I could point them out.

"They're federal fugitives, but for all I know they could have convention credentials. "Those two guys you have in cuffs are with me." I introduced myself as they led me toward Bo and Rick.

They might have been in handcuffs and drawing intense interest from spectators leaving the celebration early, but they still had their voices. The agents took me to Bo and Rick. I frantically searched for Wendy and Janet, but they were nowhere to be seen. Even with the noise, though, I heard agents' voices transmitting about the ruckus.

Two other agents blocked off the elevators, two more sprinted up the stairs with the security guards following.

"Let me follow. I can help," I shouted over the music, the cheering, and the thunderous applause.

But I was being held back. I searched again for Janet and Wendy. Bo shouted past the agent to ask me where Wendy was.

I shook my head helplessly. We stood in a cluster, the agents communicating. From what I could tell, they'd spread out on the level above us.

The sound that came next could have been balloons popping in one overwhelming explosion, but I knew better. Especially when the second shot rang out.

Chapter One

Six months earlier

I estimated the crowd to be close to two hundred people, with nearly all of them waving dark blue and white posters as they chanted "JoJo, JoJo" over and over. Not a bad showing for a frosty February day in Chicago. The group's chant got louder with every shout of his nickname, full name Giuseppe Michael Campanella. Wendy Crosbie, who liked to call herself "second in command" in my jury consulting firm, was way more political than I'd ever been. But neither of us had planned to attend this rally. We sort of ended up there on that day, the wind blowing down from Minnesota and Wisconsin to make us shiver in our home city of Chicago.

Wendy and I had left a client meeting and were walking up Michigan Avenue to grab a quick lunch over at the Park Grill. First, we had to tough out the wind and cold and walk through Millennium Park to get there.

We heard the crowd even before we saw it. An unlikely event, we agreed, but a diversion, so we went closer to have a look. Besides, I never could resist a political rally and Wendy was a lot like me.

It was the eve of the South Carolina primary in a semi-historic year when both parties had an open election. After two terms of Dean Andersen, a popular Democratic president, the party faithful were not about to buy into the bullshit about it being a Republican's turn. Turn? Who came up with that rule? Fact was, everyone had a reason to claim it was her turn or his time…whatever, and always in what we were told was the biggest, most important election in our history. Always the line, but this time it may have been true.

The Democrats had it tougher this round, though. Bad luck all around. Because of the current VP's deteriorating health, who openly admitted to have early-onset Alzheimer's or one of its close cousins, the Dems had lost its line of succession. Quiet, but popular VP Nancy Smith was forced to announce she was unable to run for the top prize. Her eight years of service in the second spot was as far as she could go. Smith promised to stay active in politics as long as she could. Everyone in the party hoped she'd be well enough to campaign for whoever emerged as the party's nominee, because she was popular on the stump.

With open primaries on both sides, this winter was shaping up to be one of the hardest fought primary seasons we'd seen since Obama and Clinton went head to head back in 2008. As we crossed the park to see JoJo, Wendy made it clear she didn't want to miss any of it.

In true U.S. tradition, the Democratic and Republican primary contenders were in the midst of a year or more long process of sorting themselves out. I was right there with them doing the same sorting. I liked a certain senator on Tuesday, but by Saturday I'd switched my loyalties to the quirky tech guy who'd thrown his hat in the ring. Not that it mattered what I thought.

Although I hadn't picked a favorite candidate, I'd had my eye on a couple of upstarts. A governor, a woman elected to that job only two years ago, was popular and charismatic. I liked her. So did a lot of people for that matter. Even party leaders said as much, usually right before they labeled her as too "mavericky." Code for risky.

16

I didn't like admitting it, but I understood. I was fine with waiting for the next election cycle to be inspired. This time, I wanted a sure thing.

The JoJo being chanted about was a young, eager, and inspiring member of the House of Representatives. He wore his Italian heritage and son of immigrants well. Locally, JoJo was popular and well-liked, but nationally he was a blip on the screen. Barely forty, Representative Campanella had that unfortunate nickname, JoJo. If his parents had thought ahead and imagined their little genius making a career in politics, would they have given their little Giuseppe the unfortunate nickname? It stayed with him as he grew into manhood and now, he was universally known as JoJo Campanella. Obviously, his parents didn't imagine their son would ever run for public office, let alone the presidency. Kind of like giving your kid the middle name Hussein, right? Of course, that one worked out just fine for Barack Obama. By any stretch, JoJo was a classic longshot, the kind of candidate who triggered the question, "Doesn't he know his chances are somewhere around zero?"

Maybe so, but JoJo still got a respectable crowd to show up.

"I like JoJo, but who's going to vote for him in this crowded field? Besides, he may be over forty, but he's still got such a baby-face," Wendy remarked as we walked to the outer fringes of the crowd. "Maybe they'd give a guy known as Giuseppe a second look?"

"Uh, oh," I joked. "I'm in trouble now. You're looking for a second career in political branding. Any day now you'll tell me some wise ass political consulting firm made you an offer you couldn't refuse."

Wendy dismissed my teasing speculation with a flick of her hand. "Nah. No one pays big bucks to have someone point out the obvious."

I laughed at that. "Since when?"

She gave me a pointed look as she maneuvered into

an empty spot in the back row of the crowd. "C'mon, let's listen."

I wasn't consulted about this detour but chose not to argue. Besides, she was already walking on the snowy grass in boots, if you could call anything with stiletto heels a boot. The rally extended south of the Millennium Park bean, a huge kidney bean-shaped sculpture, whose official name is Cloud Gate because of the reflections of the sky dominating its shiny finish. Maybe so, but you'd be hard-pressed to find a Chicagoan who could answer that trivia question on Jeopardy. I didn't even need to look up at the sky to see clouds the color of charcoal threatening to dump snow on JoJo's parade.

Suddenly, Wendy joined the chant, "JoJo...go, JoJo...go." She raised both fists in the air and let out a whoop of glee.

"What are you doing? Since when are you for this guy?"

"Since never. But I like him." She grinned. "Just getting in the swing. He's Bo's rep in Congress. He likes him a lot." She exaggerated a sigh. "But most definitely not for president."

"I get it now." When it came to romance, my employee, colleague, and all-around good pal, Wendy had a spotty record. Well, until a year ago when she started hanging out with an IT guy from a multinational company called Bradley International, headquartered in Minnesota. He spent most of his time in a satellite office in Rosemont, out near O'Hare. Sometimes he flew to the Twin Cities and back on the same day. His name was Lee Bowman, but went by Bo.

Wendy kept cheering, and I did a little people watching between checking my phone for something. I could fall into aimless scrolling as much as the next guy. When I glanced up to scan the crowd, I stopped when I saw someone familiar. How is it we can recognize people from the back? Even from a distance, I knew Rick Seymour when I saw him. I squinted so as to zero in on the figure on the edges of the crowd.

I thumped Wendy's arm. "Hey, guess what? Rick's here." I pointed to his back.

Wendy's eyes widened. "Really? Then, let's go say hello. I haven't seen him for a couple of weeks."

"I wonder if he's supporting JoJo," I said.

"One way to find out…"

Wendy and I weaved our way through the crowd, a fairly diverse group in the ways that count with Democrats, ethnicity and race, gender and age. We navigated around baby strollers and an older couple with canes. Wow, in this cold weather, too. If JoJo had other things going for him, his mix of demographics would have counted for something.

"Hey, Rick," Wendy shouted, waving her arm over her head. She repeated his name four or five times before he turned and saw her.

He didn't look pleased.

Shocked, yes.

Happy to see us, no.

Wendy and I kept moving, but Rick stayed in place and didn't change his grim expression. He turned to say something to a guy with him. Why wasn't he meeting us halfway?

Wendy picked her way through the patchy snow and last summer's grass, watching each step to keep her pencil heels from sinking into the ground.

I slowed down to match her pace.

Wendy greeted Rick with her now typical elbow bump and cheerful hello. Until we'd gone through the long haul with Covid-19, she'd have flung her arms around him in a big hug.

Still, Rick held back.

"So, are you a Campanella supporter?" I asked, puzzled by Rick's darting eyes and slight flush. Signs of unwelcome surprise.

"Uh, still making up my mind," he said.

"Like me," I agreed. I glanced at the man with him and nodded, waiting to be introduced.

The guy stood impassively.

"JoJo got in late," I said. "He should be in South Carolina with the rest of the crowd. If he's serious about competing, that is."

Rick nodded as Wendy filled him in about why we happened to be on Michigan Avenue that afternoon. She seemed oblivious to Rick's lack of response.

"Uh, nice to see you." Rick pointed at the man standing a little behind him. "This is Percy. We were just passing by. We need to be on our way. We're meeting a couple of friends."

Mile-a-minute-Rick. Why was he talking so fast? It wasn't like him.

I held out my arm to Percy and punctuated my introduction with an elbow bump. The pandemic was behind us, but it seemed the old-fashioned handshakes were slow to come back. They might be a casualty of our painful bout with the virus. Rick turned as if ready to walk away. "See you...*soon*."

Cryptic. Soon? How soon? What was he telling me?

Suddenly, four phones beeped and we all froze in place for a couple of seconds. Then the four of us reached for our phones.

Percy and I dug into our pocket, Wendy into her purse. Rick had his device in his hand. My signal was a Google alert. I usually ignored them, but not when four phones beeped simultaneously.

"What?" she said. A distressed frown instantly appeared on Wendy's face as she stared at the screen.

"Oh, my God," Rick said, glancing at Percy.

Percy shook his head. "Not good."

I read the headline. BOMB THREAT EMPTIES SENATOR TOOMEY SC CAMPAIGN HEADQUARTERS.

No wonder people claim to hate politics. One of the main—and to my mind, the worst—Republican contenders just got a bomb threat.

***

By the next day, the Republican outrage had dominated the airwaves through a couple of news cycles. It drowned out the record voter turnout on both sides at primaries in the three previous states, toss ups all. Now the Dems were competing in a state considered dyed in the wool red. Mighty Republicans were touting that no radical, terrorist-loving Dems planting bombs in their candidate's headquarters would keep them from exercising their rights, blah, blah, blah.

True, an incident involving a bomb occurred. A clumsy homemade bomb *did* explode. But not at Mike Toomey's state campaign headquarters in Columbia, South Carolina. It wasn't even in that state. The scary event took place in an empty lot a couple of thousand miles away in Seattle. No one was hurt. No one knew what to make of it.

"Democrats don't call in phony bomb threats," Wendy had insisted yesterday over lunch, and she hadn't changed her tune today. We'd kept our TV on while we had lunch in my firm's conference room so we could check the news.

Confession: Our office has become a den of news and political junkies from which there is never downtime. We were always a little like this, but as crisis followed crisis, including the long months of the pandemic, it developed into our all-day-and-into-the night-habit. At first, we offered sheepish apologies and resolutions to break the habit. We gave that up months ago. We know perfectly well cable news was invented to sink its hooks into susceptible people like us.

When an unusual phone call came in, I was out of the office doing one of my top three favorite things, walking Maude and her new friend, Quigs, well, full name Penelope "Penny" Quigley, but I started calling her Quigs for short and now she answers to that. While I was enjoying the dogs, even on the cold, off-and-on snowy day, a guy with the last name Kuhr called. No first name given.

Janet Contursi, our office manager/receptionist,

took the call and logged it into our handy computer organizer. But, while I like technology as well as the next guy, I was partial to messages jotted on one of those While You Were Away pads that ended up in a pile on my desk.

I'd started my day with a rare breakfast meeting. I usually liked my most-important-meal-of-the-day solo. I'd forced myself to change my routine—Wendy called it a rut—in order to meet with an actuary I was interviewing to be the trial consultant on a newly filed product liability case. We met at my new breakfast haunt, the famous Ann Sather restaurant on Belmont Avenue.

For years, Granny's had been my go-to breakfast home and it still lived in my heart, but in time, Granny retired and the place had closed. I proudly displayed the portrait of Granny that hung in that restaurant for decades, now a gift to me from her when they closed the doors for the final time. She appreciated my daily loyalty, and I appreciated her in so many ways.

Forced to find a new love, I discovered solace in the thinner Swedish pancake fare and accepted I'd never replace my all-time favorite deep-dish banana pancake at Granny's. I had moved a bit north, so it was an adjustment made partially out of necessity. The fact that the scent of Sather's incredible warm cinnamon rolls met you as you sat down made the move less painful.

I didn't like mixing business with pancake pleasure but this potential client, a middle-aged Italian guy named Dom Stasi, was someone I'd like to work with in any number of ways. For him, my credentials were 90% of the impression I would likely create. For me, I looked for that intangible quality of a real Chicago guy. You didn't have to be born in this city, and he wasn't. In fact, non-Chicagoans often give themselves away by referring to the city as Chi-town. Like chalk on a blackboard. That's not something a true Chicagoan would ever do. It hurts our ears. We wince in pain.

Normally quite a welcoming lot, Chicagoans never cared about things like who was born in the city. Being a *fan* of the old city and its icons counted, and this guy ordered Ann Sather's Swedish pancakes without even glancing at the menu. See? He was the real deal. I'd probably get the case.

With the meeting over, I ran over to Adel's Hair Sensation over on Pine Grove to get my haircut. The pandemic had taken its toll on businesses like hairstyling, but I did my best to get there as often as I could to help my longtime stylist Toshie Lee and the shop get through the tough times.

Then, on to the office to get my dog walking taken care of and my sweet tooth as well. A brisk walk over to Broadway and up the street to the dogs' favorite, Windy City Sweets. The owner, John "The Candyman" Manchester always greeted Maude and Quigs with a cup of whipped cream, one for each, and they knew it was coming their way! They would bark and jump once we were only a few doorways down from the shop.

Indeed, taking care of the dogs was my first order of business before returning to the office. I made sure they were settled comfortably, usually in my office, but since we'd become news addicts, they followed me into the conference room. The dogs have always been the most important members of my office staff, not to mention my family, as long as they don't bark or beg Janet for more than two treats a day. The cup of whipped cream aside, of course. Quigs, a dog I rescued from the Anti-Cruelty Society, a Chicago landmark shelter to be sure, was still adjusting to being with Maude and me, but she dutifully trotted into the office behind Maude.

Janet had made a note that this Mr. Kuhr mentioned our firm's best pal and contract researcher, Rick Seymour, as the source of this referral. That's all Kuhr would say on the call with Janet. For some reason, I had a hunch this was going to be one of those hush

hush contacts. Usually, when people wanted my services, they identified themselves with a law firm or a company. Even before we met, they wanted me aware of how well connected they were.

I put the message aside to deal with later, but before I returned the call, Rick came into the office. Through the half-open door, I heard him tell Janet he'd like to see me. I got up to wave him inside. Wendy, deep into prep for our current case, was meeting with some prospective mirror jurors in our conference room. Otherwise, I'd have invited her to join us. With any luck, we'd never need to go to trial. Hence, we'd have no need for a mirror jury. Still, our corporate client wouldn't be caught unprepared if the lawyers couldn't settle out of court.

Wendy had worked for me for many years and she was the one who interviewed Rick when he'd come in looking for a job. She recommended him as someone competent to help her with community attitude surveys and mirror and mock juries. At the time, I'd wondered if something on the romantic side would develop between them, but they evolved another way and were more like best pals. Meanwhile, Wendy met Lee Bowman, aka Bo, fell in love, and was, for once in her life, no longer on the lookout. Rumor had it that Rick approved of Wendy's new guy. Lucky for Bo. For her part, Janet played office comic and dramatically rolled her eyes at every mention of *luuuuv*. Easy for her to make fun. She'd been happily married for over thirty years to a man we all knew as Bosco.

"Tell me what you've been up to," I said, ushering Rick inside. "I see I have a referral from you. A guy named Kuhr." Rick didn't know this yet, but for some reason I'd decided—call it intuition—that yesterday's Percy was today's Kuhr. One and the same. I'm not sure why that bothered me.

Rick's hand immediately went up in a halt sign and he glanced behind him. Then he put his finger over his lips and shook his head. The cloak made its appearance, but no dagger came out yet.

I closed the door behind him. "What's the deal?" I whispered. "Why so secret?"

"Kuhr is uh, let's just say, sort of undercover."

That statement hung in the air. Actually, it had to, because Maude perked up when she saw Rick, one of her old friends. Quigs was getting the hang of things and followed her. Before we could get beyond what undercover meant in this case, Rick had to give each dog her due attention. Jowl and beard rubs, back pats, sweet talk. Rick provided it all. Priorities are priorities.

Finally, I'd waited long enough. "You mean he's undercover with law enforcement? Or the Secret Service or something? What's the deal?"

Rick shook his head. "Uh, no. With a major candidate. His first name is Percy…"

"Yeah," I quickly replied, "I figured he was the guy we saw you with at the rally."

So, was the dagger supposed to match the cloak? Somehow, I didn't think so. It all seemed like small stuff. "But it's not JoJo Campanella, I take it."

"No, no. It's Marie Kent."

"*Marie Kent*?" I let out a low whistle. "That's a major candidate, all right." Percy Kuhr hit the big time. A two-term senator from Oregon and former prosecutor, married to a surgeon and mom of one college-age scandal-free daughter. Few could make that last claim, and Marie's girl didn't have so much as a citation for underage drinking in college. Who managed that these days? A clean record and a laundry list of bragging points from her time in the senate earned Marie a legitimate shot at the Democratic presidential nomination. Her brainy sheen was a little off-putting to some. A few of her rivals in both parties called her *professorial*, as if that was the kiss of death. The glasses probably helped make that assessment. To me, it just meant she was damn smart.

For reasons I didn't get, she'd offset that image by hiring an oddball campaign manager, Steven Novak.

He had been an actual professor, but he was a little rough around the edges, but he had a great sense of humor. TV profiles liked to show footage of this Rhodes Scholar coming back from a hunting trip with his buddies in Northern Michigan. A little on the controversial side, he humanized Marie a little and sang her praises better than anyone else. And if he didn't smile broadly while he listed everything that gave her impressive bragging rights, no one noticed much. Steve hadn't had a lot to smile about professionally over the past twenty years. Be that as it may, he understood the power of television and media as if he were a director.

I liked Kent. But steady Arnold Pierson had my attention, too. Former senator, Secretary of the Treasury during hard economic times, good friend of the current president and the VP, and one-time chair of the Democratic National Committee. As if he needed more icing piled on his already rich cake, he was even an ordained pastor and shepherded a flock of parishioners in his former life. An excellent credential. The hellish DNC chair job was seldom handed to anyone and people usually angled for that title of misery. Why? Never could figure that one out.

Pierson was experienced, and sufficiently well-liked by the old guard. If Pierson actually managed to beat any possible "President Republican Nightmare," the party would demand to have his face added to Mt. Rushmore—a request supposedly made by a recent Republican president—absent a war or a major recession. At the moment, he was running slightly ahead of Kent in the polls and in the whole field of declared candidates. Most were polling around 2% nationally. Only Kent was close.

"Well, um, Percy isn't working for Kent, not exactly. It's her campaign that hired him."

Huh? I wondered how that hair-splitting worked. I chuckled to myself musing over what was one of my law professors favorite phrases—a distinction without a difference.

Now, being honest with myself, I had to admit Rick was never a smooth sort of guy. Nerdy types usually aren't. But he could string words together pretty well most of the time. Not today. In any case, I needed to be straight with him. "I haven't made up my mind who I'm backing in the primary, Rick. So, if it's money they're looking for, I'm—"

"No, no, it's not money. Not at all." Rick shook his head. "Percy is doing a project with Kent's campaign. He and the manager need information. That's why I sent him to you."

"From what I could see, your Percy guy was looking for info at Campanella's rally," I challenged. "Why? JoJo's at the bottom of the pack, around 1%, and that's generous. He barely has a seat at the kids' table."

"Oh, come on, JoJo's better than that," Rick said impatiently. "But that's beside the point. Percy got me to go to the rally with him because he's in town and is attracted to anything political. Maybe they're sniffing out JoJo for a running mate. I don't know." Rick paused. "It's not important. I dropped by because I wanted to talk to you about Percy."

"So, you know the guy." It wasn't a question.

"I used to, when we were kids." Rick stared out the window at the snow coming down. "Uh, Percy Kuhr is my cousin."

Hmm…then why not say so in the first place? "That's a fairly close connection to keep quiet about. Who is he? What does he really do?" I should have asked right away how well Rick *still* knew him.

"He's a marketing guy. Well, that's what he studied, anyway," Rick looked away again.

What was he holding back?

"He's been working at the Jewel Food Store…I mean he *was* working there before he started working on the campaign."

"You mean in the marketing department?"

"Uh, no, in the stock department," Rick said, rushing to add, "but that was temporary. You see, he's been like

27

this unpaid tactician for a lot of campaigns." Rick ran his fingers through his hair. "I don't know exactly. He kinda gets into the inner circle. But not in a public way. He's the guy waiting in the wings somewhere or off in a pub eavesdropping on voters' casual conversations over a beer or two. He's impressed Marie's campaign manager. Big time."

"What the hell, Rick?" The desk chair squeaked as I straightened up and leaned forward.

"He's deep in the inner circle this time. That's what the hell…he's not like your typical poli-sci major," Rick said defensively, "but that doesn't mean he doesn't know a lot."

"Message received." I held up my arms in surrender. I'd back off. Temporarily. "What does Percy want with me?"

Rick steepled his fingers and tapped his chin, a sure sign he was uneasy. "According to Percy, they're not just interested in oppo research, which isn't that hard to come by. And that's not where you'd come in anyway. Typically, they want to hide what they're up to. They don't want to use firms people know nationally and can easily identify with previous campaigns."

"Isn't campaign research, oppo or not, a little on the furtive side? No one wants it advertised that they're looking for dirt on other candidates." I pointed at Rick. "And isn't most everything out there on the internet just waiting for someone like you to come along and bring it into the sunlight?"

So, squeaky clean Marie Kent wants to splash mud on other people without others knowing where the pot of mud came from, I suppose. Could that be what this was about? I couldn't claim shock or anything. Not even surprise. This was politics. Hell, I was born in the city and raised on stories of the old corrupt days under the first Mayor Richard J. Daley, not to mention the continued tradition under his son some years later.

Rick shrugged. "I think they want to go a little deeper, but be undetectable."

Still puzzled, I asked. "If it's just research, like digging into the past, why don't they hire you?"

Shaking his head, Rick gestured around the office. "No, no. They want a lot more. Like community attitude surveys and focus groups. They want to pinpoint—really target—their voters. Starting now. They're looking at Arnold Pierson and who might lean toward him, but they want info on Toomey, too, which they can take into the general. They want to narrow everything they do, like match the data you produce with what kind of person buys what kind of laundry detergent or subscribes to *Guideposts*."

"What's that?"

Rick gestured across the desk and grinned. "Exactly. But it has its own demographic, the sixty-plus religious or semi-religious Southern rural woman. It even comes in a large print edition."

"Not exactly Kent's or Pierson's voter."

Rick shook his head. "Wrong. Women who watch "The View" admire Marie—a lot. Some of those women are rural religious voters."

Intriguing. It was getting its hooks into me, this idea. I'm a data loving guy. I might be persuaded to do a little work for Marie Kent. She had a real shot at the nomination and her campaign manager was sharp, if quirky. This would be a challenge because my firm had never done community attitude surveys or focus groups for anyone other than plaintiffs and defendants in civil trials—mostly. We had a few notable exceptions since I'd allowed myself to take on criminal cases again. In civil matters, our jury and community research would most often lead to a settlement without even having the trial.

"I can see us getting people in-house or on the phone for surveys that wouldn't seem like we were gathering political info. They're basically marketing surveys. Then Kent and her campaign strategists could use it to plan where she should schedule stops in certain states. They could write her speeches to target the groups we identified." I paused to catch my breath and think about the interesting possibilities. "I suppose what we did could determine how much time she spends in small towns like Minnetonka, Minnesota or the Panhandle with those "View"-watching…maybe-sorta…women who go to church sometimes. It might help her pull primary votes out of delegate rich areas like Houston or Miami."

Rick grinned and snickered—more like a hoot, actually. "I know that look." Rick made circles in the air next to his ears. "No, you're not nuts. But I see those analytical wheels turning."

"So, we'd operate on need-to-know," I said, my mind still on logistics. "Wendy and I need to know, and you, of course. We'll need you…if we take this on." I'd go farther than that. "Actually, we won't do it without you."

Rick nodded, immediately agreeing to my condition. "Look Matt, just meet with Percy. Talk to him." Rick stared out my office window, his face wrinkled up in thought. "The guy is the real deal—a political animal."

"So, do you want to set up a meeting?"

"Nope. I'll let him handle that. I don't know that much about his chain of command on the campaign." Rick paused and once again seemed to find the falling snow out the window more interesting. "But maybe I don't want to know. We aren't exactly close. He's sort of a loner."

"*You're* calling *him* a loner?"

Rick snickered and waved me off. "I know, I know. But I'm a real man-about-town wise ass, now that I have a dollar or two to my name."

I jabbed my chest. "Fuck yeah, thanks to me."

"Right, boss. Thanks to you." Rick chuckled and stood, but before walking out the door, he couldn't resist pointing to the two dogs snoozing in the corner. "But Matt, you still have the laziest dogs I've ever seen."

"Watch it," I warned, but then smiled. "Insult my

children, if I had any, at your own risk. Besides, their doggy legs walked a couple of miles in Lincoln Park this morning. They need their naps. How many miles have you walked today?"

Rick laughed and clutched his chest over his heart. "Got me there, boss. Your dogs are fitter than I am." He feigned a serious frown. "Probably eat better than I do, too."

Rick started out the door, and I glanced at my phone. "Hey, Rick." I gestured him back into my office.

"What have you heard about that bomb threat on Toomey headquarters? Any connection with the explosion in Seattle?" I had a feeling Rick was checking information in lots of places given his mastery of the internet. He looked at everything from straight up political news to conspiracy junkies. He followed all the garbage just to confirm it was garbage. He told me about one site whose members blamed every bad thing that happened on a group of families who made a pact to rule the world. Not totally unreasonable if the conspiracy didn't insist the pact dated back to the sixteenth century. Fortunately, Rick was smart and skeptical, so he had the instincts to spot wild fiction from the more boring reality.

"All I know for sure that's credible and even makes sense is that Republicans are blaming Democrats, who are, of course, denying it. No one has claimed credit for it." Rick stared into space. Deep grooves were etched across his forehead. "Kent's headquarters in Charleston is in a space across the street from another one of Toomey campaign offices."

I frowned, unsure why that was relevant.

"The TV folks keep mentioning that," he said, still frowning. "I don't know why it's important, but it could be."

I knew Rick's expression as well as I knew the uneven edges of the scar on my left arm. I earned that scar rolling across a jagged piece of broken pipe I'd said hello to playing center field in an empty lot. When

Rick wrinkled up his face again and stared into space, he was moving on to a train of thought that could prove significant.

"That Seattle bomb caught my eye. It was obviously not intended to hurt anyone. Shit, turned out that wasn't exactly an empty lot. It was a big muddy soccer field kids use for practice," Rick said. "No one around. Some young punk types who tout their white nationalism set these small explosives off now and then. But they usually claim credit."

"You mean they do that out in Seattle?" I asked.

"Sure, but lots of other places. A couple of racist groups in the Carolinas are working hard to scare certain groups of people and keep them away from the primaries. They call in bomb threats at churches or set off these homemade explosives…can't even call them bombs. The last time it happened, it was outside a beach town and the young guys ended up hurting themselves."

That was about the last thing Rick said as he went on his way. Bomb threats, white nationalism, accusations flying back and forth. I let out a cynical scoff. Rick knew he was whetting my appetite. I mean, how could I stay away? I picked up the phone and called Percy.

Chapter Two

When Rick first showed up in my office looking for a job, I thought of him as classic "down at the heel," to borrow a phrase from two or three generations ago—or maybe four. His secondhand suit didn't quite fit, he needed a haircut, and he carried his winter jacket so no one would see his suit coat hanging a foot below the hem.

I only pulled that memory out of my hippocampus because his cousin, the mysterious political genius Percy Kuhr was the opposite. Percy might have been stacking soup cans on the shelves of a local Jewel supermarket not long ago, but he obviously spent his first paycheck from the Kent campaign on a sharp navy blue suit. The fit across the shoulders was perfect. Nicely done. The yellow and blue tie flashed "pay attention…I'm expensive."

Zach, my older brother, might have sarcastically remarked that Percy was nattily dressed and he wouldn't have meant it as a compliment. I'd concede half his point. A tall, physically fit guy, Percy's thick blondish hair was maybe a little too neat. A little thicker, a little mussed up, and it would have been almost Kennedyesque. The ensemble, one of Wendy's favorite words, was a little too shiny and new for a Democratic Party operative, especially for no nonsense Marie Kent, who limited her wardrobe to black, purple, and blue. A serious woman with a trunkful of ideas, she ran no risk of being confused with the elite. If she'd been a man, she could have pulled off the grizzled, rumpled combo of an everyman meets college professor. A younger and more pulled together Bernie Sanders.

Come to think of it, my older brother Zach would offer an opinion about everything going on with me and this election. Maybe even Marie Kent's baggy sweaters. He'd spent half his life rubbing shoulders with corruption without getting too much of the stink of it on himself—at least not that anyone could see. What happened during his years of working private security for our former governor, Leo Toland, a guy lousy with corruption, was something Zach kept to himself. But my brother was a solid citizen now and making a handsome living managing construction crews for Charles Marchand's real estate development firm. Getting Zach out of the shadows of state politics was another positive development from the old Marchand case.

I'd driven to meet Percy at a diner just over the Illinois border in Southwest Wisconsin. He was keeping up the cloak and dagger routine and warned me he didn't want to be spotted in Illinois, where Marie had many campaign offices in prep for the primary. Marie Kent herself was on a final leg of her latest rapid-fire bus tour through Minnesota. She'd already survived the endurance contest of Iowa, which meant admiring butter sculptures and consuming many pounds of deep fried dough at the Iowa State Fair. She'd been photographed with farmers at pumpkin festivals in the fall, followed by tromping through the snow in the weeks before the February caucus. She came in a close second to Pierson in the caucus. Two weeks later, she walked away with New Hampshire, and squeaked out a tie for delegates in Nevada. But Pierson was favored in South Carolina.

Meanwhile, Campanella's campaign was on life support, along with a few other unlikely candidates. Most people joked that the Democratic primaries were mostly a competition for the VP slot now.

I glanced around the restaurant. "You picked my kind of place. Bet I can get a stack of pancakes here."

Percy frowned, as if he hadn't heard me. He fidgeted with the sleeves of his suit jacket, pulling them down over his cuffs. In contrast, I was feeling fine in my blue blazer and jeans. We weren't in a courtroom after all.

"I won't waste your time, Matt. My, uh, cousin, said you're busy."

I nodded to acknowledge the truth of that statement.

"He also said you're good at reading things—you know, what's behind or underneath the surface of events going on. And that's what we need."

"Profiles of voters, I assume. Maybe stats that match some districts where Kent needs to pile up votes to maximize her delegate count." I sounded savvier than I was regarding the political arena, but I paid attention to Rebekah Mathis on one of the networks. A political analyst with energy to spare, she was usually stationed by the producer at the "big board" to report polls and delegates. Rebekah was so good she could break down the probable delegate count in states that wouldn't vote for another ten weeks, and she wouldn't be far off on reckoning day.

Ever since the Obama-Clinton primary, we were all delegate counters. I don't mean to boast, but we were an office of amateur-experts who could talk changing Texas and Arizona demographics with the best of them. We sophisticates knew the nomination turned on delegate count, and votes were only a means to a delegate end. That was probably why Percy was up in Wisconsin checking out spaces to open a field office for Kent in Platteville, rather than concentrating all their efforts in Milwaukee and Madison, where fledgling operations were already underway. My guess was that the campaign was likely doing one quick Minnesota run before heading to South Carolina, where Marie polled well, but so far, not good enough.

"We want the voter profiles, yes, but we're looking at what people are thinking about the frontrunner in the other party," Percy said. "Do they believe his lies? Do they care? What do they think about the underlying ugly atmosphere at his rallies?"

"Whoa, so you want oppo on Toomey. Now?" I leaned in to whisper, "And were you really watching JoJo Campanella?"

Percy nodded and as if mirroring me, he leaned forward like he was going to share a secret. "We aren't skipping anybody. Kent is paying attention to possible sleepers." Quick frown. "Scratch that. *Steven Novak* is paying attention. Marie is focused on policy, debate prep, and her voter contacts—she's willing to do the ten-person house parties or big venue rallies. That's what's attracted voters to pay attention to her in places like Minnesota and Wisconsin. Steve handles the strategies."

"Does the left hand of the candidate know what the right hand of Steve Novak is doing?"

Percy snorted, the first spontaneous reaction he'd had. "Now that's a question no one thinks to ask."

"Which is why I do what I do. And why I want people like your cousin Rick working for me." Did I sound arrogant? Maybe a little, but I was testing the guy for something, even if I couldn't say what.

"I…no, make that *we*…have reason to believe Kent will eventually nail the nomination. And we want every bullet in the box." Percy dropped his voice to a whisper. "Plus, we want to know what ammunition is coming our way. She needs to be armed for offense and defense."

Bullets in boxes. Ammunition, offense, defense. Right. Killer information. But there was a problem with the assumption that Kent was close to nailing anything, except for maybe a couple of the early states. She still trailed most everywhere else. Not by much, a point or two here, five or six points there. It was too early for overconfidence and Arnold Pierson was a careful guy—and much better known than Kent. It was mostly his high profile that gave him a small edge over Kent. Besides, doing the kind of research we do at the firm, we'd learned never to underestimate the power of sexism, overt and obnoxious or quiet and latent.

"Okay, assuming you and your boss are right, what hasn't been uncovered already? The Republicans have their guy and Toomey is no slouch."

Percy slapped the table, but then thought better of it and scanned the diner quickly to see if anyone noticed. But the other diners were deep in their own conversations. Besides, it was a noisy place with plates and silverware clattering in the background. "Toomey is a slouch, actually. Plus, he has more baggage than the Queen."

Janet would love that cliché about the Queen. I'm not sure what prompted the judgement about Toomey being a slouch. "All well and good," I almost yelled, "but however many millions the Dems have spent on oppo research, it hasn't made a dent yet." Whoa, I heard my voice rise on every word. I'd move deep into rage if I didn't watch myself. I'd already spent too much time worrying about a ruthless guy like Toomey getting the nomination. He wasn't worth that much energy. Ha! Who was I kidding? I could tell myself not to worry all day long, but the thought of Toomey dancing at the inaugural ball made me reach for antacids I'd almost stopped using.

"Give us time." Percy said, his voice now lowered. He seemed more relaxed as he leaned back in the chair and stretched his long legs out to the side. He'd found my soft spot, fear. I was more vulnerable to losing cold objectivity than I cared to admit. Fear had a way of doing that.

"We're tracking Toomey better than anyone else ever has. Or at least we will. We already know he lies about support among farmers when he's in rural Missouri, and he tells lies to auto workers in Ohio. He's already ramping up his crusade for coal, a real loser issue for anyone else, but a winner for him. This guy is about as real as Bigfoot!"

37

"So, how will you be different?" I challenged, already aware that to voters, lying to the public goes with the territory. "Besides, Percy, you don't shock voters by exposing lies. Toomey isn't alone in not giving a damn if he's caught."

My mini tirade energized Percy. He pulled his legs out of the aisle and squared his shoulders. "This time, the party—and our campaign—has a rapid response team like no one else. When Toomey tells a big one, and trust me, we have a long list of them already, we'll be up with tweets and ads faster than people can change the channel or click off the page."

"Novak's on it, huh?"

"He's sink...uh, investing...serious cash into the immediate response shop." Percy snorted again. "Novak knows everything. Ask him about the daily change in the price of soybeans. He loves farmers. And he sees a bitter steelworker and says, "That's our guy."

The cynicism of it wasn't surprising, but there was something about this earnest Mr. Percy Kuhr I found distasteful anyway.

With a smug smirk, he added, "Marie's primary opponents won't get away with lies either."

"And you want my company to survey key communities—or otherwise gather info on what magazines they read, where they shop for clothes, what movies they watch, and what they eat for lunch. Is that right?"

"You got it. We want the data. But in secret. No one should know who's gathering it for us. I think that is why Rick thought a jury consultant might be our guy." He leaned forward and whispered. "And if you didn't already know it, he thinks the world of you."

As a matter of fact, I did know that. But I couldn't make my decision based on my friendship with Rick, tempting as that was. "I can't give you a list of recommendations of what you need from the services we offer. I'll need answers to my questions first."

Percy shrugged. "Ask 'em."

"Give me time to think about it." I chuckled at his eagerness. The guy who bagged groceries not so long ago was raring to go now. My impulse was to say yes and get started by rattling off routine and necessary projects like focus groups and a community attitude survey for sure. On the one hand, I was up for a new challenge and this could be it. But, on the other hand, I hadn't finished making up my mind about Marie Kent and I didn't want to undertake a project in the political arena with uncertainty about where my loyalties could lie. I at least wanted to know I was working for a candidate I did more than tolerate.

I was about to shift the conversation away from politics to probing a little about how well Percy really knew Rick when a loud gasp filled the room from a group of four people who were just a couple of tables over interrupting me. Seeing the look of horror on the shocked face of a guy staring at his phone, I grabbed mine, and Percy grabbed his.

"Oh, no." I looked into Percy's face. He looked more puzzled than shocked to see the headline about the mass shooting at a Columbia, South Carolina mall. Six known dead, eight wounded. So far. It wasn't over. Then, as if recovering, he shook his head sadly and raised his hand to get the waitress's attention to get the check. He looked back at his screen and nodded. "I gotta go. Novak and Marie were planning to fly to South Carolina in the morning. But he wants me to fly out tonight so I can get some advance work underway to help the team handle Marie's response on the ground. He's got somebody booking my flight right now."

My stomach lurched. Dispense with the horror show in ten seconds. Ten dead, twenty dead? Didn't make much difference if your job was to make sure Marie looked good. Unfair? Maybe. But it struck me as all wrong.

Chapter Three

It was easy to slip in and out of Marie Kent's crowds unnoticed. Surrounded by hundreds of people, many of whom were young and from the nearby college, I could linger on the fringes near the roped off press section and blend into the crowd. The kids, a misnomer for these young women and men, were believers, loud and colorful and never broke their applause as the passionate student activist introduced an equally passionate Kent.

I had to learn to stop calling college students and eighteen-year-old-army-recruits kids. Especially nowadays when those so-called kids might owe close to one hundred grand when they got their diplomas entitling them to teaching jobs starting around forty grand. Same went for the corporate coffee-runner slash marketing assistant, who could barely split a typical rent with a roommate.

When Marie took the stage to hootin' and hollarin', I checked my phone. Fifteen dead, twenty-three injured. The shooter with his AR15 and a couple of other smaller automatic weapons was on the loose. I could envision the below the fold story in the *Minneapolis Star* the next morning. Marie should have cancelled this rally. One school of thought, for sure. I wasn't passing judgement on that. Not yet. With shootings like this no longer a rare, once in a decade fluke, the case could be made that taking the stage to talk about it might be the better choice. It would have been a useful research question had there been time to get into the community for study, but that was not the case. A check of my phone showed that Toomey had cancelled his own rally. Not surprising. If he showed himself, he'd face questions about his stance against any improvement in gun safety laws.

Before I'd driven away from the diner where I'd met Percy, I checked Kent's campaign site and saw the college where she was speaking was just over the border in Minnesota. I could understand why she'd chosen to leave South Carolina for a couple of days to squeeze in stops in an important Super Tuesday state. Kent had opened up a fairly wide lead in Minnesota, but according to Percy, Pierson had started running ads. That meant Marie couldn't risk letting it melt away because of neglect.

I made the drive up to Marie's rally because I wasn't ready to commit my firm to her cause, which was the same as committing my name, no matter how secretly. I had to see her in person before I'd sign on.

A hush fell over the crowd when Marie got the several hundred people to stop their loud applause and cheering. Students dominated the crowd, but their parents' and grandparents' had come out, too, giving this rally the feel of a community and not solely a youthful campus setting. The crowd was quiet as Marie captured their attention. Good sense of timing, I assessed. Marie knew when to let the hush linger a few seconds before she spoke in a soft, somber voice. "We're brokenhearted once again, as more of our citizens, moms and dads and their kids were gunned down earlier today."

What the fuck? I was as bad as Percy. Another day, another shooting. And I was critiquing Marie's timing and mentally patting her on the back for her words. But, I admitted to myself, this wasn't the first time. In the last few years, I'd become as unshockable as the next person. And I paid more attention to the location of a mass shooting than I did to the reality that another one occurred.

Marie lowered her voice when she spelled out the need for stronger gun regulations, like the basics, background checks and a ban on assault weapons. It was like watching a rerun of an old movie, but that didn't matter because, sadly, everything she said was relevant. Then Marie segued to her health care plan with a call for coverage for all, and then moved on to improving air quality and decontaminating water in rural areas and small towns all over the upper Midwest. She laid out her plan to slow down climate change—and adapt to it—as well I'd seen anyone do it. She easily transitioned to her one hundred day plan for immigration reform.

Before she even finished, a ruckus of cheers and applause started low and built to a crescendo. Kent had drawn a contingent who shouted their support in Spanish. She answered in Spanish spoken fast. I didn't know enough to tell if she was fluent or faking it, but it impressive either way.

"When I'm president," Kent shouted, "the Dreamers and those like them will finally have their permanent home!"

Those words sent tambourines shaking and some air horns blasting their piercing honks of approval. I laughed to myself—what would a political rally be without young people and the touch of theater they brought? Meanwhile, Marie waited, letting the crowd blow off some steam. When she spoke again, it was to say, "One more thing…we have a chance to put the rise of hate behind us now. And it's up to you to help make that happen."

I knew exactly what she'd say next. All those promises would be worthless unless she got the nomination and that meant winning big on Super Tuesday, which allowed her to slide toward the end of the rally by talking about her need to get back to South Carolina. She'd be talking more about gun safety there, she promised. The mall shooting gave her license to hit that issue hard.

Played it safe there. My opinion, maybe too safe. No one wants to be accused of politicizing a mass shooting, but I wish she'd plunged more deeply into solutions and unleash her emotions, too. Her website already had her plan posted—and detailed. On the other hand, she had to eke out a win in South Carolina and follow it with big numbers in Minnesota, or it would all be moot.

No one could say Kent was timid when she ended. "Register your friends—leave no eighteen-year-old behind. And then you get them to your caucus site— drive them, drag them, kidnap them from the dorms. Just vote." She ended with a smile and a big sendoff wave to the crowd.

Kent stepped back and waited for the campaign music to start and off she went. She shook every hand in the first rows, but took no pictures as Novak himself took her arm and led her away. I was too far away to study his face, but I didn't need to do that to know something was up. Novak was looking side to side and behind him as he hustled Marie away and into the waiting van. He looked like a guy ready to take a bullet if he had to.

I left as the crowd dispersed, walking across the campus to the side street where I'd left my truck. Reality set in. Kent was one of the best retail politicians I'd seen. Ever. I wouldn't mind working for her, especially if she could beat Toomey or any of his ilk who would end up rising to the top of his party.

Percy wasn't wrong about Steven Novak's mission. If I signed on with Marie, I'd have to deal with Novak eventually, and I might not find him to my liking. And then there was Arnold Pierson. I had to make a choice. And with my eyes open. I knew that if I got involved in a tight, fierce campaign, I would be putting myself on the line. There would be no way I could keep my hands clean.

***

The rat-a-tat-tat, rat-a-tat-tat yanked me out of the dream. Startled, I sat up straight, alarming Maude and Quigs in the process. Despite being cold, I swiped beads of sweat off my forehead. The repeating, unmistakable blast of gunfire still filled the room. The AR15 noises weren't in my dream. They were coming from an NPR report on the mall shooting. The NPR reporter filled in the words to explain the ugly sound of the shots and paint a picture listeners couldn't see for themselves. The mall, a picture so easy to form in my mind: shoppers and little kids, sales associates, food vendors, the smell of burgers and coffee. And now an intruder with an automatic weapon, two handguns, and a hunting knife.

He wasn't at large for long. Knowing he was surrounded in a nearby park, he shot himself. Damn coward. The hunting knife was an added detail that pretty much meant nothing. In fact, the report gave me not one new tidbit. I'd already known all of it. Comparisons to the shooting in the landmark Charleston church back in 2016 were inevitable. At first, this shooter appeared to pick his victims randomly, but no news outlet was committing to that conclusion—not yet.

I'd slept late after driving back from Minnesota on the dark highway. I'd picked up the dogs from Samantha the dog-sitter in my building and had taken them out in the middle of the night. They weren't happy to have their sweet dreams interrupted. Now I was pressed for time. I was meeting a couple of friends for brunch at The Bagel restaurant about two blocks away. I gulped back some coffee and showered quickly. The dogs had to be satisfied with an abbreviated trip out and a promise of a later walk in the snow over near the Belmont Rocks and new Memorial Garden.

When I got inside The Bagel, my buddies were already there. They sat at the bar, but they paid no attention to the press conference showing on the TV above the bar and closest to them. But as I approached,

I saw the breaking news headline in block letters. SHOOTER'S WHITE NATIONALIST TIES.

"Did you see that?" I asked, pointing to the TV. "Not just a shooting. Another *white nationalist* shooting."

Robin Dembs glanced up at the screen. "I hadn't heard that."

"No, it's just breaking. It wasn't reported before I left my place to walk over here," I said, my voice carrying down the bar…unintentionally.

"We see it, man." Frowning, Dale spoke in a low voice.

"Hey, it's a big deal," I said, knowing I was being unfair. They weren't aware of all the connections racing through my head between the bomb threat, the maybe-maybe-not related explosion in Seattle, and Marie's campaign manager rushing her away. "The guy had an arsenal in his apartment. Legal weapons, folks, legal."

"Hey, honey," Robin said, touching my arm. "What is it? What's going on?"

I let my head drop back and stared at the ceiling. "You know me too well." True, I'd gone to law school with Robin. I reluctantly went to her first wedding to loser-guy Tyler, and happily celebrated her second wedding a couple of years ago to great guy, Dale. Right now, though, Dale had his worried brown eyes fixed on me.

"Hey, don't be concerned about me," I said, incredulous. "I was on a work thing yesterday when this news came in. I was shocked that I wasn't shocked, if you know what I mean. But the death toll is up to over twenty now."

I didn't want to belabor the obvious, but Dale, an IT manager, had the quintessential American background. His DNA was a mixture of Asian, African-American, and various European nationalities, which had resulted in a look that got him mistaken for a Latino. He thought it was kinda funny, at least most of the time. I assumed a white supremacist on a shooting spree might be one of the times Dale was less than amused.

45

"Robin and I were trying to forget this for an hour or two, Matt." Dale took a long gulp of his bloody Mary. "But we could talk about it to each other and get it out of our system."

"And I was on the road during the night, listening to cable TV on satellite radio." That was one explanation. "I wish I could tell you more about where I was and why, but I can't."

Robin, or "Rob," as Dale called her, squeezed my arm as I stood behind their bar stools. I hadn't even asked where we were on the list for a table.

"I get it. We won't ask. But we have news we want to share."

That brought me back into the room. "Really? Tell me."

Robin and Dale exchanged a look, but since they were smiling at each other with lit up eyes, I knew for sure this was good news.

"We'll tell you when we get to our table," Robin said.

After that, the conversation lagged and I couldn't keep my eyes off the TV, hit with the off-putting reality that the sound was muted and the closed captioning came and went across the screen. From a distance I could see little other than the headline that drew my eye in the first place.

When the host came, we took our drinks to a table in the back and quickly ordered off the menu of weekend brunch specials. My back was to the TV. Hmm…Robin made sure of that.

I was antsy as I waited for the lox and bagels platter. But I finally learned the big news. My two friends had applied to be foster parents, specifically taking teenagers into their home. Neither had kids from first marriages, but that could change if they took the next step to adoption. I'd known they were interested in answering the louder and louder call for foster parents, so I was happy they were approved.

"We've wanted to do this for the longest time," Dale said. "Even our families don't get it, but I assumed I'd have kids. Lots of them."

"So, when might this happen?" I asked, feeling a surge of pleasure in seeing my friends so happy. Robin brushed tears from her eyes before they spilled down her cheeks.

"It's really fantastic news," I said, focusing all my attention on my friends for the first time since I arrived. But the curtain was about to fall. If I took on this job with the Kent campaign, no matter how deeply hidden my firm would be, it would likely sequester me in my office until the conventions—and maybe beyond.

Over coffee, Dale talked about a project at the international media conglomerate that relied on the sophisticated equipment and data storage to do something as seemingly simple as reporting the latest health news.

"Are you on call today?" I asked Dale, using the intentionally mocking tone I had fun with when I acted impressed by his importance. He was such a bigshot he had to be on call, just like a doctor. "You never know when you could have an emergency." I pointed to the phone that sat on the table in front of him at all times.

He shot me a pointed look. "Ha ha. Fortunately, I'm so good at my job I have ten people in the pipeline who can fix the problem. If number ten can't do the job, then they call me to do emergency surgery."

For her part, Robin was a cog in the wheel of a big law firm. She worked primarily for insurance carriers, but she and her team also kept a couple of major not-for-profits out of trouble with the IRS. She actually *liked* the job.

After we finally forfeited our table so other people could claim their turn for brunch, we said warm goodbyes, complete with elbow bumps. Things has started to go back to near-normal after the pandemic that changed us, but we had adjusted to our new-normal, too, which meant we'd gone back to hanging out in groups, going to conferences and rallies, even half filling stadiums. But we still stayed a little apart from each other. No rubbing of shoulders in a literal sense.

I promised not to let a couple of months go by before we got together again. I wished them luck with their deep dive into foster care and they wished me luck with whatever mysterious case I had going on. My friends knew I operated on "need to know," a criterion they seldom met.

I got into my truck and looked at my phone. My twitter feed was going wild. I followed a few journalists, including the *Chicago Tribune's* Raphie Michaels, who was heading to South Carolina to cover the primary. I scrolled and scrolled and added followers, even Toomey. He wasn't the only Republican contender hoping to stop the Democrats from winning the White House for the third cycle, but he was one of the most outspoken—and the most likely to win this thing.

I stared at my screen, comparing the tweets from candidates. Did anyone go beyond the "thoughts and prayers" tripe? Certainly not Toomey. My wife and I offer all victims and their families our thoughts and prayers. Shame on those who politicize gun policy at a sensitive time like this. Those empty words garnered 440,000 likes and half that number of thumbs down.

Arnold Pierson did better. Prayer is not enough to comfort a grieving nation. We cannot wait to take action to keep guns out of the hands of those who should not have them. Those words gave him close to half a million likes and a handful, measured in hundreds, of thumbs down. He had over a million followers, more than Toomey, but that didn't mean much.

I was most interested in what Marie Kent had to say, because I'd given myself an arbitrary deadline to make up my mind if I was going to commit my firm to the frenzy of work that could last 30 or 60 days or maybe carry us through to Election Day in November. I was okay with Marie's response. Not bad at all. How much longer will we endure these massacres, this madness? We cry for families, but until we act, more tears are all we offer. Join the fight for gun safety.

I could have whiled away the whole afternoon in my truck looking at Twitter and reading comments on half a dozen news sites. Meanwhile, Maude and Quigs were alone and owed a walk.

I can't say I was disappointed that I needed to end the walk around Belmont Rocks after about half an hour. The weather forecasters liked to call the mess "wintery mix." Okay, snow is one thing, but sloppy icy rain and snow falling on the dogs—and me? Nope. I considered that a valid reason to come back home and turn on the TV. I had reason to satisfy my appetite as a certified news junky.

The breaking news banner was still up. The Columbia mall shooting was finding its place in the top ten list of mass shootings. Well, isn't that a distinction for which every city longs? Revised toll: 22 dead now.

***

I nervously tapped Percy's card in my palm. It was 10:00 p.m., a few hours past my self-imposed deadline. If it had been anyone else, I'd have worried about calling too late. Wonky political operatives are a breed of professional unlike any other. They tend to be like the cities that never sleep. Many of them sleep with a cell phone or two laid upon their chest, just in case.

In the end, the mall melee gave me the kick in the ass I needed to propel me to join the bandwagon. Maybe it was another update—23 dead now. It was getting to be time to commit to one candidate. It was clear that what happened in the mall wasn't a fluke. In covering the event, the cable networks filled empty time by bringing up the last half dozen or so shootings, including a synagogue, a mosque, a church, a school, a workplace, and a hotel. So, I had a choice, I could sink into weird despair and go back to my routine cases and let frustration nag at me, or I could break out in a new direction. Once again, Rick had started nudging me to take on a change when I'd run into him at Campanella's rally.

I stopped my musing and retrieved pizza from the microwave and turned my attention back to the TV. One of the prominent talking head historians was bluntly reminding us out in viewer-land that as much as we hated to admit it, domestic terror was a sad fact of life in the U.S.

As the guy talked, my thoughts drifted back to Percy. Something about him bothered me a little. His meteoric rise through the ranks of politicos smelled a little. But it was really Steven Novak that gave me pause. I mean, who was that guy? He'd made a fortune in politics, but when he consulted on his first race, he already enjoyed an eye-popping income mostly from well-timed investments in oil and gas. Now he was a convert to renewables. Once a Republican super-donor, Steven was now a Democrat who earned great respect for party-switching. Like a reformed gambler who turned to fighting corruption in casinos, he got more kudos than life-long loyal Democrats. Odd how that worked.

After successfully managing a tough senatorial campaign and consulting with the campaigns to elect three women in red state Congressional districts, he landed himself one helluva of a prize. Lots of people, men and women, were in the running to manage Marie Kent's presidential bid.

So, that's what it came down to. I didn't really trust Steven Novak, but I liked Kent. Even better, I liked her chances. Pierson had been in politics more than half his life. He carried the safety banner for the party. It also meant every opponent had scoured his past dozens of times. Putting aside an embarrassing frat house photo from the '70s and a couple of shady looking campaign donations that were hard to justify, Pierson made only slightly more than the usual number of gaffes and took only a typical number of suspicious votes. He'd successfully made it through every election and controversy and hadn't done anything serious enough to alienate the party—most thought he represented it with flair. Just maybe not as much flair as the younger Kent. Still, for now, Pierson was the frontrunner, the guy to beat.

I was watching the tail end of an interview with the South Carolina Congresswoman whose constituents were both the victims and the perpetrator. A loud opponent of gun safety reform, she struggled to find one original idea. Violence is bad…it has no place… the gunman had no criminal record…the guns were purchased legally. Talk about blah, blah, blah.

The sound of my phone was a relief. It was Rick. "Hey, what's going on?" he asked.

"Nothing' much. Propped up on the couch eating warmed up pizza and listening to the usual bullshit that comes with watching coverage of a tragedy. Too much time to fill," I said. "No real news, but like the army of cable news junkies, I'm afraid I might miss something, so I don't turn it off. But I'm trying out this new show called NewsNation. They say if you're tired of all spin, they'll give ya unbiased news reporting," I chuckled. "Well, we'll see."

"Look, I talked to Percy," Rick said. "Well, that's an exaggeration. Conversations are pretty clipped. He's helping Steve prep Marie for live interviews in South Carolina and working with the advance crew. She's got quick stops tomorrow out in the western part of the state. She flew in and already made two stops in Greenville today."

"I'm impressed. Really." I paused. "I was about to call Percy. I'm going to sign on with Kent's campaign, if they want me."

Rick snickered. "Making history, bro."

"You sound like Janet," I said, laughing. Oh, her legendary love of the cliché, well-timed or not.

Rick snickered again. "And I'll bet none of those reporters are even mentioning Marie's campaign, not tonight."

"Guess I'll have to help them change that." I glanced at the TV. Nothing had changed, but the motive for the shooting was getting murkier. "I know we're a little on the cloak and dagger side here, but I imagine you want to see your cousin while you're vacationing in South Carolina this week. Haven't you always wanted to see the coast?"

"I do. I hear the weather is pretty good this time of year."

"Right now it is. I'll be in touch, but go ahead and pack. Wendy reminded me in an email that you've got some data analysis to finish up tomorrow. You'll need a day for that." I pulled up one of the booking sites and scrolled fast and clicked on the button on one of the available flights to Charleston. "Janet will be in touch about your flight. I'm leaving in the morning."

I ended that call to make the second call, the one ushering me down a new road.

Chapter Four

I'd never been to Hilton Head. Since the place was all about golf and I wasn't, it hadn't claimed a place on my radar screen—and certainly not my heart. But I stood on the patio of my tenth-floor suite looking at the ocean while I waited for Percy and Steven to show up. After a delay lasting more than two hours, I'd flown into Charleston and driven around one hundred more miles to Hilton Head. That's where Steve wanted to meet.

While I was walking on the beach my mind raced with ideas, which I later expanded on the computer when I went inside. Percy was on the road with Marie, making the trip east across the state for her Beaufort rally. She was scheduled to make another appearance in the morning when she met with veterans groups near Parris Island.

For security reasons I didn't quite understand, she was staying the night at the Marriott on Hilton Head. According to Percy, trying to keep her safe in Beaufort would have meant shutting down half the town or sticking her on one of the coastal islands, where she and her campaign entourage would stick out like sore thumbs. She didn't want to risk inconveniencing wealthy folks on the islands, where the atmosphere was sleepy during the winter. Percy pointed out the obvious. Marie was already viewed with a suspicious eye. We finalized dinner plans, room service in my suite.

With some time to kill, I studied Marie Kent's record and dug myself an even deeper hole with the mall massacre story. I couldn't stay away from it. I wasn't alone. The outrage rippled through every news story, and every campaign commented on it. Some called it a hate crime, and some preferred to label the guy as deranged, the popular new word for some non-specific mental illness. Everyone with a voice, a microphone, or a computer had something to say. That's because most—but not quite all—the dead and wounded were African-Americans shopping with their families, dads and moms, grandparents, and kids. Final counts weren't in, but no less than 16 of the dead had at least one other family member killed or wounded. Everything pointed to the dead shooter choosing his victims carefully.

As the dark of the late afternoon settled in, it wasn't long before I could hear the waves gathering strength and slapping the shore. The water disappeared into the darkness and all I saw was the show of whitecaps. My heart pounded in my chest during the last afternoon press conference. The police chief himself made it clear the preliminary search of the shooter's apartment uncovered white supremacist books and flyers. White supremacist? Why didn't he—we—just say racist and be done with it? To call someone a white supremacist made it sound like a real philosophy worth debating and not a five dollar word for hate. The shooter legally owned at least a dozen firearms. They were still searching his computer to search for evidence, perhaps of accomplices and written strategies and plans.

As information poured in, candidates started elaborating on their earlier statements. Both Pierson and Kent were headquartered in the state ahead of the Saturday primary. From what Percy said on the phone, Kent would be doing some quick stops in bordering states, even though their primaries were way off. Always thinking ahead. No matter where these candidates went, they wouldn't escape the mall massacre. My word for it. Mall shooting sounded way too mild to my ears.

Since I'd made the call to Percy, I considered myself on the team, which led me to start digging around. I was curious why Kent was making a stop in Savannah this early in the game and quickly got my answer. Looking at the stats on Savannah, if the Dems were ever going to pull out a win in Georgia, that historic city was a necessary stop on their train. Muting the TV, I scanned page after page of data about Savannah, mentally putting it aside for the future. I looked at recent polls and saw most split the vote into four or five top contenders. That meant no one stood out, other than Arnold Pierson, who'd held on to his double-digit lead. But it was way too early to draw any conclusions.

I went from east Georgia stats to quick reads of newspaper pieces on the candidates from major papers in South Carolina, including *The State*, the Columbia paper that endorsed Marie. *The Post and Courier*, Charleston's paper of record went with Pierson. A couple of others went with Mullins or Greenberg, who were lucky to be in the top four in this state. They both polled below 10%. Campanella was registering under two percent. Most other major primary states had them lagging even further back in the pack.

By the time Percy texted to tell me, they were on their way up to my room. I had a better idea about what ordinary people were saying about Marie in a state where a national poll didn't say much about the race mere days before one of the most important tests for candidates on the schedule. I opened the door in response to a knock on the door, and in walked two men, two generations, in identical polo shirts, khakis, and navy blue blazers. They even wore Bass boat shoes. It had been a long time since I'd seen those on anyone.

I couldn't help myself. I looked at Percy up and down. "Do they sell those outfits in bulk?"

"We look like this on purpose." Steve Novak wasn't smiling. My little quip amused only me.

Fair enough. "I see."

"So we don't stand out," Percy clarified. He was smiling. Well, almost.

"Makes sense." I spoke while watching Steve study the room as he walked deeper into the living room of the suite.

"Shoulda booked Marie here," he said.

I couldn't think of anything to say to that. Strange guy, this Novak. I watched Percy fiddle with his phone. When in doubt, grab our phones.

"Hey, Percy," Steven said, "see what's on the menu. Make the call. Let's get started." He opened the mini-fridge and helped himself to a bottle of beer and held up his hand to offer it to me."

I shook my head. "Not now." I wasn't ready to drink with the man. It wasn't that I didn't trust him, but he wasn't a drinking buddy. Not yet. True, he was paying for that beer, or would be when I submitted my expenses, but I found him unnerving.

Steve settled on one end of the couch. He nodded at Percy, who, as if he'd read Steve's mind, rattled off some menu items. "You're not a vegetarian, are you?" Percy asked.

"No—I'm not fussy either."

"Marie won't go near meat," Steven said, still not smiling and revealing minimal inflection in his voice.

"Oh, that can be difficult on the road, I imagine." In my trip through cyberspace to learn about Marie, I picked up that tidbit, but didn't disclose that I knew about Marie's vegetarian preferences.

"Sometimes," Novak conceded. He nodded to Percy again. "Keep it simple."

"Tonight's special is beef stew…salad and bread, Steve. And, hey, chocolate cake. Red wine. Perfect pairing, right?"

Steve glanced over at me. "You good with that?"

"Sure." I suddenly looked forward to drinking

something. Maybe that beer—or the next one—would loosen up Steve. But, I reminded myself this sourpuss, one of my brother's favorite words, was reputed to be a genius. No exaggeration. But some geniuses really do lack social skills. But I'd need to see a lot more to judge how smart he was.

"I've been following Marie's statements and tweets on the mall shooting," I said. "I think they've been on target. Stronger than the others."

"Even Pierson's?" Steve demanded.

He posed the question with all the subtlety of an insecure teenager.

"Uh, yeah. I'd say so." True to a point. Marie was slightly better on an event that was critical in the moment, but would likely disappear from radios, phones, and TV screens in about 48 hours. But if I weren't paying attention for a reason, I'd have said Pierson and Kent's responses showed not a dime's worth of difference.

Percy walked to the far side of the room to call room service and while I had a minute alone with Steve, I mentioned that Rick would be arriving in the morning. "He's working with the firm on another project today." The firm. Right. All four of us. Talking to Steve, I liked sounding a little pompous. The guy brought out that side of me.

"Percy said he was looking forward to seeing his cousin," Steven said. "Guess they're close, huh."

Hmm...not exactly my impression, but mine came from Rick. I noted it, but didn't draw a conclusion.

"So, you want to shadow Marie the next couple of days? Right?" Steve finished asking the question and then drained the bottle. Definitely a gulper, not a sipper. I half expected him to help himself to another one, but I was wrong. He set the bottle aside and that was it.

"I need a feel for what she's like on the stump," I said. "We're going to wander over to Pierson's rallies at least once, although not on this trip. He's headed to Spartanburg and then on up to Western North Carolina." I paused. "But I suppose you know that."

Steve nodded, but said nothing.

I explained why it was a good idea to keep track of Pierson as well as Toomey, the likely Republican nominee. No matter who did the delegate math, it looked like Marie had a long primary road to travel to get to the nomination. Pierson was considered the front runner, but given Marie's strength and even lower placed candidates, Pierson wouldn't necessarily dominate after Super Tuesday. I suspected most other campaigns concluded the oppo on Pierson was more or less complete, although there was the chance some tidbit would surface. According to Steve, we had to rush to collect some data to tell us what kinds of voters Marie should target in California, Ohio, Texas, Maine, and a few other critical states. It was all about pulling out some delegates here, a couple more there. Enough to block Pierson.

"We're not having you work with the ad guys," Steven said flatly.

"No, but the data can help shape the target market for the ads, maybe where best to drop the money. Are you going to target Oprah's OWN network or will you pick up ad time on daytime talk shows? Or, maybe look to the demographics for different magazines— craft magazines, or even something like *Guideposts*." I pulled that off just like I knew what I was talking about.

"She's not going after only suburban women voters."

"Good thing, too," I said, "because Pierson's running strong with women in various demographics, college educated, over age 40, you know the groups. Unfortunately, Toomey is doing okay with that group, too."

I waited for a response. When none came, I added, "So, with some research, you may be able peel off some of those votes and go after the Campanella crowd. It looks small now, but in a delegate hunt, a handful of votes can swing a state one way or the other."

"She stopped at the plazas off the highway and went inside the convenience stores for coffee and snack food," Steven said, the corners of his mouth turning up. "Introduced herself and shook a lot of hands."

A smile at last.

"You should've seen the looks on their faces. She surprised everyone."

"I'll bet. Those small towns between Greenville and Columbia must not get much attention." Marie was telegenic—cameras loved her. That was a big advantage. Huge. Many more people would see her image on TV and YouTube and Instagram than would ever see her in person, let alone talk with her. She was an attractive woman in her late-50s. Wavy shoulder-length hair, warm smile. Personable. Excellent on the stump.

"Pierson doesn't do stops like that." He frowned. "He's pure gold in churches, though. He has that trusted minister look thing going for him. The kind of guy who might be standing out on a balcony at the Vatican looking out while his minions take money out of the wallets in the crowd."

I coughed to hold back a snort. Not a guy to dress up his thoughts in pretty language. "The answer to his campaign's prayers, huh?" I couldn't resist and Steve did allow himself a mild chuckle, or at least a tiny snicker.

Percy came back into the room looking mildly odd stretching his arms out to his sides and over his head. He tilted his head side-to-side, wincing as he stretched his muscles. "Hours on the bus are making me old before my time."

"Don't know why we didn't fly across the state," Steve said, rolling his eyes. "How many votes could we have picked up from some good 'ol boys pumpin' gas in towns as red as cherries? Point is, we'll never turn 'em blue."

"But *women* pumping gas are not good 'ol boys,"

Percy pointed out in a hopeful tone.

"Sounds like old fashioned retail politicking to me," I offered, curious about the change of tone. I thought he'd admired Marie's schmoozing with the gas station crowd.

"My feelings, exactly," Percy offered. "The women tell their friends, who maybe listen to Marie a little longer next time they see her on TV. Someone tells someone else about the candidate buying coffee at the Quick Trip. Can't hurt."

Steve shrugged. "You're right. Besides, she's where she belongs now—those gas stations were this afternoon. Ancient history in a campaign." He turned to me and brushed his shaggy, albeit thinning, hair off his forehead. "So, who do you blame for the shooting?" he asked, his dark eyes intense. "The NRA? Toomey and his crowd? Dean Andersen?"

Dean Andersen? The president? No way did I think he was to blame. "Since you ask, I blame the shooter. Let's put the immediate blame on the guy who points the semiautomatic at black shoppers and mows them down in a matter of seconds." My voice rose as I spoke. I didn't give a shit. The louder the better. "I'm not assigning any blame to the current occupant of the White House for this horror show. But popular as he is, apparently no one has had the power to do anything about guns over these last years."

Frustrated, I puffed out my cheeks and blew out the air. "We know Toomey and his competitors won't do anything. But today, people want to know what Marie and Pierson and the other candidates will do about it. Take Representative Campanella. It's likely he'll have to drop out, but he's still going to be in the House, and he'll still have a vote."

Percy nodded. "Right. I get that."

Steve sat in silence.

The knock on the door was a relief. I'd talked myself into a dark mood. Within seconds, the aromas of hot bread and beef stew wafted into the suite. If that wouldn't adjust Steve's attitude—and mine—nothing would. A waiter rolled the cart over to the windows and set up our dinner at the table. Percy filled the wine glasses and over the next half hour or so, Percy and I held up our held up our end of the conversation and Steve drank more than his share of the wine. I assessed Novak as the kind of guy who wouldn't know a fine French wine from cheap box wine, but he enjoyed it nevertheless.

Finally, Steve stood and Percy followed his lead. But their phones buzzed simultaneously. I kept quiet while they looked at their screens.

Steve's eyes popped open. "Shit…that stupid fuck."

"Oh, boy. Call the fuckin' cleanup crew." Percy said the words, but his expression was curiously blank.

"What? What?" I grabbed my phone and went to Google alerts, but had nothing.

"Damned Bentley. And Amanda. Why couldn't they keep their ignorant mouths shut?"

Whoa, I was waiting for Steve to start foaming at the mouth. Maybe I *shouldn't* have been shocked that Percy, and especially Steve, lashed out Marie's family, but I was pretty taken aback. What's that inconvenient word? Decorum? Talk about biting the hand that fed you. Not to mention flying into a rage in front of a relative stranger and a new addition to their campaign.

I checked my phone again and the story came up. I quickly perused it. Ouch. Yikes. No wonder. At a student event up in a college in Minnesota, Amanda Bentley-Kent, Marie's daughter made a promise the candidate hadn't a prayer of keeping. *Ever*. Amanda claimed her mom would push for a permanent ban on assault weapons—she'd start the work in the first thirty days of her term. Even I knew that was a loser in the current climate. And Parker Bentley, husband-dad, stood at her side and agreed with her. I was no political operative, but I got it. Percy and Steven weren't angry as much as panicked.

"I told Marie to get some rest. Have a quiet dinner,"

Steven said. "Fat chance now." He jabbed his finger in the air at Percy. "You, get to work on the statement. ASAP. We gotta go."

The two rushed to the door. Almost as an afterthought, Steve turned to me. "You and Rick work through Percy. He'll keep me updated."

"That's fine." I kept my voice low even as I observed their increasing alarm.

Percy nodded and looked at his phone. "Hey, hey, death threats. They've already started."

Steve let out a string of expletives that covered Parker and Amanda on a personal level, but reserved the worst for their handlers. He was still staring at his phone and swearing mightily all the way down the hall. Janet would have loved my next thought: Heads were going to roll.

A mass shooting. A major gaffe, hideous death threats against Kent—and her whole family—were streaming in. And that was just the first 24 hours.

Chapter Five

"Threats of mutilation and a horrible death aside, if there is anything that could derail Kent I want to know now," I told Rick as we drove the rental car up Route 17, the coastal highway that took us past miles and miles of new growth pine owned by one of the biggest paper companies in the country. The road was filled with hidden turnoffs to side roads, some unpaved, leading to inlets and creeks snaking through many miles of marshes. We slowed down to 30 mph when we passed through towns where live oaks dripping with lacey Spanish moss canopied the main drag. Even the dullest winter landscape had a certain beauty along the coast.

We were headed to the Waterfront Park in Beaufort, where Marie would hold her last event in that area. "It's all well and good to dig up dirt on other candidates and profile her target voters," I said, "but I want to make sure Kent—or someone on her campaign—doesn't have some rogue relative who's doing time for murder—or even worse, corruption. Or, a serial killer, maybe?" I was getting a kick out of myself, but this was serious, too. I wasn't exactly thinking of Steve, but there was an air of mystery around him.

"Or maybe he's in a weird cult, or even worse, lurking around the fringes of these stupid ass white nationalists." Rick's scoffed. "How about that for some dirt?"

Rick's sarcasm was meant to tamp down my worries.

It didn't work. "I'm serious. The primary—and the general—could turn on a mere few thousands votes in the right states. It's not like we don't have a history of that happening in our country. If you don't believe me, ask President Al Gore or President Hillary Clinton!"

I was on a roll now. And legitimate anxiety was fueling my growing anxiety. It was simple really. Death threats weren't a routine part of my work. But now, Rick and I were in the fray, even if we looked like any other voter in search of the right candidate to take over as president not long after the country had been left in chaos because a nasty virus made a trip around the globe. Before that, we'd been enjoying a fairly peaceful, prosperous time. Andersen had served a couple of productive terms. The flaw in my thinking was the scar of hate and division that had festered during his eight years. The fucking gun massacres left deep scars on those years. Historians would have a field day with the violence we'd endured. I mean, when some people hate, they hate big.

"I got it, boss," Rick said, using that boss moniker reserved for times when things were either very light or very serious. "I'm getting these odd texts from Percy about Marie's daughter's big verbal crime. But I thought Marie was for the assault weapons ban."

"She is, but she's not taking out ads about it," I said, "literally. If she did that now they'd accuse her of politicizing the tragedy."

"What the hell, they'll do that anyway," Rick shot back.

"Good point. It begs the question about what to do now. Will they waste two of the most popular surrogates anywhere in politics and take Parker and Amanda off the trail? Seems to me, the prominent surgeon husband and the soon-to-be prominent lawyer daughter are two of Marie's biggest assets. Bigger than the little sin they committed." I hoped I was right.

"Your logical mind is showing," Rick said wryly.

I scoffed. "Damn it, that happens now and again.

64

I'll have to watch it." I'd make light of this for now, but Marie's family was a big deal. "When it comes to Bentley, I have it on good authority that he's both a cutie and hottie."

"Ah, I see. Wendy and Janet have weighed in."

"Wendy likes the whole turtleneck, blazer, and jeans look. Lee—or I should say Bo—is a master at pulling that off," I said, with a laugh in my voice. "Janet likes the good Dr. Bentley's height and steel gray hair. According to the women in our lives, Parker is handsome, and tall enough to look commanding, a guy who can protect a woman."

"And he probably smells good, too," Rick quipped. "So much for scientific research."

"This political stuff really is like choosing jurors. At least in some ways." We jury consultants did the research, we matched the attitudes, we came up with models. "Sometimes we choose the old guy with a rousing lock 'em up spirit to sit in judgment of a young guy accused of reckless homicide. Somehow, your gut tells you this guy is like your old school principal, tough but fair."

"I suppose," Rick said, staring out the car window.

"I wish you'd been in my room last night when the news came in about Amanda and Parker. You didn't see how our two new buddies reacted." I described Steve and Percy jumping up to rush off even before the death threats came. "They weren't only furious. They went into complete meltdown mode. Bentley was a dumb fuck and that was for starters."

The impassive look in Percy's eyes came back to me. "Wait a second. Correction. *Steven* was furious and Percy *acted* furious. Maybe that's unfair, but he didn't seem as upset by Amanda's gaffe. He left ready to slay the dragon, but below the surface his calm nerves were as weird as Steve's rage. I don't think I read that wrong."

We turned off the highway, although calling it a highway was an exaggeration for the mostly two lane road. Traffic was heavy and slow on the way into Beaufort. At one point police directed traffic and detoured us to avoid the blocked street in front of a school half a block ahead.

"Hey, that's the Toomey event," Rick said, pointing to the crowd holding signs.

"So it is." I put on my signal and made a right turn onto a street and then a left into a hotel parking at the next light, about a block away. "Change of plans."

"You want me to check out Toomey, I bet."

"We need to split up anyway," I said. "I'm staying on the fringes of the crowd and we don't really want to be recognized by others on the campaign staff, at least not yet." I'd made the deal with the Kent campaign, but I still wanted to stay in the background.

"So, we'll meet back here later?" Rick asked, already halfway out of the car.

"Good a spot as any," I said, nodding at the windows of the lounge inside the hotel.

Rick jogged back down the street toward the Toomey rally at the school. I went the other way to get out of the traffic and detour to the Beaufort waterfront park. I parked on a side street back from the water and across from a huge clapboard antebellum mansion with turrets and balconies. A wraparound porch dominated the house on the brick street so narrow parking was allowed on only one side. I prided myself on the skill of squeezing into parking spaces that looked impossible and I managed to get into that one. Actually, it took two tries. Not my best work.

The mansion was a postcard worthy picture of Southern grandeur of a century and a half ago, but times clearly changed. The sign on the lawn made me smile. Seemed the old place had a new commercial life. It housed a salon and day spa, a yoga and Pilates studio, and finally, Stotesbury, Gerald & Kien, Attorneys at Law. Not bad digs for a law firm.

As I walked on brick sidewalks toward the waterfront, the wind picked up and I fished in my jacket pockets for gloves. The Lowcountry was famous for its summer heat, but no one told me it could get this cold in February. By the time I was a block away, older couples, groups of college students, and a couple of women pushing strollers filled the street, too, and we were all headed to the same destination. A few waved at each other and in friendly Southern style greeted me as we closed in.

I was early and checked my phone yet again and returned an earlier call from Wendy. She'd kept me updated on her efforts to set up a community attitude survey, which we'd follow up with a focus group. We used some analytics to duplicate in Northern Illinois a group of men and women of mixed ages and race, employed, self-employed, retired, disabled, single, married, kids-no kids. We balanced a small number of party-affiliated people with mostly those who claimed to be independents. Right. That was a status I doubted in these politically charged times. And I had research to back that up. Over 90% of those claiming to be political indies actually leaned one way or the other, they just didn't like admitting it to other people and sometimes not even to themselves. Everyone likes to think they are open and fair. Ha! Not a chance.

"I hear there was some big dustup about Marie promising to ban assault weapons," Wendy said, a couple of minutes into our conversation. "And Janet just mentioned Marie's death threats are on the rise."

"Well, yes to both." I sighed, suddenly wishing I'd not taken this on. I could be back home with Maude and Quigs sliding on the ice or rescuing them in huge snow piles in Lincoln Park. I could be eating cinnamon rolls at Ann Sather's and listening to the trains rattling by and screeching to a halt at the Belmont EL stop. But no, here I was in a small city dominated by antebellum homes and carriage tours lining up 50 yards from me. The waterfront smelled a lot like the horses patiently waiting for their next tour—cold wind or not.

I ended the call and while I waited, I did my own

impromptu survey of Kent voters, or rather, the kind of people who were free to come out on a weekday afternoon. A little heavy on the older demographic, I noted. Not a group that reliably voted for Democrats these days. The crowd was a little light on middle-aged folks, to be expected on a weekday afternoon. But the kids, a diverse, happy group provided the loudest enthusiasm. A few buses were parked on the other side of the horses.

Beaufort was situated on land that made up islands in bays. A stone's throw away, the bridge across the Beaufort River connected the city to a series of islands to the east. It all looked like another postcard. Or I could have been on a movie set like Gone with the Wind, absent the political conflicts that now surrounded movies these days.

When Marie's South Carolina campaign manager, Alyssa Bitty, took to the stage, she brought me back to my university days. Long black curly hair set off warm brown skin and bright red nails. As if she couldn't contain her excitement, she bounced in a sing-song voice as she spoke about the fantastic, accomplished, dedicated, honest, exciting, historic, and overall great woman, Marie Kent. No mere death threats were scaring her.

Maybe not. But I worried about this young woman, twenty or twenty-one tops, standing alone on a stage. I spotted the bodyguards. I saw Novak himself scanning the crowd. So was Patricia O'Donnell, Marie's press secretary. I recognized her from a campaign video I'd seen online. She was frowning, but even from a distance I could see she was trying to look like she was in the spirit of the rally. I wouldn't want to be in her shoes, or Steve's. Dour barely touched his expression. But with death threats flying against his candidate, who could blame him? I didn't see Percy, but he was probably around somewhere. So far, no candidate had Secret Service protection. Maybe that was about to change.

The rally went through a couple more speakers, and then finally Alyssa's introduction brought Marie to the stage to speak to the 200 or so people, my estimate, cheering and waving posters to the rhythm of her campaign song coming over the speakers. Smiling broadly, like she didn't have a care in the world, she clapped in time with the music and did what I called the politician's point, that is, pointing to people the crowd she recognized, or at least pretended to. I wondered which. When the music stopped the chant started, *Kent, Kent, Kent* and *Ma...rie, Ma...rie...Ma...rie.*

It hit me that the last time I witnessed that level of enthusiasm was at a Charles Marchand rally. After first refusing a place on his defense team, I finally relented and reluctantly took on Marchand's case. He was accused of murdering his wife, Sandra. The circumstances were murky, as was the evidence. Ever since I'd lost a case and an innocent man was executed not long before Illinois' moratorium on the death penalty, I'd vowed never to take on another criminal case as a trial attorney or jury consultant. For years I'd stuck to civil cases, in which losing was measured in dollars, not lives.

Marchand and Sandra personified Chicago's elite. He was a builder, she a philanthropist. Turned out she also had a lethal gene that brought on sudden heart failure. After Marchand was found guilty at trial, he spent months in prison before the truth was discovered. Discovered by Rick, in fact, who turned out to be the real hero of the whole Marchand case. With his name cleared and public good will toward him restored, Marchand threw his hat in the ring for a seat in Congress. He won big. Seems people don't care much anymore about candidate's criminal backgrounds whether real or not. He also sent a little money to support some of my clients, civil and criminal, who had little in the way of resources, but whose cases were important beyond their limited set of facts. I'd slipped into the back rows of one of his rallies, too, where the crowd chanted *Mar…chand… Mar…chand…Mar…chand.*

Same rhythm, different day, different candidate. No death threats for Marchand beyond the usual array of crazies who ramble on about knocking off every politician in the so-called deep state.

I did as objective assessment as possible of Marie while watching her walk from one end of the platform to another. I'd never met her, but had observed her as a senator and if I'd been polled I'd have rated her high in personal qualities—that all important favorability number.

Steve Novak stepped forward, top coat flapping open and not so much as a scarf on this cold day. It was clear to me he was trying to pretend he wasn't flanking her, but he wasn't shrinking into the background, either. Marie looked young, even radiant in this crowd that proved impressive for this smallish coastal city that usually was reliably red. Marie didn't let the red state reality stop her from wearing a jaunty red hat that contrasted with her dark hair. Unlike Steve, she'd tucked a heavy scarf under her coat making her look a little heavier than she did on TV. Marie was short, but had a compact, feminine build. I watched as she moved. Whoa. *She was wearing a vest.* Novak and Bentley were taking no chances.

As Marie spoke, delivering her Barack Obama-type "yes-we-can" message, I watched the crowd and looked around for Percy. Odd that he wasn't there, especially since eagle-eyed Steve was preoccupied with scanning the crowd.

I slipped away when Marie was urging the crowd to join her in creating real change and finished with the typical plea to bring friends and neighbors to the polls. True enough, Marie needed a win or a close-to-a-tie-second place to build momentum against Pierson.

I texted Rick and told him I'd pick him up in the parking lot where I'd left him. I suggested a drink in the lounge before heading out, but Rick sent a quick reply nixing that flat out. He didn't say why. I went to retrieve my car and navigated through unfamiliar streets until I got on the main drag through the west end of central Beaufort.

Rick was waiting for me inside the hotel lobby, and hurried out when I pulled up.

"What's wrong?" I asked. "You seem nervous."

"Go, go, get out of here. I don't want Percy to see me."

"Percy?" I asked. "I haven't seen him yet. He didn't make himself visible during Marie's event."

"Oh, I got that. Because I know exactly where he was," Rick said. "He was hanging out at the *Toomey* rally."

"*Really*? You saw him there? Did he say why?" I was now undeniably queasy, but couldn't have explained why.

"To start with, I didn't approach him. He obviously didn't want to be seen," Rick said. "I'd have hung around and followed him if I'd had the car."

All this seemed too dramatic. Didn't operatives sometimes shadow each other's events? That was a normal or expected thing to do. We headed south, this time to Savannah for our two separate flights home.

"I don't know what this is about, but it's strange to see Percy in a hoodie—hood up—and a scarf across his chin. *Inside.* I got the feeling he didn't want to be seen."

"Well, I imagine he didn't," I said reasonably. "A little extreme, but it *is* part of the political game to hang out where other candidates are—eavesdrop, get a sense of things."

"No, no, you're not getting this," Rick said, loudly. "He wasn't *in* the crowd." Rick described a gym with portable dividers and a podium on a table for the speakers. All low key, low tech. From what I could surmise from Rick's description, the crowd wasn't big, not as big as Marie's.

"When I saw Percy come in through a side entrance,

I stepped behind a cluster of people. I expected him to veer off toward the back or just step into the crowd randomly, but he didn't. He looked around and then seemed to slip behind one of the spatial dividers. I moved to my right, where I had a glimpse behind the table, and saw Percy tap Toomey's campaign manager—that guy Jeff Hoover—on the shoulder." Rick tapped the back of his hand on the window and shifted in the seat. "Then Hoover jumped out of the chair and the two disappeared deeper behind the divider. I couldn't see beyond that. But I didn't see him leave, either."

Okay. Something wasn't right, but we didn't know what it was. "Maybe Jeff Hoover and Percy are old friends, Rick. How do we know?"

"We don't, but Jeff is what, sixty years old? Percy is thirty-three, a year younger than I am. What kind of old buddies could they be? He's not a long lost uncle or something," Rick said. "I think I'd know that."

He had a point. "So, maybe he was building a bridge—civility and all that." That was weak, but it was something.

Rick was silent as we found ourselves almost alone on the road, only a few miles to go to the turnoff for the Savannah/Hilton Head Airport. "I don't see Percy being a goodwill ambassador. No way."

There was something about Percy that gave me a gut punch when I thought about him building a bridge to the opposition. And why do that anyway? "Are you saying Percy is a spy?"

"I can't say that for sure," Rick said, talking fast and obviously upset by this development. "But I don't like it. Maybe it was the damn hoodie and scarf thing, like a half-assed disguise."

"And now you want to snoop around a little." It was a statement, not a question.

"Can't hurt. I'm 99% percent sure he didn't see me. I keep thinking it was stealthy, the way he came in and got out of sight."

I had to ask myself if any of this would bother me if we weren't mired in bomb threats and a mass shooting. I didn't honestly know, but the tense atmosphere magnified everything. "The only thing we know is that he obviously didn't want to be seen."

Steve wasn't the type who would send his right-hand guy to the other party's leading candidate for the nomination. But then again, Steve himself didn't seem like the kind of guy Marie would end up with as her campaign manager. Come to think of it, Percy was an odd duck, too. "I wonder where Steve thought Percy went."

"Beats me."

We followed the GPS from the exit, and I pulled up to the curb in front of the American Airlines doors. I'd go on to turn in the rental car and go to United. "Uh, quick question. Steve is under the impression you and Percy are, and I quote, quite close. Why would he have that impression?"

Rick grabbed his bag from the backseat and slung it over his shoulder. "No idea. He didn't hear it from me," he said, leaning over to talk through the open door. "Before he called me, I hadn't seen the kid since a family Thanksgiving at his mom's house years ago—*years*—maybe five Thanksgivings ago. His mom told him about the work I do for you. That's why he called me."

Rick attempted a smile before he closed the passenger door. But he failed. All in all, he looked grim.

Was Percy outright lying to his boss about his genius cousin or was it only an exaggeration, like a little padding of work history on a résumé?

Chapter Six

I didn't forget Percy's bullshit about his cousinly bond with Rick. By the time I'd had breakfast at Ann Sather's the next morning and walked the dogs, I'd filed it away as a guy trying to impress his boss with a sure thing referral. Besides, as much as Rick's story about sneaky Percy spooked me a little, I was still focused on sourpuss Steve.

"They do everything right, don't they," Wendy said, coming into the conference room just as Patricia O'Donnell fielded questions about Marie's stance on assault weapons. They'd danced around her daughter's statement, explaining it as a young person's enthusiasm and concern. She got a little ahead of herself, you know, carried away by her passion for gun safety.

"Let's be clear. Senator Kent would like to see assault weapons off the streets—so would every major law enforcement agency in this country," Patricia said. "So do a majority of the American people. Senator Kent has been a leader in our party on expanding and refining background checks, also desired by a vast majority of Americans." O'Donnell expanded on that, by pointing out Marie's push to lengthen the waiting period to buy a weapon, not successful, and eliminating loopholes to make sure domestic abusers can't buy firearms of any kind, marginally a win.

"In case anyone questions where she stands," O'Donnell said, "the NRA likes to brag about giving her an F on their report card every cycle. That's one failing grade she wears proudly."

National reporters gathered in South Carolina shouted questions one after the other, but Patricia handled them smoothly without letting any ruffled feathers show. Wendy and I had to laugh when we realized we'd been watching so much political TV we recognized the reporters vying for attention. We'd chosen our favorites and we were fast becoming groupies. Wendy and Janet had even begun critiquing the women reporters' clothes and jewelry, all the while knowing it was most definitely not politically correct. At some point, we saw our old pals shouting questions and then heading to the network cameras to deliver their two minute spots.

"She got herself out of this mini-scandal pretty well. She didn't exactly throw her daughter under the bus," I said, grinning and holding my thumb and index finger a couple of inches apart. "Only about this much."

"You must have had quite a trip," Wendy said, quietly. I was a little off and she noticed it. Not grumpy or mad, but bothered. It wasn't just Percy. I couldn't shake my worries—suspicions—about Steve. But there was more.

"It's not the politics so much as the mall shooting that threw me, Wendy. Turns out, the guy wasn't only targeting African-Americans. He walked into that mall on the *hunt* for people of color—like immigrants or people who looked like immigrants to him, from India and Pakistan. Shooting them down like deer in the woods." I heard my voice crack. I hadn't said those words out loud before. "I mean, a scientist from India was killed. He'd been working at the University of South Carolina bio-med lab for *three* months." I slapped the table. "Welcome to America. What the fuck? And there's Marie more or less *apologizing* for an offhand remark her daughter made about assault weapons!"

I glanced over my shoulder and saw Maude and Quigs raise their heads. "Sorry pooches," I said, "I didn't mean to interrupt your naps."

Wendy snickered. "You're such a meanie."

"Yeah, well." Weary in lots of ways, I needed a nap myself.

"Pierson is for the ban," Wendy said, "so that's one thing."

I nodded at Wendy and laced my fingers around the back of my neck. In the last couple of years, after the Marchand case, really, I'd been able to go easy on the antacids, but I'd need to grab the bottle soon. "That's good, but at the moment Kent is doing her part. The advance they paid us will keep us going for a while."

"The fact is, we don't know who's going to win this thing," Wendy said. "At least on my end, I'm looking at data. Lucky for me data don't have feelings one way or another."

Good point. "Have a seat. Let's see what you've got."

Wendy waved the pages of documents. "Our first analysis looked at information that came directly from the campaign. Steve Novak sent us donor information and we have a collection of stats from her rallies."

I scanned Wendy's summary of donor information and her mailing list. It didn't take long to see Marie's small donors were primarily older white women, but she also had a fair number of older women of color. The numbers broke down in the usual ways, married or not, education, but the campaign was mostly interested in the profile of donors, whereas I was interested in voters.

"It's all predictable, for the most part," Wendy said, like a true political junky. "Except that she's weak with the millennial crowd. Theoretically, our crowd." Wendy looked stumped by this. "I don't know why."

I agreed. "Kind of hard to understand. But she had an army of college students at her rally. They were organized. To quote a pretty famous guy who also won the South Carolina primary, they were fired up and ready to go."

Wendy grinned. "Okay, Matt, I've got the Obama

message. Hope, change, optimism, energy."

"Let's just say Marie's crowd was impressive in that same way." I paused and looked at the muted TV, where Pierson was being interviewed by Chris Cuomo on CNN. I stared at the screen, but didn't read the captions. "I wonder how much the mall shooting affected Marie's support. She's actually more cautious about the assault weapons ban than Pierson."

"Speaking of Pierson, I talked to Rick earlier and he told me he was keeping track of Pierson's campaign appearances," Wendy said, "and for some reason, Toomey's."

Now I was puzzled. "Really? We haven't talked about doing that."

"*We* aren't…but Rick is. It's on his time. You know Rick. He's not happy if he's not on the computer and analyzing something."

"I suppose." Knowing Rick as I did, it wasn't hard to figure out that he'd brought up Pierson as a side issue, sort of. It was Toomey who had Rick's eye. I'd been distracted and hadn't thought much more about Percy and his mysterious visit to the Toomey rally. Rick, on the other hand, hadn't let it go.

"Is Rick due in the office today?" I asked, not recalling what we'd scheduled. Marie Kent and her campaign were important, but she wasn't our only client. In fact, I had to be in court in a week to help choose a jury in a product liability case, although we were 95% certain the client would settle once jury selection got underway. Seeing the jury pool would bring home the hopelessness of their case. We could never be sure though and prepared as if going to trial was a sure thing.

"We have a meeting scheduled late this afternoon. Is that still okay?" Wendy asked.

Still staring at the TV, I nodded.

"Okay, Matt, what is it?" Wendy asked. "I know your mood has zero to do with creating models of the typical Marie Kent voter."

"It's what happened at the mall," I blurted. That was the first half of the explanation.

"I get it," Wendy acknowledged, shaking her head sadly.

"Marie is getting death threats because of what her *daughter* said." Just speaking the words brought home how outrageous that was. "Marie had to walk that back some. Not a big deal. We all know the gun issue is center stage in this country, and everybody has to choose their words carefully. But right now, who the fuck is talking about the victims?"

Wendy took in a breath. My anger took her back. She wasn't used to me like this. Not when we were in the midst of work. Right. I kept my rage in check until after hours. "But isn't that always the case, Matt? Who's talking about the kids in the high school or the people shot dead in their synagogue on a Saturday morning?"

"I know, I know," I said, impatient with the comparisons. "Maybe so, but it's not right to forget that in some cases, like the Pittsburgh synagogue or the church in Charleston, you really can't separate the shooter from the people killed. This guy absolutely hunted people who aren't white." I had gone over that in my mind and couldn't let it go. "His apartment was full of firearms. His computer was like its own racist movement. This guy wasn't even an unknown to the hate-watch organizations. They all knew about his network. He spewed this stuff all over the internet and didn't try to hide it. That's what's missing from what Marie is talking about. Frankly, Arnold Pierson is doing a better job."

Wendy narrowed her eyes as she gave me a long, pointed look. "Tell me, be honest, do you wish we were working for Pierson?"

Taking her question seriously, despite its poor timing, I closed my eyes and tried to figure out what was really going on with me. Wendy and I didn't need to have these kinds of conversations very often. She was good at reading my moods, and I was attuned to her pretty well, too. "I'm afraid of these crazy white guys. I'm afraid for Marie, along with Amanda and Bentley. I fear for Pierson and other Democratic nominees. Is this really what this campaign season is going to be like?"

"If you want my honest opinion, Matt, then, yes, I think that's exactly what it's going to be about."

"What about regular citizens who want to go shopping in peace or don't feel like they're risking their lives going to political rallies? This fuckin' white guy with all his firepower wasn't talking to himself. He has others out there. Hell, those shoppers could have been Janet." I ran out of air before I got her name out of my mouth and gasped to catch my breath.

"Of course. Janet's front and center in my mind," Wendy said, keeping her voice low. "She and her sisters get together on a Saturday and have lunch and wander in the mall just for the fun of it."

That image of my office manager with her dry humor and her amusing clichés had gone through my mind more than once. "Meanwhile, the candidate we're working for puts herself out there in front of people every day. She mingles in crowds and stands on stages. When he's not with her, Parker Bentley is out speaking on behalf of his wife. And their daughter, too." I groaned. "It's like they're sitting ducks for crazies."

Wendy didn't respond. Wasn't much to say. It was the tragic, dreary truth.

I shrugged. "So, you asked, and I told you. That's why I'm in this weird place right now. It's been coming on all morning, even during my walk with my little buddies."

"And none of us around here can do a damn thing," Wendy finally said. "The best I can do is to leave you with data." She turned to leave.

"Wait, Wendy. One second." I didn't want to leave her with the wrong impression. "It's not about

Marie or Pierson. I'd be fine with Pierson getting the nomination, but Marie is good in different ways. She'd do a lot for the country. And I like her. I like the history she'd make, too. We committed to her. More to the point, *I'm* committed to her."

Wendy offered a sympathetic smile. "I never doubted the professional side of this, Matt."

Unable to make myself turn off the TV, I unmuted it and kept the sound on low, even as it delivered news that while not necessarily bad still unsettled me.

Around noon, I took the dogs out and came back with Thai food for everyone from Circle Sushi, which offered a mix of Asian foods from Thai to Chinese and Japanese too. Since it's just across from the Steppenwolf Theater on Halsted Street I liked to check out the latest theater offering whenever I popped in. We all loved Circle Sushi, so it was a treat when I brought it in. The fact that the food wasn't particularly expensive was a bonus. I finally muted the TV and Wendy, Janet, and I kept the conversation light.

When we cleared away the debris, Janet couldn't resist a little commentary about my apparent media addiction. "You've always had a yen for the talk shows and all the news that's fit to transmit, Matt, but this is getting out of hand."

"Fit to print." Wendy corrected Janet again. She did that way too often. "The phrase is all the news that's fit to print."

Janet rolled her eyes. "I *know* that. I was taking liberties." She flashed her signature lopsided smile. "I gave it a little cyber update."

"Hey, I only got back last night," I said defensively as I pointed to the TV. "It's my *job* now to keep up with the South Carolina primary." I deliberately injected a little laugh in my voice. "By the way, it turns out that famous Hilton Head Island is quite a place. I may just take up golf," I said with a chuckle.

The simultaneous hoot let me know my joke worked. If the success of my business depended on my talents on the greens, then I'd be looking for another career.

"When hell freezes over," Wendy said, flashing a smug look at Janet for beating her to the cliché punch.

"Well, I can read you like a book, Matt. You're fretting over that shooting." Janet gave me a "who do you think you're kidding" look. "Meanwhile, I've got matters of high finance waitin' for me," she said as she left the conference room.

"That's right, Janet, get to work," I teased. "It's payday."

Between my two employees, my two dogs, and Thai food, I was feeling a little better. That mood lasted until Rick blew in a couple of hours later.

***

Rick made something of an entrance. It was his way. Between lunch and his arrival, some serious snow was blanketing the city on that late Friday in February. I knew he'd arrived when I heard the boot stomping on the mat by the door. I went to greet him when he was shaking out his hat in the entryway. In his baggy jeans and sweater, he looked more like the old living hand-to-mouth aspiring game creator Rick than the guy with a suit that fit. I was on the brink of joshing him a little, but his tight jaw put the brakes on that.

Janet didn't have the information I did, so she went through the usual routine of waving an envelope at him and kidding him about showing up for his paycheck in a blizzard growing worse by the minute. He charmed her right back with exaggerated gratitude and a formal bow.

I led him in the conference room and something about the dark energy he came in with made me ask him if I should call for Wendy.

He shook his head. "Let's keep this between us for now."

With my curiosity taking over, I closed the door

behind us. When Rick deliberately said he wanted to keep something between us it signaled we were crossing a boundary into rocky terrain.

We started the way we began almost every meeting, with Rick opening his computer and pulling up data. I never knew whether to welcome or dread what he put in front of me. It could go either way. Placing the computer so we could both see the screen, he flopped back in the chair and propped his ankle across one knee. "I don't know what we're getting into here—"

"*We?*" I interrupted to make sure this, whatever it was he was showing, was actually related to my firm. Rick was a master at straying outside the fence on all our projects, which he blamed on his addiction to research. He was no different when it came to the already unusual work we were doing for the Kent campaign.

Rick tucked his chin as he gave me an indulgent look. "Okay. For now, I'll relate this to me, and only me. I'm not making promises, but this could soon add another layer to what you're up to with Kent campaign. I don't know yet."

"Does this all come down to tracking Percy?" I made no attempt to hide my skepticism.

His serious expression held when he said, "More or less."

"How do you—we—know it's worth our time?"

"I don't." Rick rubbed his cheeks with a lot of energy. "But it may be about something bigger than Percy. Stay with me for a second. Why does Marie's campaign end up in the same state as Toomey over half the time?"

On the face of it, that was a nonsensical question. "They're both running for president and following the primary calendar?" I opened my hands, palms up. Wasn't that obvious? I'd never given candidates' travel schedules a major thought. "Why wouldn't they end up with campaign schedules that crisscross?"

Rick raised his hand to acknowledge the question.

"Fair enough. Sure, they'd cross paths some of the time, especially early. They all packed appearances at the Iowa State Fair and pumpkin festivals scattered around New Hampshire. Same with Nevada and now South Carolina. If you run for president, though, you have to get out to other states. Like the Super Tuesday states." Rick pulled up a graphic on the computer. It was a map I could see had isolated the Kent and Toomey campaigns. He'd drawn lines connecting towns and cities in Michigan and Ohio, Idaho and Wyoming, Kentucky and Tennessee. A panel on the side of the page listed dates.

He was good. I had to hand it to him. The picture he created resembled a street map of crossing lines, like grids. I never would have connected it without the graphic. "But what does that mean? What about the other campaigns?"

Rick immediately brought up another map that was a maze of different color lines. "This is just the Dems. This is from before Iowa and New Hampshire. Everything looks about as you'd expect and it tells us almost nothing. Even South Carolina has many cross-points...intersections. JoJo has been to the state. Here's his line." He pointed to an orange line that matched the patterns of other candidates making last ditch visits in South Carolina. All the candidates trekked to Charleston and Columbia a couple of times. "But when I worked with Super Tuesday states, I came up with this." In another graphic he'd eliminated the wannabes and mapped the main candidates. "See here?" He pointed to the bright yellow and green lines. "This is just for Marie and Pierson."

"Their campaign trails track some," I said, noticing points of intersection. I could concede that, but nothing was remarkable.

"So, look what happens when I add Toomey to the mix." He pulled up another map and I had to admit the intersections increased, with Pierson, Kent, and Toomey turning up in the same regions of the same states at the same time more often than I'd have expected. But Kent and Toomey intersected so often, it almost looked planned. It looked like Pierson was the outlier. "It could mean nothing, of course."

I nodded. "Percy said an odd thing the other day at dinner. He talked about trailing Pierson's campaign on the ground in part to see if there were undecided voters—or people who could be persuaded to switch loyalties."

Rick shrugged. "Campaigns do that a lot, right? It's an obvious way to get a feel for what's happening on the ground. It's a little spying, but not malicious. Besides, most people start with one candidate and are forced to switch eventually when their candidate drops out."

"Well, it seemed to me Novak doesn't talk that way. And then the next day, you tell me you saw Percy at Toomey's event."

Rick asked. "Are you having second thoughts about Percy—and maybe about Marie?"

I snorted a laugh. "Are you kidding? I've had second thoughts about them all along." I nodded to the screen. "Not so much Kent as Steve." I distracted myself away from questions about spiffy young Percy. Trying a little too hard to be a man about town. Totally unfair of me. Besides, whether Rick knew him well or not, Percy was his family. The first time I saw Rick he was in serious need of a haircut, but that didn't keep him from having a certain genius. And he matched it with persistence. One day, he'd hit it big with a game and doing things like chasing his cousin around would quickly lose what little intrigue it had.

"It's okay if you wonder about Percy, too," Rick said. "He's a little like me."

Was Rick psychic now?

"I mean, our folks are, you know, marginal. Financially, that is. But they're smart in other ways," Rick said.

I had to laugh inside. My parents were marginal, too.

I'd barely known my dad who'd been too busy with his paper pushing job to think about us, and as much as I loved my bright, funny mom, she'd been decidedly *not* tough about her choice of men. Not wanting to ever call my mom naive, I settled on thinking of her as too trusting about the male of the species.

"It's like people in our families are brainy types. We like to study and talk about history and politics, but no one has been able to turn words into dollars. For all the good their smarts did us." Rick shook his head. "Percy and I were kind of like them, until now when we've got skills that bring in some money. I figured it out, and now Percy is doing the same."

"Working for Kent *is* a big deal—a major coup." I wanted to blurt that Percy was really working for Steve Novak, but I left that alone.

It already seemed like a two-tier deal with Kent anyway. On the one hand, we'd be doing what Barlow & Associates always did, but instead of calling it jury strategy it was a version of voter behavior strategy. The part about oppo research was another tier and less about research than positioning the vast knowledge of what everyone already knew about Pierson. It was legit to figure out ways to emphasize Pierson's weaknesses while playing up Kent's strengths. I got that. If Kent turned out to be strong with suburban women, women who are now much more accomplished than the moniker "housewives" credited them by Toomey, then she would need to court them. Nothing shady about that.

I had a sense that Marie was probably good at gently pulling people to her. She could capture them right before they could wander over to someone else. Not the most passionate voters, but the kind that faithfully showed up at polling places one election after the other.

That wasn't the same as using research and analysis to dig deep into the past. It wasn't the honest market research that bothered me. No, on the contrary, it was the ripple of something under the surface that wasn't quite right.

Chapter Seven

"In a Kent administration, exposing and combatting the rise of hate crimes, intensified anti-Semitism, homophobia, racism, and Islamophobia will not be afterthoughts. They won't be items tacked onto the long list of priorities for the Justice Department and the FBI," Marie Kent said, pointing down to the floor. "In my administration this rise of hate, this scourge, will jump to the top of our list and finally get the attention it deserves. We'll use all the resources the federal government has at hand. Our policy also will help us support the states in their efforts to rid this country of these ugly biases that continue to compromise our quality of life. It starts at the top." She raised her hand over her head, palm down.

I gave up, or gave in. Whatever. Instead of turning the channel or trying to do a couple of things at once, I went to a tiny room we affectionately called the break room, even though no one sat at the round kitchen style table and actually took a break. We used the room to make coffee and tea, store our carryout food, and heat up leftovers. If we didn't eat at our desks, we ate lunch—or breakfast and dinner on many days—in the conference room. I used to refer to the conference room as "The Wendy and Janet TV lounge," but now, compelled to follow the details of national politics, I renamed it my den. Naturally, Janet quickly and somewhat humorously morphed it into my man cave. Bears have dens, she'd reminded us. Humans have caves.

I brewed myself a mug of dark roast coffee and took it back to my cave and put my feet up on the table. It was Saturday morning, and while I didn't have Georgia on my mind, South Carolina took up residence in a chunk of it. I'd become way overinvested in the outcome of the South Carolina primary.

Marie Kent was in Georgetown, South Carolina for a quick morning stop before an afternoon launch of her newly opened campaign office in Morehead City, North Carolina. Then she'd backtrack and make a quick stop in Myrtle Beach before heading to her Charleston office to wait for returns. She had her eye on winning a big chunk of delegates in a later primary in North Carolina, even as she used her last day to convince South Carolina voters that she could beat Toomey, or whoever else the Republicans nominated.

Sometimes Marie reminded me of the old adage that Republicans fall in line, but Democrats fall in love. I saw that unfolding in this election once again as Toomey crept up in the polls and left behind the lesser known candidates. The same happened with the Dems, too, but people like JoJo Campanella managed to win enthusiastic followers and loud, if small crowds. But Marie Kent and Arnold Pierson hiked the emotion to the next level. They stayed close in the polls as many Dems sang their descriptive theme song, "Torn Between Two Lovers."

I was in Saturday clothes, jeans and boots, probably looking as comfortable as I felt. I might as well have settled in for a day of Netflix binging. Wendy stuck her head inside to remind me of a six-way video conference call we scheduled for late that afternoon. A fairly rare Saturday in the office, all because of a call about a pending medical malpractice case. Yes, real cases, real people with real problems had to move along in addition to the political game that for me, anyway, was just getting started.

"I got it," I told her. "You're talking details of the data, and I'm giving the summary."

"Good." She hesitated at the door, not backing out but not coming into the room either. "Uh, what are you doing?"

"Who, me?" I asked, laughing self-consciously. "I'm being the boss who has more or less gone on strike because I've got you and Janet. And Rick."

Wendy ignored my joke and focused on the big screen. "Is Marie saying anything new?"

"Not really."

"Then why…"

Wendy wasn't sure what to ask me, so I waved her inside the room. "Have a seat. I can't explain, but I'll try."

"Well, I thought you'd never ask." She stepped into the room and closed the door and sat across from me.

"I'm more or less taking the day off—or off from what we usually think of as work. I'm playing observer. I came in, because we have the conference call, but other than that I'm sort of glued to this primary." I shook my head. Pierson was on the screen now. Toomey and others were sure to follow. "It's not all idle time, you know. What happens in that state will influence the work the campaign wants from us. And I'm aware you're working really hard on this project and communicating with the analytics people for Marie."

"I talked to Percy earlier," Wendy said, acknowledging my attempt at an explanation with a nod. "I updated him on the major survey we're doing over the next couple of weeks. In time for the big contests in late March and April. So many delegates at stake."

I muted the TV and took my feet off the table. "So tell me, what do you make of Percy? I mean, from your dealings with him on the phone."

"Other than his marked lack of a sense of humor, you mean?" Wendy snickered. "Don't mind me. I'm being a little snarky. On the upside, he knows the right questions to ask about our work. He's reliable, which in my book means he calls when he says he will."

"Has he mentioned the mall shooting?" The death toll had ticked up again, and the primary was taking place against the backdrop of that nightmare.

"No." Wendy frowned. "Does that have something to do with why you're taking the day to follow the primary?"

"Probably," I conceded in a low voice. "Don't read too much into it, though. It's just that I can't shake it off. Bomb threats, explosions, a massacre at a mall." I shrugged. How was I supposed to react? "I think these add up to a sign of something. I don't think it's just the election bringing out some really sick folks. It's bigger than that. It's like the elections we've had when a major recession and a natural disaster collide, topped off by a mass shooting. Or millions of people sour on a war and that takes over the news cycle. Then, the next election cycle pivots on who can get us out of a war we shouldn't be fighting."

Wendy nodded knowingly. "You happened to be in the state for the aftermath, when the death toll kept rising. I'm sure it was shocking." Wendy studied my face as she spoke.

"It was. But I was more shocked by the muted response around me. Percy and Novak said all the right words and then without missing a beat, they moved on." I let out a loud huff. "It's as if we spend a minute doing our tsk-tsk and then move on."

"Be fair, Matt. They're dealing with death threats against Marie. Can you imagine what her security team is going through?"

"Maybe so." I let out a long sigh and left it at that. I couldn't shake the ominous cloud that seemed to cover everything the last couple of days. I was on edge but didn't want to admit I was waiting for the other shoe to drop.

***

Wendy left and I dutifully reviewed the summary I was due to deliver to the client. I kept a jacket and tie in my office I could slip on before we went live on a video conference or an unexpected court appearance. Probably not necessary for a Saturday afternoon meeting, but I couldn't go wrong changing out of my University of Illinois Alumnus orange and blue hoodie with the image of Chief Illiniwek on the front, an image long banned by the University as politically incorrect; I disagreed. The jeans could stay. I was like a TV anchor. No one saw the bottom half of me on a video call anyway.

This client, a law firm in Minneapolis, had taken us on for a jury selection, plus a mirror jury if we deemed it necessary in a very serious medical malpractice case. Always important in such cases. Plaintiff victims were often sympathetic, it's true. On the other hand, most people think we're a little lawsuit happy—just too many of them. When it comes to doctors, it turns out most of us are kind of protective of them in lawsuits. Plus, this client had the money to spend on those fairly expensive projects like a mirror jury. I'd head up there at the end of the week to work alongside the plaintiffs' attorneys, leaving Wendy and Rick to handle Kent's community attitude survey.

Meanwhile, back in South Carolina, the candidates either left for other states or began to wind down for the day. The state was seeing record-breaking turnout in almost every county, though. Pierson and Kent's press people gave the usual happy talk statements and try as they might, the reporters couldn't drag anything juicier than that out of either one of them. Toomey was looking to widen his delegate lead—for reasons beyond me, the Republicans were banking on this old white guy to carry them once again. They had a couple of women candidates, but neither had caught on and both languished in single digits in the polls.

With a little time left to kill, I decided to dig a little deeper into Steven Novak. I wrote off my reservations about Percy, his sneaky visit to Toomey's guy notwithstanding. But Novak was another story. The public record on him was on the thin side. Or, to rephrase, surprisingly, painfully dull. He'd been on Wall Street through his twenties, taught finance at three different universities over the next twenty years, but invested well and made tons of money. He might be a grumpy old man, but he was a rich one. Tired of teaching, he turned to fundraising for some big name Democrats, dating back to Clinton and Gore. Along the way, he managed to have three marriages and an equal number of divorces. For the last many years he'd apparently not taken another chance on love and wasn't linked with any prominent woman at the moment. Two sons in their late twenties, Jeremy and Alex, one sister named Ione, deceased parents and two older dogs. I looked up speeches and presentations with his name, and came up with nothing unexpected.

My phone interrupted me just as I was reaching the end of a list of Steve's academic publications. My new best friend had written boring academic papers titles like: *Voting patterns of Midwest farmers in off-year elections: a 50 year retrospective study*. Damn, wake me when it's over. Since he'd written that baby in the late '80s, I doubted it had much to tell us.

"I've been looking up some background on Steve," I said, when I picked up Rick's call.

"Finding anything?" Rick asked.

"Nothing much. Spectacularly boring academic papers. A try and try again kind of guy when it comes to marriage, until the third divorce."

"I knew that," Rick said with a mocking laugh. "Did you think I wouldn't do a little digging? But his kids are clean as whistles. One's in finance, the other one works for a tech company out in Silicon Valley. I have no idea what the kid does, but then no one knows what anyone actually does out there."

"Your cousin Percy is a little mysterious, but Novak seems odd. That's the only relatively neutral word I can come up with for him. I'm not convinced he's such an open book. I still don't get why Marie would choose him."

"He's smart. Whatever he's doing, it's working," Rick said. "I mean, despite being a senator, Marie started out with really low name recognition. Translated, only diehard pols knew who the hell she was. Look at her now. It's Steve's doing, too. She's not only in the hunt, she's polling second behind Pierson." Rick paused. "Um, speaking of Percy, he's in Tennessee. Supposedly to wait for returns and get ready for Super Tuesday."

"Why else would he be there?" I asked.

"Snooping maybe. Toomey's guys are in the state, too."

"Did you have that tracked on your chart?" I asked.

"Nope. This is outside the public campaign schedule. I caught a live shot on TV. Toomey is in South Carolina, but his campaign manager is in Chattanooga."

"And you're keeping track of all this. Right?"

"Let's just say I'm making more intersections in my map. I had no idea Toomey's guys were heading up that way. But that's not unusual for campaigns, especially in primaries."

Suddenly, the breaking news banner flashed on the TV screen. "I wonder what this breaking news is. I'm beginning to…" I stopped talking. "Are you watching this?"

"Yeah, and I'm wondering why anyone would want to work in politics. Not after this. There you are, young and eager making phone calls for your candidate and bullets whizz past your head because some loser fired shots into the headquarters."

Amateur video from a passerby's phone showed shattered glass all over the street of Arnold Pierson's headquarters in Salt Lake City."

"Why there?" Rick asked. "I mean it's a fucking red state. No matter what Democrat wins the nomination, the state is going for Toomey."

Paul Lisnek

I wondered whether these acts were going deeper than the race. Maybe an attempt to disrupt and unnerve the country. If the perpetrators were American citizens, to me this constituted treason.

I reached a saturation point, or so I told myself. "Great. We're down to asking about the location of bomb threats and shot up windows. You don't seem shocked. My cynical side isn't either. What the hell?" I read captions. No injuries reported.

"I'm *not* shocked," Rick said, "and I hate that. I wish I were surprised by any of this. All I can do is keep track, check the campaigns, Google threats. I'm finding out where all the candidates are and what kind of harassment or true threats they're getting. Whatever I can pick up from twitter, blogs, Facebook."

I wasn't sure I wanted to know, but I asked anyway. "And?"

"Lots of shit happening and not everything makes the news. Pierson, Kent, and Toomey suck up all the oxygen, but they aren't the only candidates targeted."

"Are they all Dems?"

"No. But on the other side, they're all *not* Toomey. I mean, he'll get a threat, the news covers it, he gets attention, but no damage is done," Rick said, "and his office is still in one piece. Makes you wonder what's up with that."

I parsed that sentence and put two and two together. Jorge Santana was a mid-level Republican. Vanessa Torres was not quite mid-level. Both had received death threats, but no bombings or bomb threats. At this point, there was no way to tell if the death threats were the garden variety run-of-the-mill threats all politicians learned to live with. And lawyers and jury consultants, too. And judges. I'd had a few threats on my life over verdicts that didn't go someone's way. Breaking news. People can be irrational. And sometimes, irrationality leads to actions that look like pure idiocy. Some are so driven by emotion they lose their ability to distinguish right from wrong.

94

"My theory of the case is that someone wants to scare Jorge and Vanessa out of the race," Rick said. "Maybe a particularly hateful anti-immigration group, with all of six members, show up every day at noon to insist they go back home to wherever they came from."

"Home? Jorge's parents are immigrants and now their son is running for fucking president." This was too much.

"Exactly. And his home is *Boston*," Rick said. "Born and raised there. On the other hand, Vanessa has religious fanatics spouting nonsense about women in power doing the devil's work and pushing abortions on everyone. No wonder women in the Republican party are so scarce."

"How is that different from the nutcases in every election?" I asked. "But wait, wait, why are we even paying attention to that kind of crazy?"

"You mean as opposed to the would-be mall shooters?"

"Exactly." My own grim tone made my head hurt.

"It's probably about atmospherics," Rick said. "Toomey, and I'm not accusing him of anything like bomb threats, spends a lot of time talking about shutting down the border and deporting millions of people, putting the kids back in cages," Rick's voice rose on every word. "He's a hardliner on what he calls religious freedom, code for anti-choice. In any other time, he'd be considered a right wing fanatic. These days, he has a seat at the table."

"Maybe so, but that doesn't mean he'd kick his Republican buddies over the border. Hell, if Toomey gets the nomination, and he's got the best shot on their side, Santana could be his running mate. Or Torres." I took a breath and read the breaking news on the TV screen and told Rick the shooter in Salt Lake was taken into custody.

"Maybe he'll spill some information."

"Do you think these incidents are isolated? Just a

random uptick in threats and violence." It was a logical concern. We'd been living in the era of daily mass shootings, most of which we no longer heard about. After all, if a shooting killed less than three people it wasn't worth reporting. Or so it seemed.

"Could be," Rick said, "but I don't get why more journalists aren't digging a little deeper and writing stories about it."

"And the campaigns are downplaying it," I pointed out, "or not saying anything at all. Politicians like to talk tough, don't they? Like nothing scares them." My suspicion that Marie was wearing a vest crossed my mind. How many other candidates were doing the same?

Was Steve behind that move? Marie's private security team? Who? "Keep doing what you're doing. Consider it part of our contract for this project. There's something odd here."

Rick quickly agreed, as I knew he would. I ended the call and took the dogs out for a quick walk in the neighborhood park down the street. I swapped out my shirt and tie for the hoodie and forced myself to think about anything but when the next breaking news story was another bomb threat or an attack on a headquarters. I didn't have to wait long.

Chapter Eight

The next bomb threat of the weekend was phoned in early Sunday at Mike Toomey's headquarters in, Coeur d'Alene, Idaho. The morning shows were filled with screen images of local law enforcement, the state explosives unit, the FBI, and at least fifty reporters covering the second bomb threat against the Toomey campaign. Threat, I reminded myself. Not an actual bombing. Toomey and his spokespeople, all white spokes*men* in his case, spread their outrage across every network, successfully sucking up the airtime Pierson would have claimed—rightfully earned through months of work to come out the victor in South Carolina.

Pierson would have had bragging rights to put to good use because he bested Marie in the South Carolina Saturday primary by three points. Not a devastating rout, it was about what Marie hoped for, given the crowds she'd gathered and the attention she drew. Still, Steve had to add South Carolina to the loss column all the same, although through the magic of delegate allocation the gap in the delegate count had stayed about the same. I tried to remind myself that Marie hadn't lost delegate ground, and she lost in a state the Dems hadn't won in the general election for decades. Still, I was surprisingly frustrated by the outcome.

Even worse, attention flipped from both Kent and Pierson to Toomey in a matter of minutes. Toomey couldn't have planned it any better. I channel surfed to note the shows that devoted a block of their hour to the primary. Despite disliking Toomey at a deep gut level, I had to hand it to him. He sure knew how to milk a story. So aggrieved. So indignant. The images of yellow crime scene tape and bomb units added to the drama. You'd have thought something actually had blown up.

I muttered to myself to quit being an effing hypocrite. Of course, he'd act aggrieved. I would make the same statements about the disappointing lack of civility and violence having no place…and on and on. I believed that, of course, but who didn't? Well, maybe I'd answered my own question. Toomey was no Mr. Rogers. Definitely not a role model in an anti-bullying program. He reveled in his reputation for a nasty edge, claiming he was only parroting what he heard from his supporters, who could be not just rowdy, but angry and threatening.

In Toomey's eyes—and in supporters' opinions— Kent and Pierson weren't worthy potential opponents. No, they were tools of the communist underground doing the devil's work inside all our institutions from universities to the IRS. Devil's work, I got, because Toomey had garnered great support from the evangelical wing of the Republican Party. But who called anyone a communist anymore? Had we really traveled back in time to the 1950s and 60s? I guess anything goes in conspiracy theory land.

I'd laughed when some politician pointed out that "politics ain't beanbag." Maybe not, but it shouldn't be bomb threats and bullet proof vests, either. Something about Toomey's indignation seemed more than a little staged.

I startled when my phone chimed and I saw Percy's name. He quickly gave me a workman-like rundown on the results in South Carolina, telling me where Marie had shown strength, mostly within Charleston and suburban women outside a smattering of other key smaller cities. Dry facts, no emotion. No surprise there. Pierson edged out Marie for the minority vote, meaning Marie's inroads there were modest. He was precise about how the delegate count would shake out. It was a relief to know I'd been right about that. So, being grateful for small blessings, I pointed out to Percy that in reality Marie's investment in the state blunted potential damage. She could legitimately claim she'd lived to fight another day.

But as I listened with another part of me, I heard the canned quality to every word Percy said. He might as well have been spewing his talking points to Chuck Todd or Chris Wallace on their Sunday morning TV shows.

"Percy…Percy," I interrupted at the point he started reciting poll numbers by district and precinct. "I'm not interviewing you. You don't have to spin this. She lost, but not big. The pre-primary polls looked better. The delegate count worked in her favor. I got it."

Percy cleared his throat. "I didn't consider this spin."

Ooh, his voice was tight. I could almost see his jaw clenching and the vein in his temple pulsating. I'd noted that telltale vein before. He was under way more stress than he showed. It was probably fairly hard to pull an A out of good 'ol Professor Novak. "So, what are Steve's thoughts about the outcome?" I asked.

He cleared his throat again. I filed that away as one of his stress responses. Jury consulting involved being a bit of a wizard at interpreting body language, and I considered myself pretty damn good at reading the signs and signals. Meaningful moves aren't obvious and broad; they're mostly split-second and micro. This wasn't the first time Percy gave himself away.

"It's part of the game," Percy said. "Not easy. But we're with Marie in Massachusetts and Vermont today, and we'll have two quick stops in Alabama tomorrow morning and a big rally in Texas tomorrow night."

I jotted that information on a notepad, while I casually remarked, "I suppose the candidates tend to cluster, so I guess Pierson will be in the same locations. And Toomey, too, huh?"

"Why do you ask?" Did I note suspicion in Percy's voice?

"Just going off what I see on TV and from being down in South Carolina." *Where Rick saw your ass at the Toomey rally.*

"Since you ask, Pierson is in California, but we'll cross paths in Texas—I don't think we'll trip over each other." In business mode now, Percy wasn't prone to forgetting I was an employee. "Not sure about Toomey or the other Republicans. The Dems are pretty spread out and some are hoping for a miracle finish."

"I bet the Toomey folks are sick of these threats."

"Oh, yeah." He spoke fast. Then he paused and cleared his throat again. "Like we all are."

"I imagine you know his campaign manager and some of his crew. Seems like a small political world. You probably all end up winding down in the same hotel bars."

"I know a few people—but only from being in the business," he said quickly. "Jeff Hoover's a good guy." He paused. "For a Republican." He allowed himself a snicker and that was all.

Never one to say an extra word, our Percy. Kind of like Steve, who spoke more when he blew up over Bentley and Amanda than at any other time during our exchanges in my hotel room. But I knew from a few remarks Charles Marchand dropped that all these candidates and their crews, both in the office and their campaigns, crossed paths more than any of us lay folks realized. They really did end up having a beer in the same hotel bars in the same cities, usually late at night with their cell phones at the ready. A certain honor code prevailed, too. If someone said a war story was off the record, it was considered a betrayal to talk about it outside the small circle of operatives. Besides, the war stories told from both sides sound remarkably similar. Charles had struck a fairly close friendship with a Republican from Alabama, because that guy lost his wife, too. That's why I wasn't buying Percy's quick dismissal.

We ended our call and I left with the dogs for a fast walk on this freezing cold day. At least it didn't threaten snow or sleet—or our March Midwest special, both. By mid-afternoon I'd made up my mind. I didn't like to bother Wendy on Sundays if I didn't have to. But this time I called her to ask if she could spare Rick on the survey work. She didn't ask the reason. She didn't have to. She understood this was about more than working for Marie's campaign. I can't say Wendy was thrilled, but she'd already started hiring temps from an agency to organize phone banks. The in-house focus group was scheduled for later in the week, anyway.

Then I called Rick. "I'm sending you to Texas."

"O…kay, what's the mission, Boss?"

"It's complicated." I kept my voice neutral, but I admit I was amused by Rick's response. He didn't show surprise, but he had plenty of questions about the heart of it. "Easier to talk about it in person. Book a flight to Houston. Tonight, if you can get one. Let me know whether you're flying out of O'Hare or Midway. I'll meet you there."

Catching my hesitancy to talk on the phone, Rick squelched his curiosity and kept his questions to himself.

Just under five hours later, I pulled my truck into a space in the lot for hourly parking at Terminal Three at O'Hare, where Rick would catch his American flight to Texas. But first we could grab a beer and a burger at a pub on the concourse. Rick was already in a booth with a mug in front of him and reading something on his tablet. One of his fantasy/sci-fi favorites I imagined. Basketball games were on the TVs with the sound muted, but country music filled the place. Rick looked like a casual traveler, but since I'd told him to nix the suit on this trip, I'd expected that. We didn't want him looking like a businessman.

There might have been a time when the two of us would have made easy jokes about our snooping. We had a good sense of each other, Rick and I. Thanks to him, we'd not only overturned Charles Marchand's conviction, we more or less ended Governor Leo Toland's political career by digging up dirt about one of those ugly college incidents that sent shivers up the spines of politicians. In Leo's case, a classmate, a girl he'd not treated well in the first place, died of alcohol poisoning. And the future governor himself had moved the body. Marchand ended up in the wrong place at the wrong time and got roped into staying silent. The secret the two shared. Funny how no one had made a connection between Marchand and Toland, at least until Rick discovered they both attended a small Illinois college few people had heard of.

The Marchand case had built trust between Rick and me inside and outside the work of the firm. Rick still considered himself a video game designer, a creative type. That was probably true, but I saw him as a guy with great instincts, who could look at a bunch of facts and pull together all the odd threads. But then again, he needed that trait to create games, too.

I slid into the seat across from him. "Thanks for doing this."

Pushing his tablet aside, Rick shrugged. "I consider myself on call."

"Good," I said. "I wish I could say for sure what I want. I just know you need to be invisible. Those campaign location maps you've done showing the convergence of campaigns is triggering something."

"For me, too," Rick said, turning his head to scan the restaurant. I'd done the same when I walked in. Chicago is hardly a small town, but I was surprised how often I ran into people I knew in places like airport restaurants.

Rick nervously rubbed his chin. "I've been looking into Steven Novak."

Puzzling. "We're not done with him?"

"No. I'm looking in a different direction." Rick leaned forward, but pulled back fast when the waiter came to the table.

Keeping it simple, I ordered whatever they had on tap, like Rick, and we ordered burger platters. Food hadn't interested me all day, but it did now. Rick's train of thought got my attention, too.

"Uh, let's eat and then walk around," Rick suggested, once again looking around the over half-full restaurant.

"Do you think we're being watched?" I asked.

Rick shook his head. "Not really. But I don't want to take any chances." Keeping his voice low, he ran through a list of possible coincidences. The bomb threats, the still unexplained explosion in Seattle, the mall shooting, the shot through the campaign office window. "Somehow, with the exception of the mall massacre, everything comes back to the Kent, Pierson, and Toomey campaigns. I'll tell you the rest later." He checked his phone. "I'll have thirty minutes to kill." He frowned. "Scratch that. I'll have an hour. I got an update. The flight's delayed."

As if by instinct we both looked outside. Then we laughed. "No snow, no ice," I said, "so it must be something else."

Over the burgers, Rick and I talked about movies and TV series we could stream, an interest we shared. We couldn't get enough of those grisly European crime series with disheveled detectives, the men and the women. Our other common interest was politics.

But when we walked the concourse and stopped to chat by the windows looking out on the runways, Rick confided what was really weighing on his mind.

"It isn't all about Steven Novak," he said, "or even Percy, although there's something off about my cousin." He flashed a pointed look. "There, I said it so you don't have to."

Good. Who wants to raise questions about someone else's relatives? In fact, Percy and Steve made an unlikely pair. Something didn't add up about either one of them. "So? And…"

"I think somebody's got something on Marie?"

"Are you kidding? Marie? What do you mean by somebody and something? Who and what?"

Rick scratched his cheek. "If I knew, boss, I wouldn't be spending your money in Texas," Rick said.

"Good point. Remind me," I joked, "why am I sending you to Texas?"

Rick snickered. "I didn't say all this is unrelated. You know me. I'm looking for clues that lead me to connections that lead to new clues."

Suddenly impatient, I blurted, "Looking for… whatever…on Marie Kent is a little nuts. A waste of time."

With a firm nod, Rick said, "I agree. Based on what we see on the surface, that is. But I think this might be a little more complicated than it looks."

Since Rick was never one for wild conspiracies, just small, logical ones, I trusted him. If he was wrong, that was okay. "If you're looking for my go ahead, take this where you need to."

We stood side-by-side and stared out the window.

When my phone signaled an alert, so did Rick's. Like robots in sync, we both reached into our jacket pockets.

"Holy shit," Rick said. "This changes everything."

I closed my eyes, not wanting the words I was reading to be true.

***

I left Rick at security and broke into a jog to get back to my truck, where I listened to updates on the latest bloody crime. We seemed to be in the grip of something new. And close to home. Like Rick said, it would change everything.

There was nothing random about any of this.

Everything was orchestrated. This time, it was an actual office bombing, more accurately, two. But why? What would motivate anyone to bomb the offices of two candidates polling at less than 10%...well, less than 5%? Neither candidate, our local guy, JoJo Campanella, or Republican Alabama Governor Diana Briggs, had gained any traction with the voters. That was the polite way to put it. They'd likely be dropping out soon, having finally faced reality. Neither had a chance in hell of being the nominee.

JoJo Campanella wasn't well known enough, and to be glib about it, it wasn't his turn. Unless you had over-the-top charisma or pockets full of money, you had to bring a thick résumé to the presidential horse race. As for Diana Briggs, from what I heard, she was despised on both sides of the aisle. It would never be Diana's turn, because bigger fish in the pond held all the tickets.

I detoured off the highway and headed to the northwest side of the city to take a look at Campanella's campaign office, or what was left of it. A sea of red, white, and blue flashing lights came from dozens of cruisers. Firetrucks and ambulances blocked access to the street. Two ambulances screamed behind me as they headed to the scene. I pulled over to let them pass. Three were already in front of the office in the middle of the commercial street. Mayhem.

I stopped my truck down the block, but I could spot firefighters in full gear clustered in front of the burned out storefronts. One carried a woman out of the rubble and another led two people slowly to the waiting ambulance. Walking wounded. A cynical thought. Another siren muffled the sounds of firefighters barking orders, shouts for help in one spot on the sidewalk and another from the street. Paramedics were rushing in and out. How many dead, I wondered.

I moved the truck and willed myself to fit into a barely legal spot on a side street. With the wind blowing hard, I pulled on my gloves and turned up my jacket collar as I approached the edge of the crowd. But I was still cold. I didn't want to be noticed if I could help it, especially since I had no reason to be here other than idle curiosity. Well, not exactly idle, considering what was going on.

I guesstimated that about 100 or so people were hanging out on the fringes of the crowd. I eavesdropped on a couple standing near me. They were chatting with other bystanders, who like them, had been in the Italian restaurant next door to the headquarters when the explosion blew through the wall in the office and into anyone in its path working in the kitchen and the servers' stations. The diners in the front of the restaurant were able to rush out the front door to the street. Now with their phones in hand they were waiting to see how many others weren't as lucky. My phone was telling me at least six were killed, four known injured, and two of the deaths occurred in the restaurant. The other bystanders were probably getting the same information from their alerts.

I scanned the crowd, which was being pushed way back from the street. I was about ready to walk away, knowing I'd get faster updates on the cable networks. At least I'd be warmer while I heard the bad news. I was beginning to feel guilty about Maude and Quigs at home and needing to go outside. I swear I was *always* worried about those dogs no matter what was going on.

Deep in my own thoughts, the sound of my name came out of nowhere. I turned quickly, but damn it, I'd tried not to call attention to myself. Well, well, if it wasn't Lourdes Ponce. Blogger, tweeter extraordinaire, Lourdes now had a regular gig with *Pol-alert*. It was a relatively new online news source giving *Politico* and *Huffington Post* a run for their money by sending out up-to-the minute stories even faster—and even more abbreviated. Coincidentally, Lourdes also had a baby now named Maddie. The baby wasn't with her that night, but Lourdes occasionally came to mundane press conferences with her little Maddie safely tucked in a pouch. In fact, her tweets were often accompanied by photos of that kid on Instagram. She couldn't help herself.

I stopped and waved. I had no choice but to stay put while she weaved her way through the crowd and got to me. "Hey, Matt, what brings you here?"

I shrugged. "Saw the Google alert. I was in the neighborhood." In the neighborhood? Doing what? "Visiting friends." That made sense, even if it was a lie.

I liked Lourdes well enough, but she was a dyed in the wool gossip journalist. She found ways to mention people as if there was some significance to running into them in various places. Oh, why was the mayor's top aide in Macy's? Or wheeling a cart in Trader Joe's? Why was a certain alderman talking with a certain alderwoman in Grant Park? On the other hand, her tweets were potentially powerful. Tweets about a fundraising event became evidence used *against* Charles Marchand, as if a fairly public argument led to a conclusion that Charles must have murdered Sandra. I didn't want to be egotistical about it, but ever since that high profile trial, I was one Chicagoan who turned up now and again in Lourdes' twitter feed. This political crime scene was likely worthy of a mention.

"I suppose I don't need to ask you why you're here," I said, "but I imagine you never expected something like this on an ordinary Sunday night in February."

"No," she said, looking at the scene. Even from a distance, the building was a hideous wreck, bodies still not removed. Carnage, really, like a war zone. "I just filed a preliminary story. I'll update it through the night. Sam is with the baby."

We both stared at rubble. Then Lourdes spun around to look at me and in a surprisingly confrontational way.

"Were you expecting anything like this during this cycle?" she demanded.

The election cycle, she meant. I had to say no. Play

dumb. She had no reason to speculate that I had any stake in the primaries, let alone a fledgling role. "No, did you?" That was the solution. Turn the question back on her.

"I didn't last year, but I do now. We've seen bomb threats and random explosions. A mass shooting that at the very least was racially motivated and on the eve of the South Carolina primary."

"True, but that horrible mall massacre was probably not related," I said, as if I knew that to be a fact.

Lourdes cast a skeptical glance my way. "Really? I'm not so sure."

Interesting. Had the two of us picked up the same scent?

"Oh? What are you hearing?" I asked.

"Buzz."

I snickered. "C'mon Lourdes, you always hear buzz. That's your job."

She pressed her lips together and looked away. I let the silence hang in the air. Finally, she said, "This is different."

"Oh? How?"

Her very expressive face sent a message tinged with suspicion. "Who's the journalist here? What's with the questions?"

"Why wouldn't I throw out some questions? You're the one in the know," I said, only a little sarcastically.

She scoffed. "Dammit, I don't know anything about it, not really." She let out a discouraged sigh.

I knew that cost her. In her position, she'd hate admitting she was in the same boat as everyone else and didn't have inside knowledge about what was happening within our political system. Suddenly, another siren screamed. An ambulance and the cruiser following it down the street brought our meaningless banter to an end. She wasn't giving me information, and I wasn't revealing why I cared to know.

"I gotta go," Lourdes said, staring at her phone. "I need to get to the hospital. I'll be sending out updates."

"I'll be looking for 'em." I was just happy to get a quick escape. I didn't know her well, but I knew she had the ability to gather information and selectively spill it out in dribs and drabs. She also liked to tease readers with questions. I was 80% certain she was going to tweet about seeing me, even though I wasn't a Chicago star of anything. She'd phrase it in a way that invited the questions about why I was there, which would then lead her followers to think, "Who's he?"

"Are you headed there, too?" Lourdes asked.

"Uh, no. I'm going home." I fought back the urge to ask why she wanted to know. Why would she think I'd head to the hospital?

Lourdes didn't respond but glanced down at her phone. "Bye, then," she said. "See you around." She didn't simply hurry through the crowd. She rushed away and broke into a jog when she freed herself from the cluster of people on the edge at the same time a fourth ambulance and cruiser went by and a fifth was right behind.

All I could think of was the number of bodies turning up. Despite it being a Sunday night, JoJo Campanella's headquarters had been busy. Phone banking maybe? Bagging up campaign literature for an upcoming mail drop? Organizing campaign flyers was typically a job for the older volunteers, not the young energetic ones who could knock on doors.

I got to my truck and again looked for messages. Something had driven Lourdes away fast. Sure enough, the police had taken a young guy into custody. A twenty-year-old shaggy-haired white guy wearing camouflage. What a cliché. The lawyer in me bristled. Being a walking cliché wasn't the same as committing a crime. I was immediately suspicious of this quick arrest.

Damn it. If Lourdes hadn't rushed away from the crime scene, I'd have headed to police or FBI headquarters and hung out a while. See where the bank of microphones was set up and wait for updates.

But I didn't want to run to Lourdes. I had a feeling she wasn't headed to the hospital. She was on her way to wait for the police presser. She and every other reporter in town.

Idle curiosity might have worked as an excuse as long as I'd happened to be in the neighborhood, but hauling my ass downtown to the press conferences would only trigger questions. Besides, I could watch it on TV.

What exactly was I waiting to hear? I couldn't have explained it. In any case, I went home to listen to the same news everyone else had access to. I'd pay extra attention to Lourdes' feed. I opened my front door prepared to take the dogs out for a quick walk. No wonder I loved them. Who else would jump for joy at the mere sound of my footsteps? My key in the lock was enough to create a frenzy of activity. They had no guile, no pride. Their tails went wild. I let them jump all over me and when their walking and sniffing the sidewalk was over, they curled up with me on the couch while I turned on the TV.

Split screen, pretty common right now. Two press conferences were underway. One I expected, one not.

Chapter Nine

"I see no path to the nomination now," Alabama Governor Diana Briggs said. "As for recent events, my campaign was lucky this time. But JoJo Campanella's staff wasn't as fortunate. It was an evil act. Pure and simple."

So, the bombers got their way. Briggs dropped out of the race. I felt some rage on her behalf, nasty piece of work or not. Only last week, she refused to delay an execution even in the wake of new and possibly exculpatory evidence. That's the biggest, most significant reason I loathed her. Her action reminded me of Joey Haskell, my innocent client.

Not only did I lose Joey to execution, I'd permanently lost a piece of myself. For a couple of years I suffered from alternating lack of sleep and when my body finally succumbed, I startled awake from crazed nightmares. I lived on antacids, but fortunately my need for them lessened over time. Things like mass shootings and campaign office bombings brought back some of the same tension—even anxiety—and I'd started reached for the antacids again. Overall, though, just like the cliché, time helped me get over what I perceived as my failure to save Joey. Eventually, I'd adjusted, the word I used to describe the way I learned to live without that small part of me that died with Joey. The rest of me finally adapted to the gap left behind.

I'd sworn off criminal law for years and kept that promise to myself up until the Charles Marchand case. Winning that one—or, I should say watching the reversal of a guilty verdict—pushed me around a corner and back into the fray of the world in which I'd once thrived. My jury work still was mostly for civil cases, but I'd allowed a criminal case or two in the door.

If I pushed my disdain for Briggs out of the way, though, I could empathize. She was a longshot, her campaign marginal, and maybe she really hoped to be the VP pick, but no matter what, she'd put herself out there. Her headquarters was empty when the bomb went off. A closed insurance office was a building away. No one got hurt, let alone died. The office was a shell, rubble. Luckier than JoJo, Diana had not one casualty on her conscience from this travesty.

Reporters shot questions at Briggs, some implying she was giving into terrorists. Or, in that post-9/11 phrase, "letting the terrorists win." Only this time, it was domestic terrorists.

Sounding more like a Democrat than an anti-immigration Republican, which is the foundation she'd cynically used to advance her career in politics, Briggs's voice rang out like a preacher railing against hate. "That's nonsense. I won't entertain it as a serious question."

"Is this a decision you would have been forced to make anyway?" a reporter from Buzz Feed demanded.

Ooh, cheap shot. Still in single digits, she didn't need her face rubbed in her failed campaign.

"That remained to be seen," Diana said, pushing her hair back with her fingers, and not cracking a smile. "We've had a mere handful of primaries. As I said, though, based on both public and internal polling, I believe it's time to coalesce around a candidate who can win in the fall and get the country back on track. We need to recover from the last eight years."

This was the part that galled me. The stats on the country's progress in the last two terms didn't match the other party's rhetoric. People were always talking about getting back on track, as if anyone could define that with anything other than the most biased and partisan terms.

"Do you think your message subtly conveyed approval of divisive rhetoric?"

I winced, bracing for her to blurt out a condemnation of the question asked by a guy I knew to be a conservative commentator. I expected her to lash out at the journalist and the whole profession. I waited for "how dare you?" indignation.

It never came. Instead, she shook her head and said, "I've called on everyone involved in politics to cool our language. I include myself in that." She paused. "We had two dozen people killed in a mall last week. By all indications it was a racially motivated crime. We've had death threats and bomb threats. Now we had two actual bombings. So far, ten deaths from tonight's melee. This has to stop." She paused a second or two before adding, "And I don't mean by passing empty gun laws that don't have a prayer of stopping violence."

Not letting the moment hang in the air, another reporter shouted, "Should JoJo Campanella drop out of the race?"

I had to admire the withering look Briggs shot the reporter's way. "Why would you ask me such a trivial question at a time like this, that's none of my business in the first place? Go talk to JoJo."

With that, her aide stepped up and called the press conference over.

I couldn't say I blamed the aide. I'd had reporters shout at me that way, too. It was frustrating. And I more or less liked journalists and, truthfully, they liked me back. I knew they were doing their jobs. If information was going out to the public, I wanted it to be as accurate as possible. But, sometimes a reporter's timing could be pitifully off.

"What do you think?" I asked the dogs. I scratched necks and jowls and made cooing baby noises at them.

113

All to distract myself from the broken face of JoJo Campanella. His image now filled one side of the screen. The press conference at the hospital filled the other. Eleven dead, fourteen wounded. Man, that was a deadly bomb. Most victims were on the young side.

JoJo Campanella had missed being in his headquarters when the bomb went off by no more than twenty minutes. He'd done a round of interviews and then visited the office with his wife and little kids to give the volunteers a pep talk. Then he'd gone home, but he was making his statement in the street in front of the rubble of what had been his headquarters. The restaurant was almost as damaged as JoJo's storefront office.

I opened my iPad and looked at the intersections on Rick's maps. According to Rick, Campanella was scheduled for an event in San Antonio the next morning. He was then due to fly to Fort Worth and on to Oklahoma for a primary day appearance. All so futile. Maybe Briggs wouldn't say so, but I would. JoJo should take himself out of the line of fire. Shut the campaign offices—not that he had many across the country, anyway.

If Rick knew the whereabouts of all the candidates in both parties, then the information was at least semi-public through campaign announcements and press releases. JoJo's office was bombed when it was full of volunteers, and Diana Briggs was in the Governor's mansion in Montgomery and her Huntsville office was dark. JoJo had plans to be in Texas on Monday, like most all the candidates of both parties.

Did the bomber know Diana's office would be dark? If mayhem and disruption was the point, why not wait until Diana was in the office, or her troupe of volunteers had gathered? Was the intent to kill? To scare? Was the intent to discourage voters from going to the polls? If the intent was to scare only, then why bomb Campanella's office when it was full, but spare Governor Briggs?

I didn't believe this was the work of anarchists who dismissed both sides as part of the corrupt political class. Ironically, the anarchists weren't so well organized. It took significant planning and subterfuge to pull off simultaneous incidents like this. No, for the moment, this seemed much more personal than random anarchist violence. This was terrorism and maybe treason on this country. I made notes of the states affected, the names of the politicians. Who was threatened, and where? So far, one campaign dropout traced directly back to the bombing. A candidate who had little influence on the race, let alone win it.

Restless, I made myself a drink, two shots of bourbon poured over ice. It was a bourbon kind of night. I settled on the couch again, tablet open, phone at the ready, TV on. Something familiar settled over me as I sat in my multimedia world. Would I sleep at all?

***

Wendy and Janet were in a mood. Dark and dreary and a little suspicious. It happened now and again, and I knew it the second I walked through the door. I could feel it in the heavy atmosphere that hung over the office like a blanket. Wendy would tell me our office was crawling—well, not literally—with the wrong kind of ions. The air was charged with positive ions, which were bad. If we wanted to lift the mood, we needed negative ions floating around. I think that's how it went.

Ions or not, I wasn't in the best spirits on this early March day, dark and dreary like my mood. Janet, in her blunt way, greeted me with a cool nod before turning her attention to Maude and Quigs. Like the trained dogs they were, they ran from me to Janet, where they sat like little goody-two-shoes pups waiting for Janet to give them each a treat. This wasn't a habit I'd encouraged, but I didn't have the heart to change it.

Not so much for the dogs, but for Janet.

Coming out of her office, Wendy looked close to six-feet tall in her completely impractical purple boots with ridiculously spindly heels. She loved them. But why? She leaned against the wall and crossed one ankle over the other, for balance I assumed. Oh, hell, she folded her arms across her chest. I knew the stance.

"I'm going to need a couple of hours off later in the week," Wendy said, "for a *funeral*. I went to school with a campaign volunteer at JoJo's office. He died in that blast."

I closed my eyes as if that would make me not hear the news. "I'm so sorry, Wendy. Of course, take whatever time you need." It was indisputable that Wendy was a networker extraordinaire. She knew so many people in town and in all the burbs of Cook County. Unlike most of us, she'd actually kept up with her high school classmates.

"Yeah, well, we don't have much time around here. Rick says he's off 'on assignment', like he's a damn journalist now. You're not exactly around. Meanwhile, Marie Kent is running neck and neck…"

"I'm here now," I said, not allowing my annoyance seep into my tone. Or, maybe it was the guilt talking. "What do you need right now?"

"First, of all, you have a bunch of calls. Your head might be in the election, but Nick Kachiroubas called about his case's mirror jury." Wendy gave me a long look.

"That's handled, Wendy. You and I finished the recruitment." I was saying things that didn't need to be discussed, at least not under normal times. "We're set to go at the end of the week."

"I know, Matt, but he was just checking in."

That was Wendy's way of reminding me, as if it were possible I'd forget, we could have jury selection begin in a few days. "Nick is still hoping to settle. I acknowledged his text a few minutes ago in my truck."

"You workin' from your truck these days, kinda like

workin' from your home away from home away from office?" Janet teased me in her folksy way.

"You gotta problem with that?" I teased back. Maybe we could lighten the mood.

"Not with that. If I got a problem with something, it's you and your *other* sidekick snooping around campaigns. You think that didn't grab my attention."

Almost as if we were afraid the walls had ears, Wendy and I tapped our mouths with our index finger to shush Janet. I gestured to have them follow me into the conference room. Maude and Quigs followed the two women so our staff was complete. Well, almost. We weren't really complete without Rick.

I shut the conference room door and shook my head. "I'm getting a little paranoid, I guess. What with all that's going on."

"This election is getting more dangerous every day," Janet said, no trace of teasing in her tone now. "I don't like it."

"Me, neither," Wendy said in a firm tone, "but we're committed to Marie Kent." Wendy gave a quick rundown on how effective the preliminary data appeared to be in the Super Tuesday primaries. "They targeted ads to certain key spots, where no one else was running ads and now she's neck and neck with Pierson in the final polls. We think Marie will continue to poll well with women, among other groups."

"She's almost even," I added. Marie was still a little behind in delegate counts, and how she did in the next group of primaries was going to either keep her going or knock her out of the race for delegates. Meanwhile, Toomey still dominated the Republican side. No one was getting close to him. There was almost a cult-like following of supporters that nothing could break apart.

"Can you tell us what you're looking for, Matt? Why is Rick out on the road?" Wendy pointed to the blank TV screen. "That bombing we had yesterday was no joke. Janet and I were watching the coverage when we first came in and grabbed our coffee, but we forced ourselves to turn it off. It's so, so close to home."

What to say? Rick and I weren't sure what we were looking for. Did I want to tell her that I didn't trust Steven Novak, and Percy was a little strange? Nope. And I wasn't ready to share the campaign maps that may or may not mean anything.

"Rick is on the ground," I said, "because we wanted to get a feel for Marie's crowds. Who shows up and how committed are they? Who will follow through and actually show up and vote, plus what strategies the campaign can use to reach them?" I paused and thought about Beaufort. "When people go to rallies and town halls this early in the primaries they may be shopping for candidates. Maybe they haven't made up their minds."

"So, what we're doing here in the office is the more scientific end?" Wendy asked the question in a flat tone, but eyed me with suspicion. She knew something else was going on.

Janet knew, too, but didn't say anything. At least not about what she probably considered some mysterious trips.

"Jeff Hoover, Steven Novak, David Scheffler—nothing but a bunch of old white guys running a bunch of white guy campaigns...except for Marie Kent." That was Janet's unvarnished take on the state of the race.

"Don't forget Alice Bresloff," Wendy teased. "The *youngish* white woman running Diana Briggs's ill-fated mess."

"Ran, as in past tense. And Al is young in years, maybe," I interjected, "but in spirit, Alice Bresloff is just like the old white guys."

The two stared at me. It was written all over their faces. They each had a sarcastic remark waiting in the wings.

"Okay, okay, I know what you're thinking." I let my smirk linger. "But no matter how old I get, I will never be as stuck in my ways and crotchety as those guys."

"That's one piece of good news today," Janet said.

"On a serious note," Wendy said, "why is it so many of this cycle's campaigns have these older men running them? It looks like a full employment program for old pols. Maybe this year is their swan song?"

I shrugged, unable to give her an answer. Then I laughed out loud. "No matter who is running them, all presidential campaigns are mostly unsuccessful. The dropout rate is likely to take a steep climb after tomorrow's primaries. These are like the playoffs in sports. A process of elimination. Each primary is its own tournament."

When the office phone rang, Janet turned to pick up the call on the phone on the credenza. A couple of seconds later she said, "Hey Matt, Cooper Julien's on line 1."

Coop…nosing out a story, no doubt. "I'll take it in here."

Wendy and Janet left and I greeted Coop. I liked to think I was among a select few who called him by that nickname. He had a way of making people feel like having his good opinion made us part of an elite group. On the older end of TV journalists, Coop had one of the longest running legal shows on cable. I used to be one of his regular guests, before I lost Joey Haskell's case, that is. But Coop had played a key role in uncovering some of the dirt on Governor Toland for the Marchand case.

"Hey, Coop, it's been—"

"No time for small talk, Matt, I'm in a rush," Coop said in a gruff, yet refined voice.

"Okay, what's up?"

"I want to know why your man is following candidates around. First, South Carolina and now Texas."

"My man?" Had we dropped into a British colonial drama?

"You know exactly who I mean," Coop said.

"C'mon Coop, Rick has lots of clients."

Exaggeration, but not a lie.

Coop scoffed, long and loud. "Do you take me for a complete fool?"

"No, of course not," I responded in exaggerated resignation. Hmm…now he had me curious about what tidbits he'd come across. "Okay, let me put it this way, Coop, why do you ask?"

Coop was famous for seeing things others didn't. He was a lot like Rick that way.

"Because I've seen Rick, but he hasn't seen me. He slipped in and out of Toomey's smallish rally in Beaufort. I just saw him in Dallas hanging out on the edge of the Kent rally—impressive gathering, I might add." Coop spoke in a matter-of-fact way, not his normal tone.

"Why were you there? Are you broadcasting from Dallas tonight?"

"I am, and I'll be up in L.A. tomorrow. The usual Super Tuesday fare."

"You've been doing some traveling this campaign season, huh?" How much? It was only luck that he hadn't seen me slinking down the cobblestone streets of Beaufort.

A little less matter-of-fact now, Coop said, "But I'm less interested in the politics than some other things."

I grunted in frustration. "Don't be coy, Coop. What are you watching?"

"Shootings and bombings. *Patterns…connections.*"

Now he really sounded like Rick, making connections and studying data for patterns. And Coop wasn't being especially cryptic, at least not to my ears. No wonder we got along so well. We were noticing things along the same lines. I responded with a quick, "Tell me more."

Coop started with the standard questions asked by anyone looking for coincidences and patterns. He was steering his queries toward a possible connection between the primary in South Carolina and the mall shooting. And JoJo's headquarters. Was the shooting part of scaring people enough they wouldn't venture out to vote?

"I thought of that, Coop, but the numbers don't bear it out. We don't know about Illinois, yet, but looking at past primaries and all that, if anything, it brought out the 'no one will intimidate me' voters."

"I still filed it away to be watched. But I wonder why anyone would bother to knock out Briggs and your local guy Campanella from the race. The campaign grave diggers had already marked the plot for those two."

I hooted at that. "So tactful. But true. I asked myself the same thing."

"Who benefits from them being out of the race, Matt?"

"I'm not sure. What do you think, Coop?"

"It's neither here nor there to Toomey. Doesn't hurt a bit. But what about Senator Kent? Where are Campanella's voters going?"

"Most of the professionals and the analysts on TV are calling it a draw. They could as easily go to Pierson as Kent, maybe a 50-50 split."

"That sounds like what they say when they don't have the clue but don't want to admit it. Hmm... you could argue that, but it remains to be seen. The delegate race is close." Coop cleared his throat. "What do you know about Marie Kent?"

This was getting too close for comfort. Could Coop have figured out that my firm was working for Kent? Emphasis on *for her,* not *with her.*

I swallowed hard. "I know she's declared by all as squeaky clean and if you're asking me the question, you must know something I don't." This was making me jittery. Coop wasn't wrong very often. "You're not linking her to the campaign threats and bombings, are you?"

"No, no, of course not," Coop said in a raspy voice. "I need to stop talking. I have to go. By the way, I'll be broadcasting from Illinois in a couple of weeks."

"In Chicago?"

"The network prefers Springfield actually. More of an America's Heartland atmosphere and a distinction from everyone else. Maybe you can come down and join me for dinner. So much to talk about."

What the hell? What didn't we know about Marie Kent?

Chapter Ten

"The way you're acting right now, I'm still watching for your cloak and on the edge of my seat waiting for you to pull out the dagger," Rick said as we wandered down one of the paved paths toward the water. We'd spoken a lot about cloak and dagger tactics in the last few weeks. "And why this detour on a freezing cold March day? Are you keeping secrets from Wendy? And Janet?"

"That's exactly what *we're* doing," I said. I'd waited to tell Rick about Coop's call until Rick and I had polished off Ann Sather's pancake platters and we were more or less isolated in the park. Maybe I was being over-the-top careful but running into Lourdes had made me double down on caution.

"Coop saw you," I said, "but his suspicions started before that. He's like us. He's convinced that everything that's happened, all the chaos, is probably way bigger than we thought. Like you, he's big into patterns and connections."

I'd wanted this meeting to start away from the office. But did I really *believe* we were being watched? Not really, but Coop spooked me. Rick had caught on when he'd called to say he was back and made remarks about so much going on. Exciting campaign and all that.

This year, March's Super Tuesday had done its usual job of filtering out the candidates viable enough to stay in and had a prayer of raising money. By the next morning a few marginal candidates dropped out, having made no traction, none, from the sixteen states in this cycle's big bundle of prizes.

Percy was jubilant over Kent's performance. Over the phone, he went on for a good long while about it. She'd picked up the states she had in the bag, her home state of Oregon, of course, but she'd come in big in Washington and a couple of Western states, whose delegates were small in number but added up enough to narrow the delegate gap. "We've got time," Percy had said, "to gain delegates, especially now when the difference is only nineteen. And lots of big states to go."

Now, talking to Rick face to face, I told him that according to Percy, Super Tuesday was a huge success.

Rick agreed they had to be thrilled. "But Coop must suspect whatever is going on is bigger than an old frat boy or even a professional bond between Percy and Toomey's guy, Jeff Hoover. And maybe even bigger than our hometown candidate's campaign ending in a total tragedy."

"One of Wendy's friends was one of the casualties."

Rick's eyebrows shot up in surprise. "Fuuuck... I wish you were kidding."

"Me, too. Now I wish we hadn't gone to South Carolina and you hadn't seen Percy with Jeff. And now again in Texas."

Rick had let that drop in an earlier conversation before I changed the subject. I was almost 100% certain we weren't being watched or bugged, but I was careful anyway.

"See what I mean by chaos?" I asked rhetorically. "It's hard to know where to start sifting through everything?"

"Well, for starters, I'm creating more data banks," Rick said, "if you know what I mean. I've got a chart dedicated to my dear ol' cousin Percy and his known contacts with Jeff Hoover. I also have dates and times for all the bomb threats called into campaigns and law enforcement, and, of course, for the ones that someone made good on."

I stopped walking and tugged on the leashes to stop the dogs. "Great idea—by now, you're keeping track of meetings here, sightings there, and intersections across the aisle. Percy and Jeff started that."

Rick squatted down and gave each dog a pat and beard scratch. "I don't have a clue what it all means. Maybe nothing." When he stood, he looked down at both dogs, who were in turn gazing at him through adoring eyes. "I need to get myself one of those."

"They're fun, but can you manage it when your boss sends you out of town on a moment's notice?" I was all for Rick rescuing a dog, but they were a lifestyle, more or less. I had to consider Maude and Quigs in almost everything I did, from going out to dinner to taking cases that involved a lot of travel.

"How do you handle it?"

"A woman in my building is a dog and cat-sitter and on-call dog-walker for a bunch of us. If I'm going to be late, I call Samantha Briscoe and she takes them out. If I need to leave town in a hurry, I leave them with her for however long it is. She's a little older and it's how she brings in extra money. Maude and Quigs adore her."

Rick's gaze lingered on the dogs, but not for long. "Are you sending me somewhere now?"

"Not right now, but Coop led me to something. I believe he did it on purpose. He asked me how well I know Marie. It was like a challenge."

"And you didn't have a great answer, did you?" Rick shot back.

"No. To be honest, I was counting on the typical press vetting and other campaigns' oppo research to have it covered. I mean, Marie announced a year ago. She's been a serious contender all along. Whatever embarrassing audio or video—or rumors—that exist on her was likely already out there."

"I'll dig. But what are you thinking? An affair.

College cheating? Plagiarism?"

"All of the above. Might as well include them. Hell, include her husband in the search, too." I looked at Rick. "I wonder if Coop was trying to lead us to him without spelling it out."

"Why would Coop do that?" Rick asked, clearly annoyed at the notion of any information deliberately withheld.

"Lots of reasons," I responded as I started walking again. "He may not trust the accuracy of what he hears from his own sources. Dropping hints to us gives him a way to verify what he's heard. He's had to make very few retractions or apologies over the years." I came to an abrupt halt and checked the direction of my own thoughts. "I still can't believe this. In normal times, I wouldn't be snooping around into a political candidate's background. But then again, my firm wouldn't be secretly working on a political campaign."

"And Coop's suspicions were fed when he saw me hanging out in Texas?" Rick asked.

"He recognized you from a piece in the paper," I said nodding. "The one after the Marchand case." I'd second guessed myself about letting an Illinois business journalist profile my firm after the case, but because Rick had made the connections that unraveled the guilty verdict, it made a good story. The public had to recognize the rush to judgment that occurred when Charles Marchand was so quickly charged with murdering his wife—and quickly convicted. Turned out it wasn't a murder at all, but a natural death caused by a rare heart condition.

Rick nodded. "I'll hang out in the conference room, me and my computer, that is. I hope I don't find anything that justifies Coop's curiosity."

"I get it—we want a worry-free past." I laughed, knowing what Rick was going to say next.

"Not a chance in hell of that. With public people, especially politicians and celebrities, angels are so rare I can't think of anyone off the top of my head. And

Marie falls into the category of celebrity politicians. Think of the following of women she has." Rick's tone brightened when he added, "She could break a huge glass ceiling once and for all."

"Or break a bunch of hearts," I countered. Objectively, gender was the difference between Pierson and Kent. Their policies were practically identical, varying only slightly around the edges. Kent inspired people, though, where Pierson was the safer choice. That was the perception, anyway.

Rick and I drove back to the office. I stood at the reception desk to read through a few messages. Rick waved to Wendy and went into the conference room. Almost in one smooth action, he opened his computer and turned on the TV.

"Wendy!" I called out. "I need to see you in the conference room."

"Got it." A couple of keystrokes later, she was out of her chair and following me inside and around the long table. I looked back at Janet and nodded to the dogs.

"I can tell something big is going on," Janet said. "I got the dogs, Matt. Don't worry about 'em. I'll let them gorge on treats. They won't miss you at all."

I gave her a long-suffering look and closed the door.

"I've made up my mind," I said, glancing at Rick. "I want Wendy in the loop on all this…whatever this turns out to be."

Rick grinned at Wendy whose attention was split between the TV and Rick. "Fine by me."

"Matt, isn't that Stephanie Rungee?" Wendy asked. "She's with the center that tracks hate groups."

"It is." I unmuted the sound to hear what one of my favorite law school professors had to say.

The reporter interviewing Rungee, or Steph, as I began calling her once I'd graduated, was the network's senior legal analyst, Gryphon Finn. She had a lot of leeway on choosing her guests. They didn't have to fit into neat little ideological boxes and she wanted independence. No pressure to say what other people, including producers and network execs, wanted to hear.

"From what I understand, you're convinced a link exists between the shooter in the South Carolina mall and the political violence taking place," Gryphon said. "You've suggested the bombing in Chicago is connected to some of the other threats."

"That's correct," Steph said, "direct or indirect. At the center, we've tracked bomb threats, actual bombings, and racially motivated mass shootings that we can all see have scarred our electoral process." Stephanie's hands were gesturing in rhythm with her words, leaning forward in the chair for emphasis. "We believe the South Carolina shooting and the bombing in Chicago are part of a well-planned effort to intimidate voters."

"Are you blaming one party over the other, Dr. Rungee?"

"This is beyond party politics for sure," Stephanie said, an obligatory attempt to be even-handed. "However, the voter intimidation element tends to affect certain populations more than others, and as we saw with the Campanella campaign office incident. Representative Campanella was appealing to younger voters. Indeed, the majority of victims of that office bombing were under age forty, including those killed or injured in the restaurant next to the office, also popular with young people."

"You see this as an important factor, then, in this round of political chaos?" Gryphon asked.

"I do. It hasn't been widely reported, but it's part of the statistical information we're tracking here at the Center, so age may be one factor." Steph held up her hand to indicate a pause. "On the other hand, we must allow for the possibility the demographic breakdown is coincidental."

My gut spoke loud and clear, only not through the burning acid making an appearance, but in the sudden uneasy churning. Coop was seldom wrong, and my former professor had a pretty good track record, too.

The interview ended, but I still stared at the screen.

"She has such cool hair," Wendy said with a wistful sigh.

Stephanie, probably well over seventy by now, could pull off the thick halo of long white wavy hair, blond at one time, but for as long as I'd known her, it hung past her shoulders. And she was always holding a chocolate bar in her hands. I smiled thinking of the way she proudly walked around campus in loose, flowing clothes, reminiscent of the hippie era. Quite the contrast with the buttoned up suits so many women lawyers wore today. Stephanie could wear jeans and T-shirt and still be a presence. She only had to enter a room, even with her signature chocolate in hand, to command attention. Plus, even all those years ago, she'd been focused on the rise of hate.

"She's probably right," Rick said, glancing up at me.

"I know. And I hate it."

***

I groaned. Sure enough Lourdes couldn't resist.

> …looks like chgons stand together over the tragedy at campanella's headquarters. hearts breaking over this. I visited the site on the nite it occurred. witnessed the carnage. I wasn't alone. Matt Barlow, attorney and jury consultant in our midst was there as well…he's seen it all… and now this.

Why, Lourdes, why? That tweet was about a lot of nothing.

It was a relief when Janet told me my client was on the phone, I went into my office, hoping for good news. The client was Nick Kachiroubas, who, regardless of his name, I like to tease about coming from a tiny village in the North of Sweden, knowing he came from a small town in Northern Minnesota. A place with the reputation of being the coldest place in the continental U.S. Lucky him. He checked in often to see how his research project was coming along.

"Watcha got? Good news, Nick?" I asked the question with a hopeful lilt in my voice.

"The best news, my friend. We settled. Thanks to a fine piece of reporting in the *Minneapolis Star*. Apparently, the company decided it would be cheaper to settle the suit rather than have any more bad PR about the lax safety standards in meat packing," Nick said with a chuckle. "Turns out consumers like the people who butcher their meat to stay alive and well on the job."

"Aw, really, Nick? Even those tough Minnesotans?"

"*Especially* tough but very civilized Minnesotans." Nick let out a hearty laugh. "It was a good settlement, too. I'll send you the details, you'll send me the invoice. And by the way, I've decided journalism really is a noble profession sometimes."

"I agree." I was half listening and half thinking about Stephanie Rungee's interview, where Gryphon created the path to get important information out.

"The series of three articles exposed the 57 safety violations in the last five years and the way Tomasulo Meatpacking got around them." Nick laughed again. "But then, you already knew that."

I knew that inside and out. Tomasulo was not likely to win the good corporate citizen award. I had my own reasons to be relieved the case settled. Not that I didn't love the challenge of jury selection. No matter how much research we did, there were trade-offs and educated guesses. The pressure to make good decisions never went away during any phase of a case. In a water poisoning case that involved suppressed data, I had to ask myself if the middle-aged-gun-owning-veteran was really a better choice than the older guy with a bunch of grandchildren. That grandpa leaned a little toward a "tough it out" attitude. He thought the whole country was getting a little soft. In that case, we chose the vet—turned out he had a thing about powerful people hiding the truth.

So, one part of me had been eager to head to Minneapolis, while another was raring to get on the campaign trail, figuratively for sure, but maybe literally, too.

When I went back to the conference room, Rick nodded at the TV. "Is this our new normal? The TV stays on, but muted." He smiled sarcastically. "Oh, and Lourdes tells the world she saw you somewhere. Does that pass for news?"

I shrugged. "Apparently. I was hoping she'd resist the urge to mention bumping into me. It wasn't like it was yesterday, either. We can unmute it if you want to," I said, looking at Wendy, too. "I'll be honest with you. I can't turn it off. Too much has happened lately. I want to see it as it happens, as much as possible, anyway. Maybe I can't shut my mind down right now. It's like I'm always looking for connections."

Rick smirked sheepishly. "Blame it on me. I like keeping an eye on the news. Whole lot of shit is going down, and I don't plan on missing the thud of the next shoe dropping."

Wendy opened her mouth as if to speak, but stopped abruptly and leaned across the table to pick up the remote and unmute the TV. I knew why. The breaking news banner indicated a press conference outside the Federal building downtown. She probably also wanted to offer her two cents about Lourdes, not her favorite person. Wendy liked gossip, but not so much the people who started rumors.

"Maybe they have something on the bombing," Rick offered.

"I hope so," Wendy said, "I'm getting sick of the crazies blaming everyone from Al-Qaeda to ISIS for killing all those people."

We stayed silent, while JoJo Campanella himself announced that two of the injured were released and on their way home and one had not survived. Good for Campanella. I didn't like being so crass, but he was racking up points in the good will column. He was a standup guy. Chicagoans and people across the country would credit him for not slinking away. I could almost write the newspaper story about the way he honored his young staff and volunteers. He and his family missed the bombing by less than an hour. JoJo thanked all the right people, including law enforcement and showed his concern for the restaurant owner and patrons before turning over the mic.

The FBI spokeswoman said that information had leaked that the same kind of explosives were found in the South Carolina mall shooter's apartment and in Campanella's campaign office. They were homemade devices, she said, not exactly bombs in the technical sense, but they could do a lot of damage.

"Big news," Rick said with a groan. "The conspiracy websites are filled with that meaningless tidbit."

"We can confirm this information is accurate," the spokeswoman said. "However, it's also true—and we won't name the substances—that these are the most common materials used to construct homemade explosive devices."

She was good, this FBI public affairs officer. She confirmed no suspects were in custody, several people had been interviewed, no one claimed credit.

"She's covering everything," Wendy remarked.

"Everything of nothing," Rick added. "She's being thorough about telling the public that law enforcement doesn't know the first thing about this bombing. Not one fucking thing."

"Jeez, Rick, tell us how you really feel," Wendy said.

"I intend to." Rick let out a grunt of frustration.

"What is it?" I was surprised by the cynicism coming over Rick.

"I'm sick of this." He pointed to the screen. "Do you know that since the mall shooting in South Carolina, there has been at least one mass casualty shooting every day? Where's the news about four family members killed by a relative? Turns out the guy went out the day before to buy the gun he used to kill his parents and his two brothers." Rick's voice boomed in the closed conference room, but gradually fell by the time he got to the end.

"I get it, Rick," I said, nodding. "It's frustrating, but that's nothing new. I wish every guilty verdict overturned would be announced every day. But it doesn't work like that. Whether we ignore those shootings—I hate to call them typical—at least we know about them. But bombs exploding in campaign offices are not everyday events. Neither are the threats."

With his eyes still focused on his screen, Rick nodded, "I know." Suddenly, his head jerked back. "Holy shit."

"What? What?" Wendy said.

I braced for bad news.

Rick explained.

I finally exhaled.

Chapter Eleven

I laughed, inappropriately and with unholy glee.

"What does it mean?" Wendy asked, looking over Rick's shoulder and frowning as she pointed to the lines of text on his screen. "So, Toomey was caught cheating in college. Decades ago. He wasn't expelled over it."

"But he could have been," I said for no particular reason. "What else?"

"So, HuffPo is reporting that he applied to a shitload of law schools and got into one, Rennie College of Law—out west somewhere, like Idaho or Wyoming, maybe.

"I can't remember exactly," I said, "but wherever it is, Rennie is legendary for being the worst law school in the country. Ha-ha!"

"The article says Toomey's dad went to law school at Duke," Wendy said. "Even with the legacy admission advantage, he couldn't get in. The reporters are listing a few of the schools he applied to."

My shoulders drooped, all my joy over someone else's semi-failure proved so short lived. "Oh, man, what have we really got here? A potential cheating scandal that went nowhere, and some screw up kid graduating from a low-level law school."

"Still, it's something." Rick scrolled the screen. "Took the bar in Ohio three times before he passed."

"Like JKF, Jr.," I said dryly. "No one cares."

"I knew JFK, Jr.," Rick said, imitating a low,

commanding voice, barely able to suppress a laugh. "I worked with JFK, Jr., John Kennedy, Junior was a friend of mine. And *you*, Senator Toomey, are no JFK, Jr."

Rick allowed himself to laugh out loud at his own reference to Sen Lloyd Bentsen's historic 1988 comment to Dan Quayle in the infamous vice presidential debate. Wendy and I joined him, and it broke the tension.

"But his law school doesn't matter. Toomey never practiced law, anyway. He couldn't get a job in firms in Ohio or a couple of other states. That's when he was hired by one of Daddy's friends running for mayor of Cheyenne, Wyoming." Rick scrunched up his face. "Cheyenne?"

Out west again. "Did he stay out west?"

Rick nodded. "He stayed in politics, too, until he went back home to Ohio and ran for state senator and then U.S. Senator, where he's serving his third term. But a lot happened in between." According to Rick, Toomey had detoured to Northern Michigan, to help a buddy running for state senator there, and then he was in Mississippi for two years, working there as an aide to a Congressman.

Toomey had a curious history. No one would care, but for the fact ambition had shaken him out of a Senate stupor and into presidential politics. "Funny what matters when you run for president, isn't it?"

"Did he think no one would discover the cheating?" Wendy asked, mystified.

Having worked with me on trials for years, Wendy was painfully aware of the kinds of tidbits that turned up about people. Things like freshman year essays filled with naïve language about wanting to make a difference in the world and right all the wrongs. Sure, the person was fourteen, or, maybe eighteen and an idealistic college student. But in this anything goes privacy-starved climate, embarrassing school papers had the power to make a candidate blush forty years or more later. Or, now and again some guy wrote a snarky editorial in the school paper expounding on the evils of admitting women to the prep school dedicated to grooming the natural leaders of tomorrow.

As if reading my mind, Wendy said, "Remember William Kissinger the Fourth?"

"I was just thinking about him." I grinned. "Rick would have loved him."

Wendy filled in Rick about Kissinger, CEO of Pappas Pharmaceuticals, the defendant in a class action suit filed by our clients on the basis of discriminatory hiring practices, among other allegations against them like major water pollution. "He'd apparently forgotten about a certain editorial. He was a senior in high school when he wrote ridiculous nonsense about nature—biology—designing women to be followers, not leaders."

I winced. "Ouch. Those words hurt my ears."

"Now, *technically*, he was still a kid," Wendy said, "but it became clear those attitudes stuck when the Pappas stats were exposed. The salary charts, the mysterious numbers of employees around age 60 whose positions mysteriously needed to be eliminated." Wendy shook her head. "Matt came up with the phrase, 'Sexism was the entrée, but ageism was the dessert'."

"Good one," Rick said.

"Turned out the leopard hadn't changed its spots." Wendy mocked the tone of a guru offering wisdom. Or maybe just offering a Janet imitation.

I told Rick the nasty tone of the piece wasn't exactly our icing on the cake, speaking of dessert, but it was one of the final impressions the guy left with the jury. It didn't decide the case, but it magnified the stakes. "Juries are unpredictable," I said with a shrug. "And this one small mistake cost the company millions."

"So, is Toomey toast?" Rick asked in semi-disbelief. "All because of a cheating incident that didn't even get him expelled? Could we be that lucky?"

I shrugged. "Remains to be seen, I guess. I would have thought toasting his demise would have happened long, long ago." But voters were tricky and what they cared about had a tendency to change with the times. That was the point. "Since he hasn't been driven out of any race he ever ran, it depends on what the voters consider important right now. This isn't the first thing Toomey has gotten away with."

"Jeff Hoover overlooked it," Rick said. "Assuming he knew when he took the job of managing Toomey's campaign."

Coop convinced me we needed to look more closely at issues that could have an impact on Marie, but something interested me about Toomey. I turned to Rick. "This guy looks like the shoo-in candidate, mainly because he's out on the right-wing fringe. The voters who want that won't give a damn about his mediocre law school." Thinking out loud, I added, "Let's piece together a list of Toomey's schools, jobs, elected positions. The usual background. But I'm curious about the candidates he worked for. Who was the guy in Wyoming, and the one in Michigan? And the guy in Mississippi. Seems like odd locations, and he had to relocate to work for these candidates running for relatively small-time offices."

Rick flashed a devilish grin and rubbed his palms together as if eager to get going. "Sure—I'll start with the basics, Wikipedia and Toomey's campaign website. And from there we'll trace these jokers."

"What are you looking for, Matt?" Wendy asked.

"Patterns," I said, glancing at Rick.

Rick glanced up at me and then added to my answer. "Your boss wants to see if there's a common denominator lurking about, Wendy."

"Exactly." I hesitated but decided to go ahead anyway. "I'm really curious about the guy he worked for up in Michigan." I sighed, not liking what I was about to say. "No matter what else this guy is, he's made a career in the senate playing on fear. Fear of immigrants. He voted for every increase of millions of dollars to pour into deportation efforts. He stokes racial fears and tries his best to ignore women's rights."

"Guess he's not a big fan of diversity," Rick said. "It doesn't take much to figure that out."

Wendy changed the direction of her gaze from Rick to me. "I assume you'll fill me in. I need to go. We've got a phone bank ready to start."

"I'll let you know what we find," I assured her with a nod. "Meanwhile, I'm going to do a little digging on Marie." That was the takeaway with that otherwise insignificant meeting with Coop.

As she walked out the door, Wendy reminded me that she'd need the next afternoon off to attend her high school friend's funeral. She left before I could respond. I wondered if Bo would go with her. I hoped so.

"She's said good-bye to a lot of people," Rick remarked when the door clicked closed.

"That's true." They weren't all her best buddies, though. She once went to her former alderman's funeral, just because he was a good public servant. "She attended a gathering to honor a teacher who'd been shot and killed trying to keep the shooter away from a group of kids. Wendy didn't know the teacher, but went to pay her respects, anyway. She likes to honor people for their lives."

Rick looked up quickly and as if he'd never thought of that before. "I hope she doesn't have too many more lives to pay tribute to."

I'd been thinking the same thing.

***

An hour later, I was staring at a story I discovered online without breaking a sweat. When, I wondered, were Arnold Pierson's people going to drop hints about Parker Bentley? Or, were they going to leave him out of the campaign, unless Marie kept gaining

138

on him? If Marie got the nomination, and I believed she was gaining steam, not losing it, Toomey's people would jump on Bentley's malpractice suits, even if Pierson's campaign left it alone.

I rubbed my eyes, strained from these long hours at the computer, or reading texts, not to mention constantly going from small print to refocusing on the TV screen. But a little eye strain couldn't be helped. Since I knew a little something about medical malpractice, I could rev up some sympathy for surgeons, especially the innovators and experimenters. They were vulnerable, often shouldering the blame for bad outcomes, which could crush a reputation in nothing flat. The brilliant surgeon one day was the cocky cowboy the next.

Bentley wasn't one to settle quietly out of court, at least in a couple of cases that went to trial. Won one, lost one. No surprise or shock there. The article in front of me was filled with a lot of medical mumbo-jumbo, but from reading between the lines, Bentley, an orthopedic surgeon, was both a brilliant innovator and a risk taker. Suddenly, the text in front of me started to shrink. Shrink in importance that is.

If anyone wanted to turn Parker Bentley's professional story into a negative, then they'd have to do that without me. Mentally, I put it aside as an item to mention to Rick, but not to belabor. It wasn't as if this digging around would bring surprises.

I swiveled my chair away from the screen to give myself time to think. Theoretically, Bentley shouldn't matter one way or the other. He was brash, maybe a little arrogant, but so what? All that really mattered about Bentley is his support of Marie—enthusiastic support for a woman who could make history by crashing through a tough glass ceiling. He'd have to accept becoming First Gentleman, or whatever designation would stick for the presidential spouse. This First Lady moniker didn't have a prayer of lasting much longer.

I talked myself into my accepting Bentley and his

swagger even if there was something that bothered me about him a little. On the other hand, in election gossip magazine polls of potential presidential spouses, he got rave reviews. Women took to him—swagger had its appeal. But I had my doubts. Was he patient enough to keep his cool through a long presidential campaign? Wendy and Janet might admire his affectionate ways with Marie, but Parker hadn't even tried to soften the stance on automatic weapons. He used his medical background to justify talking about gun violence and health. I had to admit I admired the skillful way he played the physician-healer card.

Despite my sense that Parker himself was a neither here nor there factor during this primary, that probably wouldn't hold in a general election. Hell, what Parker ate for a late-night snack would be scrutinized in the general. He had a couple of celebrity clients, stories written about surgeries that weren't so successful. I sensed all that was going to be an issue, but doubted Steve Novak was prepared for it. Still, Steve might not have the greatest personality, but he'd ushered some happy winners to the victory stage on election nights. For the moment, I saw no alternative but to put aside my doubts.

Odd, in some ways, Parker was better known than Marie, the senior senator from Oregon, primarily because for a time he was a regular guest on sports' medicine segments on ESPN. Would the pitcher's arm recover or would a blown-out Achilles end a basketball career barely underway? How much more important could climate change be than that?

All the digging around for irrelevant info on Parker had one positive effect. It made me remember why I admired Marie, a relatively obscure senator when the campaign started. But not to a news junky like me. I'd seen her on the PBS Hour and lots of cable shows numerous times. She was one of the greenest of the current crop of pro-environment senators and staked out a commitment to do everything possible to make sure every American had healthcare. These were wildly popular, if expected positions for the base, but equally wildly unpopular with Toomey supporters.

I leaned back and rubbed my eyes, like I always did after reading a whole lot of text on my screen. I laughed to myself thinking that at least Parker hadn't turned up on a notorious madam's client list. Not yet, anyway. To confirm that, I googled Parker Bentley alleged infidelities, Parker Bentley sexual harassment, Parker Bentley employee complaints, and Parker Bentley womanizing.

One gossip rag had him having an affair with his celebrity lawyer on one of his malpractice suits. The doctor-and-his-attorney-story had legs, but very short ones. Bentley had other mentions, as a side issue, more or less. Like a politician, he cut a ribbon or two when a new clinic opened. He got a humanitarian award. Okay. Good. Whoa, wait a minute. The doc also got a divorce. I scanned the clip. Hmm…could be nothing. Probably was nothing. Unless it was something.

Feeling like a creepy voyeur, I texted Rick and a minute later he was in my office carrying his laptop.

"What's up?"

"What do you know about Parker Bentley's divorce?"

"Huh? I hadn't come across it. But I was focused on other stuff."

"Me, neither, until just now." I shrugged.

"Who gives a rat's ass?" Rick asked.

I let out a hoot. Rick could be so logical sometimes. Unfortunately, logic could be the kiss of death in politics. "Okay, let's see where the rats' asses are," I said. "Now, good 'ol Mike Toomey probably could care less, since he's on his second marriage. Arnold Pierson doesn't care, but you can put one rat's ass in the David Scheffler column under the label Family Effing Values."

Rick gave me a hoot right back. "Okay, Matt, we like Arnold. We might end up voting for the guy. But his campaign manager has a different agenda. David Scheffler probably keeps track of what Marie eats for breakfast. If she eats cereal, he'll make sure the egg lobby knows it."

"Egg lobby, nothing," I teased. "The protein shake crowd will have them both on the ropes."

Rick threw back his head and laughed really hard. He sure got a kick out of all this sometimes. "David's probably discreetly asked around about the first Mrs. Bentley—or whatever name she went by back in the old days."

I pushed back my chair and went to the window— my favorite feature of my office. In the distance the sun was glancing off one of the spire of one of the oldest churches in Chicago. Coop's words, his question about what I knew about Marie Kent came back to me. Was it possible he had info about her husband's first marriage? I massaged my forehead, where what had been a dull ache was now starting to be distracting. Suddenly, I pivoted toward Rick and blurted, "This is the part of politics I detest."

Rick nodded to the screen. "Maybe so, but as we speak, I can guarantee someone is out goading a gossip reporter to write about Marie and Parker being married the same year the divorce from the first wife was final. In fact, we're talking mere months."

"Shit. You know that's not good. Now Marie is going to look like the other woman," I said with a groan. "The homewrecker."

Rick shrugged. "Maybe she was."

"Thanks for pointing that out." I laughed. "I still don't give a rat's ass."

"Are you going to ask her about it? Well, not her, but Steve?"

I noticed he jumped over Percy's head and went straight to the boss man. "Oh, hell, I don't know. I'm not going to rush in with the info. Let's at least make sure we get the dates straight first."

Rick focused on his screen, his fingers racing across

the keyboard. Then he abruptly stopped. "What the fuck are we doing?" He looked at me with an expression of disgust, every feature scrunched or distorted. "How is this helping Marie? It's not like we're snooping on good 'ol Arnold or fuck-face Toomey."

"Don't mince words, Rick," I said with a laugh. "Oh, and if we do bring it up, I'm not above telling a little fib about one of our respondents leaving a question about Parker's first marriage in the comment box on one of our surveys. We can honestly tell Steve we're obligated to bring it up even though it's distasteful and not the dirt we traffic in."

"Right, except when we do." Rick shook his head. "I'm sorry. It's just sometimes I really do wonder why anyone would run for office."

"I get it, believe me. But somewhere, someone is looking at the same pages we are, Rick." I waved to his iPad, the symbol of every fact known to anyone anywhere in the world. "Only they're doing it on offense. We're on defense."

I turned and stood with my back against the wall of windows. I folded my arms across my chest. "They're picking up the tidbits they can put in ads and press releases. It's what they can drop to reporters in 1:00 a.m. phone calls. They hope little seeds of doubt will wiggle their way in. Right wing news anchors and pundits will conveniently drop innuendo and irrelevant facts into their stories."

"The plan is to blindside Marie or Parker. You know they hope they'll slip up during interviews." Rick launched into one of his theatrical imitations, this one of a TV interviewer. "Why did your first marriage end so quickly in divorce, Dr. Bentley?"

I couldn't say Rick was wrong, so I suggested we talk it out, come up with why we had to follow leads. "You know I took this job to gather data. My company has chosen sides and we owe our clients the best we've got."

Rick nodded. He knew I was talking to myself as

much as to him. He gave me a wry smile. "Well, when you put it like that." He paused. "Seriously, though, right now, Marie and Parker look like a fun couple—they have an almost grown up kid, who put her foot in her mouth over guns. Big deal. I feel like a vulture picking at their lives."

"It makes me sick," I added, propping my hip on the corner of my desk. "On the other hand, Toomey and Pierson would have the same feeling if they uncovered dirt on Marie like we had in the Marchand case. As gruesome as it was, we were pretty pleased with ourselves when we happened upon a link between our then governor and the body of a girl found on a river bank." I shook my head. "We were practically high-fiving over it."

Rick waved me off. "Okay, okay. I get it." Looking at the public records on Marie, she and Parker married three months after his divorce from Adrienne Shire was final." He counted on his fingers. "Divorced from Adrienne in Mid-January, married to Marie in Mid-April."

"Where?"

"Where what?"

"Where were they married? Out in Oregon?" I asked.

"Yep, Portland. In a civil ceremony." Rick laughed. "You'll be happy to know their only child, the one Amanda June, was born more than two years later in, you guessed it, June." Rick clicked around and filled in other basics. Parker and Adrienne had been married for a total of only 14 months.

"No wonder it doesn't come up," I said. "Any links to Adrienne?"

Rick typed and frowned. "Oh, shit, this is even worse. And it comes right up so I'm guessing these questions have been raised before. Adrienne died a few years ago. The obituary doesn't list a cause. Survived by a husband and a stepson. I'll note the names."

I looked on as Rick added to this file. "I don't want

to bother those people. Why don't I ask Percy, in an offhand sort of way, what Marie and Parker have said about other campaigns sniffing around in the past? Maybe he'll tell me what they've heard from other people."

I expected Rick to readily agree. What was the downside? But he didn't. Instead he went quiet on me. "What? You don't approve?"

"I think we should go to the conference room and work on this where we can spread out." Rick stood and stretched his arms to the side. "Not to minimize your hard work, boss, but I think what I found is a whole lot more interesting than malpractice lawsuits and a short-lived first marriage. Or even the second presumably happy marriage that started in a quiet courthouse ceremony."

I picked up my laptop. "I don't know if this is good news or bad news."

"In terms of Marie's campaign, I honestly can't say."

"You had me at a 'whole lot more interesting'. Let's go."

Chapter Twelve

A few minutes later, I burned my tongue on a cup of dark brew coffee and wondered how Mike Toomey slipped through the cracks of media scrutiny. "His campaign slogan should be 'Leave No White Supremacist Behind.'"

Rick guffawed. "And people thought Governor Diana Briggs was a horror show. She looks like Mother Theresa next to this guy."

I sat back and watched Rick create a flow chart of Mike Toomey's life. He was dragging this or that fact around like a jigsaw puzzle and showing me the guy's chronology. "Funny how he managed to support a lot of hate without letting too much stick to him."

Another Teflon right wing guy. I had no explanation for this phenomenon. "Democrats nitpick over every little slip of the tongue and apologize for every possible offending remark." I slapped the table in frustration. "But a guy like Toomey is allowed to mingle among civilized people." I laughed at the ludicrousness of what I'd just said.

As Rick filled in the flow chart, a picture emerged of the Republican front runner as a man who'd spent a career skirting the fringes of most every fringe group around, starting with the time he tried to help elect a small town mayor who wanted to require men to carry guns and defend the town against marauders, the exact word, the guy used. Marauder wasn't defined, though, so it covered a lot of ground.

"Toomey's guy was quirky—and loaded with cash," Rick said, "but running on arming citizens and an open carry policy in a small town in Wyoming isn't revolutionary."

"And he won with that platform?" I asked.

Rick ran his finger down the text without actually touching the screen. "Nope, he lost to a popular incumbent. Looks like Toomey hung out in that area for about a year but didn't stay long after his rich guy lost."

I leaned back in my chair and put my feet up on the conference table, not something I particularly approved of, but what the hell. I was settling in to get a real earful about the Republican frontrunner.

Rick shook his head. "But get this. The guy he worked for up in Northern Michigan lived in a survivalist compound, Matt. He ran on an exaggerated state's rights platform, including the right to form a militia to protect the state from Federal control." Rick kept running his finger down the text, his frown deepening. "How about this? The guy wanted checkpoints at the state line and advocated for the right to turn away people at the border to keep undesirables, his word, out of the state. No new immigrants were to be allowed in the state for five years and after that, immigration would be limited to people from Europe. End national parks, the EPA, and the right wing favorite, the Department of Education. English as the official language, and Christianity the official religion." The guttural noises coming out of Rick reverberated through the room.

"What a peach," I said, "but he fits the profile of the typical separatist. And? What happened to him?"

"He lost, too." He looked at me with priceless glee. "It says here Toomey's former client is currently serving time in prison for tax evasion and threatening the life of a federal judge—*three* times." He waved three fingers at me.

"Don't shed too many tears," I said sarcastically.

"Oh, I won't. The joker is filthy rich. No wonder the IRS went after him. He made a fortune in packaged food for the coming apocalypse," Rick read with a straight face. "He was a Michigan State alum—started out a high school history teacher. At least the kids' impressionable minds are spared."

All well and good to laugh, but how was finding out about this compound-dwelling-tax-evader helping Marie? "Sadly, Toomey isn't a survivalist himself."

"No, but this is the kind of stuff Toomey was spending his time on out of law school with no job prospects," Rick pointed out. "His job history is spottier than mine."

I chuckled. Rick had spent a few years out of college designing games and barely paying his studio apartment rent working temp jobs. Being a good data analyst meant he could land these now and then, but the assignments rarely lasted long. A couple of months tops. But after the Marchand case, he'd turned his starving artist image around pretty well.

I was about to ask about Toomey's detour down to Mississippi, but a knock on the door broke that train of thought.

"Break time," Wendy said, holding a large white bakery box. "I stopped for goodies—my treat."

I waved her in, and she called out for Janet to join us.

"How was it?" I asked in a low voice as I put aside my tablet and a legal pad.

"Sad. But interesting. Things to mull over. JoJo will never be the same," Wendy said. "That's for sure."

About the time we started drinking coffee and eating jelly donuts and buttery muffins my head started pounding. Janet, Wendy, and Rick chatted about the rain, the Bulls, and the Mexican restaurant due to open a couple of blocks away. Janet and Rick compared notes on the newest of the Icelandic murder mysteries on Netflix. Janet remarked about the hardy people who wore nothing but sweaters and hooded puffy coats.

I offered little but a nod here and there. I wasn't a headache kind of guy. Burning acid, I could handle. I had the remedy at hand for that. Not so for this dull ache.

"Tell us about your friend," Janet said, turning to Wendy. "It must have been a sad occasion."

Wendy nodded. "Afterwards, I pulled JoJo aside and told him about coming upon his rally a few weeks ago. He didn't want to talk about any of it. He had hate groups on his mind. He sees them as traitors, and he's not wrong."

Rick and I exchanged a quick, spontaneous glance. "I'll bet he did," I said. The League of True Americans, TLTA, pronounced "tilta" had finally come forward to claim credit. Odd, though, no one could dig up anything about them. Few people actually believed there was such an organization. It sounded more like someone pulled a prank than a serious group coming forward to taunt the public.

In my mind it was legitimate to ask if JoJo would ever get over what happened at his campaign headquarters. Would he give up his seat in Congress? No one would blame him if he did. On the other hand, would he dig in and become an expert on hate groups and domestic terrorism? As a Congressman, he could own that cause, make his mark.

"Since it's just the four of us," Wendy said, "I think it's okay to throw stuff out. You know, speculate a little."

"About what?" Janet asked before lifting the mug of coffee to her lips.

"I think JoJo is having a hard time accepting this bombing as an isolated incident," Wendy said. "To him, the real question is how whatever group is behind the bombing managed to pull it off."

No shit. I would have said as much. I could see Wendy just warming up.

"Did you get the impression this is going to be JoJo's cause now?" Janet asked.

"I was wondering the same thing," Rick said.

Wendy nodded. "I think so, but at the moment, he's concerned about beating Toomey and his crowd."

I caught Rick's eye again, but we both quickly looked away.

"What does this have to do with Senator Kent?" Janet asked. "I thought you all were focused on research for her."

"We are," I said. It was up to me to try to define what we were doing and why it could be directly related to helping Marie. "As it turns out, though, it isn't quite as straightforward as we thought when we started. The ongoing threats and violence have changed things. We have to be on alert for anything that shifts public opinion one way or the other."

Wendy took in a deep breath. "Okay, here it is straight. JoJo admits he has no definitive evidence, but he believes something else is going on here, that people are hiding something. He thinks these incidents could be linked to one of the *campaigns*. He thinks that's where law enforcement should be looking for the answer to all the threats and violence. And this is no conspiracy theory, I can tell you."

"Did he say who?" Rick asked.

"You aren't surprised by JoJo's suspicions," Wendy said, giving Rick a long, pointed look.

"Nothing about this campaign season has the power to shock us, I guess." I blurted that hoping it sounded as good as any other response. For the moment, I wanted to quell Wendy's curiosity. But she already suspected we knew more than we were letting on.

"The congressman thought it could be Governor Briggs," Wendy said. "He's not convinced her hands are clean in all this, even with her campaign suspended now."

"No kidding?" Rick acted like he didn't buy it.

I hid my surprise on purpose. I wasn't about to knock down that idea. No one else had a better one. Apparently, Janet shared my feelings because she looked expectantly at Wendy and asked, "Go on. Did he explain why he suspected Briggs?"

Rick and I exchanged another quick glance.

"He doesn't trust Briggs' campaign manager. He has some kind of old connection with a separatist group in Alabama—not like those militia types, though. But JoJo talked about a network of groups that he thinks are involved in this election, but not necessarily linked to only one campaign."

"Of course, campaigns would try to hide this, if they even know," Rick offered. "I mean, no one wants to be called a racist or seen as biased against gays or women."

"Unless that's their M.O.," Janet said. "Some people like that way of thinking. People say one thing to their neighbors and coworkers and then vote another way in the voting booth."

"Yes. That's what JoJo said, too. He's going to follow up." Wendy popped another chunk of a chocolate chip muffin in her mouth. "Oh, and JoJo's holding a memorial service at one of the big community churches, where he'll raise some money. And he's planning a fundraiser at a bar in his district. He's worried about the families—he promised to cover medical expenses for the uninsured restaurant employees. He's not letting this go."

Good for JoJo. Not to be crass about it, but his fast, empathetic response to the tragedy could potentially change the outlook for the young Congressman in the long run. Could be his turn will come up after all, maybe a cycle or two from now.

It was too early to offer my two cents about JoJo's future, but down the road it might be a good idea to talk about his concerns about the networks he thought existed. One thing for sure, white nationalism was showing up under every rock.

"Did he say anything else?" I asked Wendy. "Any other insights?"

Wendy closed her eyes and shook her head. "I've

never seen anyone as broken as JoJo. Or as determined to do something. It seemed half the cops in Chicago were standing guard over the funeral."

My head still pounding, I rubbed my temples and found a little relief. But something was eating away at me. Unintentionally, I let out a long groan.

"What is it, Matt?" Wendy said, looking ready to jump out of her chair.

"We're falling into a trap of thinking of hate as some kind of attitude problem," I said. "But that's bullshit. We can't forget we're talking about crimes. The serious, violent kind that land people behind bars. Stay at home and talk hate with your friends and you're covered by the First Amendment, but call in bomb threats, blow out a window or kill people in campaign offices and you're a criminal. If we can catch these people, we can put them away for a long time. You can't get rid of hate." I groaned again. "Damned if it seems to lurk in the background until it is able to rear its ugly head."

Janet pointed to the TV. "Where's the breaking news banner about arrests and perp walks and bail hearings over that?"

"Good question. We're still waiting," Wendy said.

"Well, except for the hapless guy in camouflage they picked up for the JoJo bombing," Janet said. "Poor kid ought to think twice about wearing militia gear when he doesn't know a gun from a tank."

That was an embarrassing early arrest that led nowhere fast. It was particularly embarrassing for the police. They'd picked up a guy from central casting, but it turned out he didn't know his fashion statement made him look like a survivalist at best, a militia warrior at worst.

"Matt's right, damn it," Rick said. "So far, the real investigation for the JoJo bombing has led to nothing."

"Bet you wish you never heard of Steve Novak," Wendy said, almost as an afterthought and not linked to anything we were talking about. "I wouldn't blame you."

"Just my opinion, and nobody asked me," Janet interjected, "but you should go home, Matt. It's obvious you have a bad headache."

Best idea I'd heard all day. "But Rick and I weren't quite done."

"It'll wait 'til tomorrow," Rick said pushing his chair back. "I'll make this easy. I'm going home, too. I'm beat—this stuff makes my head buzz."

By the time I'd gathered the dogs and my laptop, my head was pounding even harder. Janet's last words to me came in the form of a series of orders: Drive carefully. Take your temperature. Get some sleep.

***

I hated being sick so much I rarely gave into it. At most I'd stretch out on my couch, but I never stayed in bed. It was a point of foolish pride to tough it out. I'd lived with acid burning holes in my gut, and unrelenting insomnia for months after I lost my fight for Joey Haskell, ironically, cruelly, right before the governor declared a moratorium on the death penalty in Illinois. So how could a mere headache bring me down? Instead, I stuck with a cliché…I was under the weather.

After my employee-pals sent me home, I took my under-the-weather-self and made the couch my headquarters. I'd suffer in silence, but in twenty-first century comfort. I had the dogs, my phone and tablet, cable TV, the remote, and the coffee table covered with bottles of water and soup from Trader Joe's.

By the time I rifled through a bunch of drawers I found the thermometer that delivered the bad news. Janet was right—straight up 101 degrees. High for an adult, or so I'm told. I slept hard for several hours. It was dark when various dings and rings and buzzes finally got through and put me into action. Nothing more strenuous than looking at devices, though.

Sitting up and stretching my arms over my head, I took a few deep breaths and confirmed I still had a pulse and a thinking brain. I sent texts to my three Musketeers to let them know I was following all orders. I even went so far as to admit I felt like I'd landed in hell, but thanks to soup and crackers I planned to live. The last thing I wanted was a bunch of Good Samaritans stopping by with chicken soup. I wanted my cave all to myself.

I took the dogs outside, but not for long. It was too cold to enjoy a walk, anyway. Then I dozed on and off while listening to the news. I'd missed a few hours of it, so what had gone on without me? As I watched, my own words haunted me, realizing that I'd been like so many others, including my three pals. We'd been viewing these crimes through a political lens. I'd put aside the raw lawbreaking, the disregard for life, the randomness of the terrorism, which from where I sat was leaving scars all over the country. We didn't need any foreign interference to ruin our so-called way of life. We were doing a fine job of it all on our own.

Given my foul mood and fuzzy brain, I almost missed the breaking news story about an arrest in the Toomey campaign South Carolina bomb threat. That seemed so yesterday, but it was mere weeks ago. It came in the middle of Coop's show, so I hauled myself up and sat on the edge of the couch so I wouldn't doze off while he talked.

I called Rick and told him to turn on Coop's coverage. Then, I put him on speaker.

"A Toomey campaign volunteer from Florida was taken into custody about an hour ago," the local network affiliate reporter said. Her image filled half the screen. The other half rolled video showing an older woman being walked from her apartment with an officer cupping her elbow. "So far, this appears to be a case of an overzealous supporter doing this on her own."

Overzealous, my ass. You don't do what she did

without having a screw loose in your head.

Coop reiterated the early statement from the Toomey campaign that this was a lone actor. Toomey himself had never met the volunteer, but she was known by local campaign staff. As the saying goes, he was deeply saddened by the volunteer's actions.

"That doesn't tell us much," Rick remarked.

"No, I suppose not. Do we believe the explanation?" Everything in me urged me to believe it. It wasn't unique, this idea of a mentally unbalanced person doing something because of a distorted notion of loyalty. No doubt, the woman thought a bomb threat would help Toomey's campaign by making people sympathetic to the poor candidate who has been unfairly threatened.

"Oh, hell, I guess I do," Rick said. "I know it's a crime, Matt, but frankly, do we want to send Grandma to prison? What's the charge? Twisted thinking?"

I laughed. "I agree. The only question is whether someone put her up to it? If that's true, it'll come out soon enough. I'm writing the story in my head right now. This woman is going to talk about Toomey as a religious man, whose enemies surround him. She'll be talking about Satan before all this is over. It's almost like a return to QAnon stuff."

"What are you? A psychic journalist? You really have this figured out, Matt." Rick was sputtering his laughter, knowing as I did, this wasn't really so funny.

"I've seen too much. I don't need to be psychic." I was resigned to the fact that this was nothing more than a dreary campaign season story. It just happened to coincide with a slew of political violence. "Doesn't it seem strange that with all the threats and the violence going on, no one is taking credit for any of it? Usually, it's the quickest way to notoriety."

"True believers in movements or causes usually boast about their power, don't they?" Rick asked, rhetorically. "Or, maybe I'm thinking of ISIS or Al Qaeda."

"It usually works that way." I let out a heavy sigh.

"By the way, I forgot to tell you and Wendy that I'm driving down to Springfield next week. Coop is broadcasting from down there."

"And?" Rick asked. "What does that have to do with the Kent campaign work?"

The question wasn't as challenging as it sounded and I took it as a sign "I don't know yet. But I'm going to find out." I sighed. "With a little digging, by that time you'll have told me about Toomey and his years in Mississippi. Right?"

"You got it, Boss. Go back to sleep and take of yourself, will ya? We'll talk tomorrow. Don't worry about any of this," Rick said. "I mean it."

Fat chance.

Chapter Thirteen

It's an odd process to create a life of working for oddball candidates in campaigns who stood little chance of winning. Even if they win a squeaker in their district, it was usually short-lived. True, Congress had a few radical, obnoxious types that preached what sounded like the politics and policies of the 1950s— or the turn of the century, the twentieth century, that is, not the current one. In some of those cases, for whatever reason, these folks were popular enough to eke out wins one election after another. There was just enough opposition to these politicians to give the other party hope that next time they'd throw the crazy guy— or in a few cases, the woman—out. Primary election at whatever level, have become a race to the extremes. Republicans want someone who makes the tea party look liberal and democrats are after the candidate to the left of a unicorn.

This was going through my mind as I sifted through information on Toomey's early clients. Fringe types to a man. Never a woman. Toomey's time in Mississippi was spent working for one of these fringe Representatives. Based on my fairly superficial browsing, at least at first, Scott—better known as Scotty—Tabakin was the worst of the worst of the group of reactionaries Toomey gravitated to.

Like other shrewd twenty-first century racist types, Tabakin left his white robe and pointy hat at home and he cloaked the ideas in polite, if patronizing words. Still, he'd written articles and columns about codifying separatism that appeared with regularity in a southern history magazine and even a few respectable newspapers. He spoke to the so-called Southern heritage groups. They liked to claim they were more like genealogical societies and research scholars than white supremacy councils, which were deemed so twentieth century. Scotty was a little vocal, a little blatant, and a lot blunt, which made the party establishment nervous. As the current adage goes, he was fond of saying the quiet parts out loud.

I clicked through all the links Rick sent, and he'd not included much of his own commentary. But he added a note saying: Tell me what you think.

It didn't take long to start making my own connections and using arrows to point in all directions. Wow, what a life. Rick called just about the time I was reaching a dead end in connecting the dots.

"I'm here, still breathing and working now," I told Rick. "I'm starting to get my oomph back, which is why I began sifting through these links you sent… about as much dirt as…"

"Uh, I better stop by," Rick interjected in a firm voice. "You probably aren't contagious."

"No, at least not anymore." I told Rick he could stop by anytime with the results of the attitude survey for our new client. My way of asking if we had any data on Marie. But Rick's interruption also reminded me we were watching ourselves on the phone. Given what had been going on, we were getting more paranoid than I'd ever imagined possible.

"I'll bring food. I'll see you in an hour or so." Rick ended the call before I could object. I was feeling well enough to go out, but I didn't have to if Rick was willing to put something delicious in front of me without any effort on my part.

I used the hour I had to clear away debris from the coffee table and stand under a hot shower until I felt almost like myself again. Rick and I muted the

TV while we filled up on the spread of Thai food he brought. My appetite was back, at least I couldn't turn down Rama Broccoli with chicken. Love that peanut sauce. Extra sauce in fact.

"I'd forgotten all about being cautious on the phone," I said, although in some ways it was sort of a joke. If anyone was actually listening, it wouldn't be that hard to figure out what we were doing. The question came back to who would care about our snooping, anyway? Maybe we were flattering ourselves and exaggerating our importance. And yet…

"I suppose we should talk about Marie, huh?" I joked. "The woman who's paying the bills. Are we sidelining Parker and his first wife for now? So far, no one seems focused on him."

"Toomey and Pierson are, sort of," Rick said, "but they've got a couple of skeletons themselves that they'd just as soon not become topics of drive time talk radio."

The buzz of my phone took me by surprise. "It's Percy," I told Rick before I picked up. Damn it. I wanted a chance to talk to Rick about good ol' Scotty Tabakin. I'd have to take my chances.

"I hear you've been sick," Percy said when I answered.

"I was, but I'm apparently over it. Almost, anyway. Must've been some kind of fast flu bug." I glanced at Rick. "I'm glad you called. I was just thinking about you."

"Oh, yeah. That's good. I've got some news. It's about our ad buy."

"Tell me more." I stayed focus on Rick. "So, Rick is here with me. Brought me dinner. I'm going to put you on speaker, okay?"

"That's cool. He never buys me dinner by the way, cheap ass," Percy said with a chuckle. Percy went through some details we really didn't need to know about their ad buys, which didn't sound especially logical to me. Instead of going after some new voters in favorable demographic groups, they seemed to be trying to lure Pierson's voters away. It could work, but seemed a little late in the game for that.

Rick had the same reaction because he jerked his head back and frowned. A couple of seconds later, he was tapping his screen where graphics appeared. He broke in with questions about cyber ads, and still appeared puzzled. Rick glanced at his screen and frowned again. "That's where our first analysis and the initial attitude survey led you? Curious," Rick said.

Something seemed off to me. "Sounds like you're competing for the voters in Pierson's strongest group," I said. "Was there something in the data that led you to compete in Pierson's stronghold?"

Percy let out a harrumph. Testy, maybe? Clearly, not welcoming anyone challenging their decision. But my question was logical enough. We flipped the calendar to April now, and although the weather hadn't changed much, a big round of the spring primaries was coming up. Marie still had some gold to mine where Arnold wasn't strong—she was better with the college crowd and younger women and the younger Hispanic vote.

I signaled to Rick that we had to drop it. This wasn't what we were being paid to do. No one asked us to make decisions. We delivered the data and analysis, but that was the end of it. I wasn't the campaign strategist. "Don't mind me. I was only asking out of curiosity. My firm is providing the numbers, but the campaign has the expertise."

"A lot of this has to do with reliability," Percy said, sounding like the pro who could school us on strategy. "This late, we need to target the people who show up to vote, not those who tell pollsters they *intend* to vote, but something gets in the way when election day comes."

Keeping my voice light, I told Percy we'd keep going on our end.

Rick cast a skeptical look my way. I wasn't quite ready to let Percy go. "I know we're all watching the primary polls for Marie, but what do you see going on with the Republicans? Toomey is hanging on to his lead."

"I suppose," Percy said, a little suspicion coming through in his voice. "The guy hasn't had competition to speak of. Toomey probably expected Briggs to give them some headaches, but everybody else's campaigns blew up fast." He quickly added, "At least as far as I can see from the outside."

"Well, sort of surprising, but kind of a relief, really," I said. "It looks like the Democrats will have an easy time of it."

"Why?" Percy challenged. "Why would you say that?"

Rick gave me a big thumbs up of approval. He sensed what I was about to do.

"Well, c'mon. Toomey's got a past only a mother could love." I looked at Rick for approval, kind of proud of myself for catching Percy off guard.

"We wish," Percy said, innocently.

That was the best he could come up with? "I mean it," I said. "Do you know if that guy…" I waved at Rick "…what was his name again? That guy from Mississippi."

"You mean, Scotty, uh, was it Tobacco?" Rick matched Percy's innocent tone and then some.

Silence.

"Close, Rick. *Tabakin*, yes, that's the guy. What a loser, huh?"

"I…I wouldn't know," Percy said. "I've just heard of him…not really someone I know."

"He's fairly famous. He fools around with white supremacy, that sort of thing. I'm surprised no one's asked Toomey about Tabakin's role in his campaign." Surely, someone in Marie's campaign would have started piling up interesting facts about the company the Republican frontrunner keeps.

"If he's that notorious, someone will eventually grill Toomey's campaign," Percy said.

"You know Jeff Hoover, don't you?" Rick asked.

It took a couple of seconds for Percy to answer. "Sort of, we're both in the business."

In the business—right. From shelf stocker to high flying political strategist in ten easy lessons. "Well, when you run into him you could name drop, bring up Tabakin. See how he reacts."

"I suppose I could do that." Percy spoke fast, like he wanted to say his piece and go. "But hell, I don't expect to cross paths with anyone in the Toomey camp anytime soon."

"I see. I'm not sure how you can avoid it. The candidates on both sides seem to cluster in the same places." Rick held up a piece of paper on which he scrawled the words, *Toomey in Pittsburgh on Fri and Sat.* "Well, I should go. Your ad strategy sounds good. We'll get going on that Florida demographic in the next few days. I suppose Marie will be pretty busy in Pennsylvania, probably Philly and Pittsburgh, maybe some suburbs I'll bet. And Delaware, too."

"She'll be in both states Friday and Saturday morning, and then it's a quick trip out to Montana. She's big with the kids at the university in Missoula. It's weeks off, but her organizer wants to put her in front of some students. That's how Obama put Montana in his win column. I'm sure you remember that."

I smiled at Rick who was already searching for Toomey's stops in Montana. "Now that you mention it, I do recall that," I said, as if just reminded of that fact. Percy and I ended the call with the usual promises to stay in touch.

Rick looked at his screen and shook his head. "Well, if cash on hand gets tight, Kent and Toomey could save a lot of money if they just shared a plane."

I pulled up a photo of Tabakin shaking hands with the head of a white citizens' council and turned my screen toward Rick. "Did you see him in Beaufort by any chance?"

"Not gussied up in a suit like that," Rick said, looking grim as he spoke, "but I saw him. The man in the photo is clean-shaven, but the guy I saw behind Toomey's curtained divider had the start of a beard... like he hadn't shaved in four days. He had big plastic glasses and longish white hair."

"But you're sure it's the same guy in the picture."

"Ninety-five percent. The rings give him away."

I studied the photos, and saw both a wide wedding band and a pinky ring on Scotty's left hand.

"For some reason, they stuck out when I saw him in that little campaign enclave." Rick tapped all four fingers on the coffee table. "But still, I only noticed the guy in passing. He caught my attention because he tapped four fingers on a folding table the whole time I was trying to get a good glimpse of Hoover and Percy. Like I'm doing now. That's why I noticed the rings."

Suddenly tired, I rested my head on the back of the couch. "I don't get it. This guy was *traveling* with Toomey. Maybe still is."

"Or, he shows up now on his own steam in a low profile sort of way," Rick pointed out. "The glasses and the long hair could have been a disguise."

"But isn't that what reporters *usually* look for? The things that aren't so obvious? What is oppo research for if not to uncover real stuff like this? Why didn't Diana Briggs send a fucking reporter on a mission to expose Tabakin? If she had, she might still be in the race."

"She's a bad example," I said. "She had plenty of shit like this in her past—don't expose what can be thrown back at you. She'd end up just as muddied."

Rick and I fell silent. I'd muted the TV and now we had no noise to drown out our thoughts. Finally, I said, "A major candidate for president of the United States spent over two years of his life as an assistant to a state representative who espoused separatism. He spoke at groups who toyed with the idea of redesigning the country to create white and black regions. No more

United States. We'd live in the *Untied* States."

"A fucking kick in the teeth, isn't it?" Rick said.

"Yep, but I don't work for him. I didn't put my firm's skills behind his efforts. If I hadn't signed on with Marie's campaign, I'd probably still be making up my mind between her and Pierson. We're steeped in delegate math and getting ads in front of women who buy running shoes and crockpots. Meanwhile, since no one is paying attention, a white supremacist is advising a guy some people think is a run of the mill conservative Republican. But we know he's a guy with a political rap sheet."

I flopped back on the couch and raked my hand through my hair.

"Uh, oh, I see wheels turning. What's up, boss?"

"I think a trip to Montana is in order."

Rick shook his head. "I wanted to see the place in April. I hear the mud season is lots of fun."

I grinned and said, "Pack your boots."

Rick hung around my apartment and booked tickets for the two of us to head to Missoula, although Pierson wasn't investing much time or money there. This time, I decided Rick and I could both follow Toomey to a stop or two in the bright red Montana counties and lose ourselves in what were sure to be big crowds for Marie in student strongholds.

"I have to admit Toomey is smart to do one of those folksy bus tours," Rick said. "We can shadow him in a rental car."

I stood up and raised my arms over my head and bent from side to side. Happy to feel like myself again, I suddenly wondered what kind of maze I'd gotten myself caught in. I started pacing around my living room, not exactly set up to be a walking track.

"What the hell are we doing? Flying out to a state that has a county named Glacier, in early April, no less, to tail a miserable excuse for a human being I don't even work for?" I glanced at Rick and laughed out loud. "Why, why?"

"You ask a whole lot of questions," Rick said in a loud snicker. "But you are on to something. Frankly, so am I."

I rolled my hand at Rick. "Go on…"

Rick launched into a detailed rundown of the election-related violence since the day we signed on with the Kent campaign. As I spoke, investigations were going on in hotspots all over the country and in Congress as well.

"JoJo is making a name for himself. The only good thing to come from all this." From the look on Rick's face, he knew exactly what I meant. "With a little help from a terrorist, or someone claiming to be a terrorist." I wasn't being ironic. Once someone claimed credit for the bombing of JoJo's office the door to an investigation opened.

It turned out this wasn't the first time TLTA claimed credit for a violent act, adding some line about the glory of America's past—like two hundred years ago. They no longer put up a pretense of advocating the peaceful return to a national policy of segregation. If separatism didn't occur peacefully, then forming armed militias to forge a revolution was the next step. But JoJo was proposing—demanding—more funding for investigations into these hate groups.

"Exposing TLTA and the other groups like them is his new life's work," Rick observed. "His speech on the floor of the House the other day is on YouTube now." A couple of commands later, he repositioned his computer so we could both see the screen. He increased the volume so we could hear JoJo reading the names of the dead and wounded in the bombing of his office. Then he read the names of the dead in the mall massacre. He wanted the FBI to designate TLTA as a domestic terrorist organization, just like all the terrorism watch groups had.

"You mean it's not already on the FBI's list?"

Rick shrugged at my rhetorical question. "Guess not. But that's because they haven't been able to trace them back to an actual person or a location. It isn't clear who to watch."

"By the way, what are we telling your cousin about our trip to Montana? I'm assuming he'll be out there with Marie and Steve."

"I'm one step ahead of you. Looks like the whole family will be there. Parker and Amanda are being freed from lockdown," Rick said with a smirk. "They love Marie in Missoula. She's way ahead of Pierson there. Toomey is going to hit Billings and Great Falls. Marie is adding Helena, another Dem stronghold. We can assume this is a full-out campaign trip with Steve and Percy."

That video of JoJo ended, but the TV screen now showed him being interviewed at the Capitol about his earlier call for funding hate group investigations. In an ominous tone he warned of more violence ahead. "Candidates of both parties should be on high alert. We need a thorough investigation to root out the bad actors in all these incidents. Hate groups have been poisoning our system for too long. We find ourselves not even knowing who the operatives in TLTA are. They're almost completely under the radar. And undermining American values."

JoJo walked away from the media area of the Capitol, where reporters were available to Representatives looking for coverage of their issues. No guarantee their statements would be broadcast live or replayed later, but JoJo's message stood a good chance of being picked up beyond the Chicago markets. What had happened to his campaign was still talked about even weeks later.

"I'm going to talk to Steve about meeting Marie," I said. "We can keep slipping in and out of her orbit for a little while longer, but our low profile surely has a shelf life."

"Aren't you curious about the ad buys? It's almost as if they misused the data you provided?" Rick asked.

"Nah, we can keep an eye on it, but I have to let

that go. It's a judgment call, and Steve is good at what he does, but I don't think he'll reveal the secret of his success yet. I'm more interested in how defensive Percy was about it. In any case, I'd like to meet Marie and her family."

"Will we just show up?" Rick asked.

"No, we'll text Steve and Percy and let them know we're on our way to Missoula when it's too late for them to discourage us. Did you reserve a car?" I paused. "We'll need rooms, too. I hope we're not too late. The place will be crawling with reporters."

"Not so much for Toomey; I mean the guy has all but locked up the nomination," Rick said, waving me off. "Yeah, I got us a car."

"What are you up to?" I asked. "You haven't looked up from the screen since we started this conversation."

"You're not going to believe what I'm focusing on."

I groaned. "Great. Now you have to tell me."

"I went back to Scotty Tabakin," Rick said. "Well, to the Wikipedia version of his life, anyway. We'll dig deeper later."

"I see. I think."

Rick flopped back on the couch, stretched his legs out and crossed his ankles. Then he laced his fingers behind his head and stared at the ceiling. "Mr. Family Values, Scotty Tabakin, is on his fourth wife."

More unholy glee. It was a big source of daily pleasure. "He's not the first of the super-religious people who love marriage so much they can't get enough of them. And how else could he be so judgmental of others without hypocrisy? Goes with the territory." I laughed at my own joke, knowing it was a long running joke and not even *that* funny.

"Well, Matt, while you were speculating about the ad buy and wondering if we'd be welcome on the campaign trail, I've come across a juicy tidbit about the third Mrs. Tabakin, first name Lori, birth name Hochberg.

I'd heard that name. Just recently, too, but I couldn't

quite place it. "Why does that sound familiar?"

"Because she's the newly named Assistant Director of Communications for the *Pierson* campaign—the white supremacist's ex-wife hitched her wagon to a flaming liberal Democrat—and still the presumed winner of the Democratic nomination." Rick looked up and grinned. "How do you like that?"

For a couple of seconds, I didn't know what to say. "Well, it shows me I still have the ability to be surprised," I said. "Lori Hochberg versus Scotty Tabakin."

"I'm looking up some more fun facts to fill in," Rick said sarcastically.

I was more than annoyed, not at anyone in particular, but in media coverage in general. "Try finding out why we're hearing about this for the first time now."

While Rick did his search, I combed Pierson's campaign site and scanned some of his recent campaign emails. They'd not made much of a splash with their announcement of Hochberg's new role. She'd been on Pierson's legislative staff in D.C., and then ran the communications shop for his campaign in South Carolina and Nevada.

"Hey, Rick, it says here that as Lori Hochberg worked for the governor of Mississippi and then for the state Republican Party, before going quiet for a few years. Then she switched her party affiliation." I mulled that over for a minute. "So, with those other jobs, she must have been a true believer. I'll do a search of that period. And find out who replaced her... as Mrs. Tabakin, I mean."

"A woman who died a year after they married," Rick said. "Scotty-the- grieving-widower now. Still wears that wide band I saw in two photos and in Beaufort."

"Aren't we kind," I joked. "Just listen to us. Let's show Lady Lori some respect. Maybe she left Scotty because she got tired of his plantation owner attitudes."

"Could be." With his hands still, Rick stared at the screen and then at me. "But why do we care? What does she have to do with what we're up to now?"

"I'm not sure, but let's take note. A former bigwig in segregationist politics had a conversion of some kind and now is prominent in a major presidential campaign. Her ex is some kind of stealth supporter of a right wing Republican." I shrugged. "For all we know he's the brains behind TLTA."

"Correction," Rick said, holding up one finger to make his point. "We believe he's connected to Toomey's campaign. We don't know that he's on the payroll. We only know Jeff Hoover is, and he's the link to my cousin."

"I wish we were in the office," I said. "We need the white board."

"Tell me what you want. I can create a white board right here on my screen."

I thought for a minute. "Something about all this seems a little too convenient. A little pat."

"How so?"

I began trying to connect the dots. Meanwhile, Maude and Quigs were sending their own brand of clear signals, namely parking themselves by the front door. They looked longingly at me, and then Quigs lifted her paw and offered up a quiet "woof."

Rick laughed. "I think your little mutts are telling you they need to go out."

"Yeah, and I need to text Samantha to let her know I need her to dog sit yet again." I grabbed my coat and the leashes and told Rick I'd be right back.

He waved, but never looked up. He knew I was on to something.

Chapter Fourteen

The next day we landed in Billings and picked up the rental car. Rick drove and I checked the news on the expected crowd size at the Toomey rally—we were in deep red country and it could be huge. Montana wasn't a monolithic state, but this might be the only chance to see Toomey. In the general election, it wasn't likely the campaign would need to court voters in this state. It was too reliably red to spend precious campaign money needlessly defending.

I still wondered why Toomey bothered to make this stop in a place with miserable April weather. Maybe he wanted to deepen his footprint and use it in the fall to drive turnout and run up the popular vote. It might not mean anything legally, but Republicans wanted their win to include a hefty popular vote count, as well as a decisive win in the Electoral College. According to Rick, a tiny chance existed for Marie Kent to pull off a statewide win in November and rob Toomey of a reliably red state. Interesting, though, if Pierson won the nomination, the state wouldn't be up for grabs, but would go back to its constant red status.

We checked into a hotel near the airport, fairly far away from the rally site in a high school near Billings, but even deeper into Toomey country.

"So, what will we do if we run into Percy?" I mused, letting us both into my room, not exactly like the place in Hilton Head, but serviceable. Rick could settle into his when we finished our conversation. I reminded

Rick I wasn't alerting Percy or Steve to our arrival the next day.

"Your call," Rick said. He sat at the table and opened his computer. "I kinda thought we should let them know."

I pulled back the homely green drapes to let what light there was into the room. I had to turn on every lamp to give us enough light to work. If the room lacked charm the mountain view made up for it. Incredible. I didn't have to say it out loud but I understood Rick's thinking. My firm was being paid for attitude surveys and data analysis, not for spying on the leading Republican candidate—or even for visiting Marie's campaign stops.

On the other hand, I looked at what we were doing as value added. Wendy delivered the digital equivalent of reams of data about Marie's likely voters versus Pierson's cache of supporters. When we'd analyzed the data, it was clear this was a practical Democratic electorate this time. That's why Pierson was doing well with the "don't rock the boat" crowd, but Marie was popular with working people with improvement on their minds—no big revolution, just better jobs, schools, retirement. Oh, and by the way, what about those green jobs we've been promised for years? Hell, looking at it that way, I was becoming one of Marie's biggest fans myself.

"The country's been through a lot in the last few years," I said. "A pandemic, natural disasters, hurricanes, fires, washed out dams, economic fallout over all of it. Andersen has done about as well as anyone could, but the voters want another president who will try to put the broken parts put back together."

"My parents prove your point. They accept trees coming down in a storm, but not unreasonable delays in getting the debris off the road and repairing the damaged houses." Rick sighed. "But that begs the question at hand. What would lead someone to make the effort to show up at a Toomey rally? What is he capturing that the other candidates couldn't?"

"I don't know. Maybe we'll get some insight when we see him in person. In terms of the work we're doing, I can justify wanting to get a glimpse of Toomey up close," I said. "And if that catches Percy or Steve off guard then so be it. Besides, I'm aware this falls outside the mandate for regular expenses."

"If they want to spy, they have plenty of people to send to the Toomey rally," Rick said. "Besides, Billings is a long way from Missoula and Helena."

I pointed out the window. "No wonder people love it here." Snow covered almost everything in the distance, even though the fields and side roads we'd passed were broken up with patches of snow and muddy earth. This street itself, though, with its auto parts store, fast food restaurants lined up in a row, gas stations, and supermarkets could have been anywhere in the country.

"Assuming we don't get spotted tonight, we'll drive over to Missoula and then I'll text Percy and Steve when we get there. It will be a done deal. It's time I apply a little pressure to meet Marie." I'd made up my mind about that.

My phone signaled an incoming text. "Who knows? Maybe that's the campaign…oops, nope." I laughed. "It's even better. Samantha sent photos of the three dogs snoozing, kind of curled up together. She's got a big Irish setter with her for the week." I turned the phone so Rick could see the photo. "She's never sent me pictures of the dogs before. I wonder what prompted that."

"Cuteness. Plain and simple. Everybody takes pictures of their pets," Rick said. "I'm surprised she didn't send a video of them eating their dinner with napkins tucked into their collars." Rick tried to hold back a hearty laugh. "You could post it on the firm's Facebook page."

"All right, all right, I get it. I'm over the top. But I can't change, or maybe it's that I won't change." My pups were part of my being. "I love my dogs!"

"Changing the subject," Rick said, smirking, "let's not forget we still have Parker's first marriage hanging out there."

"No, no. Let's forget that," I said. "He had a short first marriage. They divorced, both remarried. He has a daughter. She *died*."

Rick smirked. "What's your point?"

"Who gives a rat's ass?" I pretended to shiver. "It creeped me out to dig around a man's life for no reason. Besides, if anything from Parker's past could be controversial it's more likely to come from his practice."

"Right you are," Rick said. "Besides, we'll stay plenty busy keeping track of the former Mrs. Tabakin. I think we can leave Parker alone."

"Right, we can't forget our convert," I said.

"We'll see if that's true."

I scoffed. "Okay, what now?"

"I'm not convinced," Rick said. "Seems like a conversion of convenience."

I glanced at Rick, whose fingers were tapping the screen of his tablet. I kept quiet, but I knew in my gut, another set of dots were begging for connection.

***

"What does Senator Kent know about you?" Toomey boomed to the crowd. "I'll tell you what she knows. Nothing! When she's not hanging with radical leftist professors, she's collecting money from the richest women in Hollywood."

Wild cheers erupted from the mostly male crowd. The few women present were as loud as the men.

Most everyone in the high school gym wore jeans and heavy jackets. Not everyone had gray hair, but most did. No firearms were allowed inside the rally. Good to know. Volunteers at long folding tables were handing out yard signs, but for the price of signing in with name, address, and the all-important email addresses and cell numbers.

It had been easy to slip into the crowd unnoticed, but for the friendly greetings we got from nearly every person we saw. Rick kept his eyes on the group standing behind Toomey while I scanned the crowd. Some part of me couldn't believe I was spending a freezing cold spring winter evening in a gym outside Billings, Montana. Reflecting on all that had happened since Percy dropped by the office, it occurred to me that almost from the first bomb threat, the job was nothing like I'd imagined it. The mall shooting was still under investigation because of the shooter's ties to right wing groups. Investigators had only weak leads about the person who murdered mostly young people in JoJo Campanella's office. No one knew if the isolated, thankfully harmless explosion in Seattle was connected with anything, everything, or nothing.

None of it, not even Parker's irrelevant so-called scandals had made me sour on Marie. She put in the work every day and so far nothing bad had come out to make a liar out of her. Having my behind-the-scenes role in her campaign only solidified my support. She was proving to be a resilient candidate, too, which is why I was eager to see her the next morning at her rally. And hopefully I would get to talk with her. If I could find a way to get around Steve.

Collectively, the data had become the elephant in the room, but I still couldn't say for sure that anyone was sabotaging Marie. On the other hand, the campaign was making what my gut told me were bad choices. I really wanted to be wrong about that.

An elbow jabbed my ribs, snapping me out of my reverie. I quickly joined in the applause just like everyone around me. I cast a grateful look to Rick, but he was already turning his attention to the stage and the doors.

When Toomey started talking about running up the vote on primary day, Rick and I edged toward the door.

It was the best time to slip out and get to the rental at the far end of the lot. Icy rain was falling, and we hit the defrost button and put the wipers on high speed to be able to see anything. Our hotel was 35 miles away. Whose bright idea was that? I didn't like admitting it was mine.

"Most people come to this area and go to interesting places and see all the General Custer stuff—you know, that damned Little Bighorn Battlefield," I said. "History. Wild mustangs and a canyon. But no, not us. We're on some fucking wild goose chase to spot your cousin doing stuff he shouldn't. Not that we know what it means—this shit he's fooling around with all the time."

The words were barely out of my mouth when the car lost traction and made a 180 degree turn. "We could go back where we came from," Rick grunted, expertly turning the wheel and avoiding the temptation to slam the brakes.

"Right."

"In case you hadn't noticed, we're in trouble here," Rick snapped "I can barely see through this rain or ice or whatever the fuck it is. And no taillights to follow."

I was hungry but kept that to myself while we inched along at about 30 mph and finally slowed even more when we came up behind a semi that was doing no more than 20. An SUV appeared from behind and more lights appeared.

"Nothing to do but follow the truck," I said with a sigh.

"I need a beer," Rick said. "Two beers. And pizza. Oh wait, make that a steak. Isn't this steak country?"

I snorted. "The whole U.S.A. is steak country. It's woven into our flag somewhere."

We inched along in near silence. The only sound was ice hitting the windshield and the blower working to keep up with the fogged up windows.

"This trip was my idea, wasn't it?" I said.

"That would be a yes," Rick said irritably.

"So far, part one was a big zero," I admitted, "but there's always tomorrow."

Rick watched the road and checked his mirrors and tightened his grip on the wheel. "Maybe so, Matt, but I can't think about tomorrow when I'm hoping we make it to that ugly ass motel in the next hour."

I couldn't argue with that, so I kept my mouth shut for the last miles until we saw the exit we were looking for. The truck's exit, too. We followed it off, and the SUV exited behind us. For half a second, I was a little paranoid. Was the SUV following us?

"Why do I feel like we're doing something slightly shady?" Rick asked as he glanced in the rearview mirror.

"I don't know. It's like being a kid sneaking around behind our parents' backs." I gripped the handhold on the passenger door as we made a quarter turn on the ramp forcing Rick to fight with the wheel again. Meanwhile, the SUV behind us went into a skid and Rick steered into the right turn lane instead of the left so he could get out of the SUV's way and roll to a near stop before easing onto the road. The SUV had room to maneuver without slamming in our rear end. Good move, Rick. We could turn around later. I exhaled. "Aren't you glad the primaries are more than half over?"

Rick laughed, but at the first stoplight, he made a left into a parking lot where we could come back out and make another turn and drive in the right direction. A steakhouse with a giant steer's head came into view. It was across the road and down half a block from the motel.

"Looks like we're having steak for real," I said. "Eat there or carry out?"

"What's the worst that can happen?" Rick said, impatient with me by now. "We see my cousin with Hoover? Or alone, or with a woman. Luckily, the chances of that happening are slim to none. The Kent campaign is across the state."

We'd been so careful to hide ourselves. But what the hell. Rick was right. This time, saying we were in the middle of nowhere was actually true. At least nowhere to us.

The place was quiet, but I didn't know whether to attribute that to it being a weekday night or the miserable weather. The host seated us at a table opposite a private room. We heard the muffled buzz of conversation inside, mostly in low tones, but occasionally laughter pierced the air.

"Private party, huh?" Rick remarked when the combination host-waiter, a burly guy with tattoos covering almost every inch of his visible skin, handed us oversized menus.

The host smiled. "A big night in here. That's Senator Kent's campaign. A little fundraising dinner, I'm told."

I choked back a hoot of laughter as I met Rick's eye, but quickly reassembled my casual face and added my comment. "I guess a lot of candidates are roaming around the state."

"We've seen a few come and go. This was the first chance I've had to meet Senator Kent, though. Her family is with her. They seem to be having a good time."

My heart pounding in my chest, I said we'd like a couple of beers, whatever was local, and the waiter walked off. Rick and I still hadn't done more than exchange a glance.

Since the place screamed steak, I settled on it. "I'm keeping it simple. What could go wrong with a Custer steak, medium rare and whatever comes with it?"

Rick agreed and when the waiter came back with our beer, I soon learned ordering the steak was the easy part. What came with it got complicated. Before Rick got his turn, I had to choose between classic, curly, waffled, or sweet potato fries or baked or mashed potatoes, plain, cheesy, or garlic. And that didn't count the hot bread options or the salad dressings.

Meanwhile, I tried to figure out a way to make sure I

got my chance to meet Marie. If I ruffled feathers and forced the issue, so be it.

Our beer arrived quickly, but Rick hardly noticed. He was busy checking messages.

"Anything I should know?" I asked. "I'd prefer not to deal with a crisis and a medium rare steak."

"Not at the moment. But, tell me, how are you planning to deal with Marie?" he whispered, and scanned the room to make sure we were alone. Only a few people were at tables. Most people had the good sense to stay off the roads.

"We have to be underway early tomorrow," I said, as if it mattered one way or the other at that moment. By the time I'd gulped down some beer, I'd concluded that if it weren't for the immediate chance to meet Marie, I'd have written off this leg of the Montana caper as a waste of time. And it would be entirely my fault. Maybe the purpose would end up being the chance to meet Marie.

"Maybe it's not Marie you—I mean, we—need to see," Rick said. "Maybe it's Steve."

I swallowed another mouthful of the cold beer. "I'm aware I'm being vague. Somehow, it feels like we're back in South Carolina with the threats and the massacre. A white nationalist massacre at that," I scoffed. "Damn you, anyway, it's all your fault."

Rick jabbed his finger on his chest. "My fault? How's that?"

"You and your formulas and maps and connections about campaign stops. See? You started it," I teased. "Then Toomey's past and the people he surrounds himself with began raising more flags."

"We really don't…"

Rick stopped talking when the door to the private room opened and about a dozen people filed out. We simultaneously got to our feet and walked toward the group. I spotted Steve, and Rick waved to Percy to grab his attention as the two of us got closer. If Rick had reservations, he didn't show them.

Percy's mouth dropped open before his brain had a chance to hide his surprise, maybe shock. Then he remembered and pasted on a neutral expression, followed by the start of a genuine smile. Steve stared at me, and not giving a shit anymore, I took two long strides and planted myself in front of him.

"Good to see you, Steve." Under different circumstances, I'd have extended my elbow for a post-pandemic bump. I held back and so did he. Instead, I turned to Marie and her family, and introduced myself.

That's when Steve took over. He infused a little energy in his voice when he said, "Matt is the Chicago data guy I was telling you about."

Marie looked puzzled at first, but ever the professional she looked me in the eye and smiled cordially. "I expected I'd have a chance to meet you one day." She pointed down to the floor. "I hadn't thought it would be here. Why are you here?"

I avoided the question by introducing Rick, and we both met Parker and Amanda.

Finally, I said, "I could give you a long technical answer, but the truth is I like a hands-on approach, Senator Kent. We can do our work better when we get a sense of the candidate. And the major opponents, too, of course."

"Matt was in South Carolina to get his first look at you in person," Steve interjected. He sounded smooth, but he shifted his weight from one foot to the other.

Percy, standing a little behind, ran his hand over his mouth. Wiping away beads of sweat over his upper lip? Why?

"We'll be in Missoula in the morning," I said, glancing from Marie to Parker, who stood next to his daughter. He smiled pleasantly and looked mildly interested. "We'll slip in and out of your rally, like we did here."

Suddenly, Rick spoke up. "I get a really good vibe from your campaign," he said, grinning at Marie and then at Percy.

Percy apparently decided it was the right time to interject some new facts. "I'm not sure if I mentioned this, Senator, but Rick is my cousin."

Steve rolled his eyes, but the information seemed to pique Marie's interest. "Is that so? And you work for Matt?"

As if she wanted to be sure we knew she was in control of her campaign, Marie squared her shoulders and turned to me. "So that's how we got lucky enough to find you."

"The luck is all mine." I sounded like a gentleman, a throwback to a more civilized era. "Rick works for himself, but he's signed on with me as a contractor for some important projects. Like this one." I caught myself in time not to use the word "cases." I didn't want to wear my jury consultant hat too obviously. It was also clear to me I wasn't going to have a chance to probe around Marie's opinions of her campaign, and certainly not her advertising.

Parker pointed with his chin toward our table. "Looks like your dinners have arrived."

"Don't let us keep you," Steve said, extending his hand to shepherd Amanda and Parker toward the door. "We were leaving anyway. We've got rooms in a hotel downtown."

Percy was leading the others away. They nodded cordially, but we weren't introduced.

"What a lucky coincidence," Marie said as she inched away from us. "Wish us a big crowd tomorrow. The staff is working hard in Missoula." She pivoted away, but then turned back to us. "Oh, and drive carefully."

"We will," I said, as if her words demanded a response.

Our food was still hot when Rick and I sat down. Keeping our thoughts to ourselves, we dug into the giant platters of food, including a mountain of sweet potato fries so high I thought it might topple over. I didn't know what to make of what just happened, other than happily discovering that it was easy to talk with Marie. If the circumstances had been different, I was confident she'd be ready to engage in serious strategy conversations.

About halfway through the second beer and three-quarters of the way through the steak, I pushed back in my chair and declared myself done.

"I'm right behind you, Matt," Rick said, putting down his steak knife and fork and splaying his hands across his stomach. "I feel like my dad. He was always patting his stomach when he'd overeaten. I swore I would never pick up his habit."

I laughed at the image, but every time Rick pointed out the little flaws of his quirky dad, I envied him, sometimes so deeply it hurt. He had a dad who was no wealthy mogul or even successful by corporate boardroom sense, but he'd been a real dad. He hung out with his kids because he liked them. I'd had a dad who was mean to my mom and couldn't hold a job. Once he left us, I rarely saw him again.

Deciding it was time to change the subject—fast—I mused about the restaurant. "I'm wondering how soon we can get one of these places into my neighborhood," I said. "You have to go to the burbs to get a pound of nearly raw beef tossed to you."

Rick almost choked on his beer. He knew exactly what I was talking about and got a big kick out of it. Sure enough, he leaned back in his chair and rubbed his stomach.

"On that note of fun, I suppose we need to hash out what just happened," I said.

"I guess." For some reason, though, Rick kept right on laughing as he said, "My cousin might as well have been wearing a muzzle for all he managed to say. As for Steve, he acted like a sheep dog or maybe a collie. Whatever kind of dog people use out in these parts to keep cattle all together."

"These parts, huh? I think the Lassie dogs are good at that." The whole scenario, the two of us in fucking

Billings, Montana stuffing ourselves with steak and fries seemed over-the-top funny. I laughed until Rick started checking out the room to make sure we were more or less alone. No need, really, since the only people left in the restaurant were the employees and one lone couple who'd moved to the bar.

"The next time I need to herd sheep or cattle," Rick said, "I'll be sure to remember that."

I shook my head. "It struck me how wildly unlikely all this seems. You and me, here. And Marie and her entourage landing in this same steak joint, too."

"True, I have to remind myself why."

Having finally stopped laughing at this theater of the absurd, I leaned forward and plunked my elbows on the table. "If Percy is secretly working for Toomey through his friend Jeff Hoover, then his nervousness makes perfect sense."

"Matt…come on, that's a stretch."

"Is it?" I challenged. "But okay, this is all hypothetical, anyway. But hear me out."

"I know what you're going to ask. If what you're saying about Percy, my cousin, let's remember, is true, then what's with Steve?"

"Is he in on it?" I couldn't get there. I shook my head. "Nothing points there…well, except those ad buys that still puzzle me."

"Here's something that can get us part of the way to making sense of Steve." Rick paused. "He hired my cousin. I mean, I know Percy is good at this political stuff, but before this he worked on other campaigns as a lowly office runner."

"Ah, coffee boy? Is that what you mean? You yourself said he was smart and people saw it." I gave the table a couple of gentle whacks with my balled up hand. One possibility loomed. I didn't like to bring it up, but it'd been bothering me.

"You weren't in the room, but the night I met Steve, he and Percy were talking about Marie driving across South Carolina and pumping gas along the way—

or at least stopping in the plazas." Why did I even remember this? "She took some selfies with people she chatted with, like informal photo ops. Percy saw it as great exposure, but Steve was much more grudging about it. Your cousin understood why one woman telling another woman about greeting Senator Kent in the plaza was a good thing. Percy was counting votes one at a time. Steve sort of agreed, but to tell you the truth, I don't think he demonstrated Percy's savvy about exploiting moments like that."

"You're saying Steve is a saboteur?"

I shook my head. "Nope. Not at all. For whatever reason, and I can't name it, I trust the guy personally. Steve is brilliant in the ivory tower sort of way, and maybe he'd be the best man for certain campaigns. I don't think he's that smart when it comes to Marie."

"A little elaboration, please."

"I've been wondering why, with such enthusiastic supporters, she can't overtake Pierson," I said. "Arnold and his crowd have painted Marie as a risky choice. Steve hasn't countered it—not well enough. I don't think he was that great a choice as campaign manager for her."

Rick stared at me, silent until he gathered his thoughts. "You have a point. If it's true, then sabotaging Marie would be child's play."

I didn't like interpreting his words, but I had to do it. "So, you're speculating that your cousin really isn't exactly what—or who—he purports to be?"

Rick shook his head. "This is me thinking out loud. I'm not there yet. All we really have goes back to Beaufort. The Percy-Jeff Hoover spotting."

It was my turn to be silent. Too many questions. Too few answers. "Now we have the Scotty Tabakin mystery, and figuring out how his ex-wife landed a job working in the Pierson campaign. We can't claim any connection between Lori Hochberg and Pierson as far as we know, other than their career in politics."

Rick and I looked at each other and simultaneously scoffed.

"See what you got me into?" I joked. I took one more gulp of beer before pulling out my credit card and signaling the waiter. "And tomorrow is another day."

Chapter Fifteen

It was still dark when my phone rang, and rang…
At first, I thought it was the damn alarm due to go
off any second. When I picked it up, Wendy's name on
the screen grabbed my attention. I got out of bed fast.
"What? Is everything okay?"

"That's what I called to ask you? It's early there, but
have you seen the news?"

"No. What now?" I said with a cynical scoff.

"More bad news, that's what. Someone shot out
Marie's windows in her Missoula headquarters a few
hours ago. Dark of night and all that."

"Anyone hurt?" I asked. I didn't even have the heart
to start scrolling through my phone. "Just tell me."

"No injuries, but that's not all. The same thing
happened to Pierson's office. Get this, Toomey's office
was hit, too. Not just a threat this time. All three of
those offices were in Missoula. Not that far apart."

"Did you text Rick?"

"No, not yet. I figured you could tell him, or he'll
get an alert on his phone. I heard about it because I
turned on the news when I got up. I have to go in early
to finish up some reports. Steve texted me last night
to see if I could get everything to him this morning."

"Speaking of that, will you take a look at the
questions we embedded that rank the safest choice,
down to least. And, this is important, let's revisit the
female demographics."

"Really? That came out of nowhere," Wendy

185

declared, clearly confused. "Aren't you more concerned with who shot out the windows?"

"You have no idea how concerned I am," I said, feeling more sad than angry. "I just can't explain…"

"Is this 'need to know' or are you piecing something together?"

I had to laugh. "It's the latter. But I'm going to ask you about someone I'd like you to search. Look at sites about women in politics, not candidates, necessarily, but leading staffers—emerging leaders— for candidates running right now. See who comes up more than once or twice. You know how that goes. A woman gets one mention in a piece about women in politics and suddenly her name comes up in every list."

"Anything special you want me to look for?" Wendy asked.

"Not really." I wanted to hold back any hints about a major political conversion. "It's not a secret project. You should see the same names in all kinds of media. I'll figure out how it fits together later."

"Sounds a little mysterious, Matt." She sighed. "There's nothing new about mystery around here."

The knock on the door brought my talk with Wendy to an end, and the beginning of a new conversation with Rick, who had two giant cups of coffee in his hand, courtesy of the hotel breakfast room.

"I thought you'd rather take in the news here," he said.

"Unlike what happened to Campanella's crew, and the restaurant workers, no injuries that we know of," I said, "at least according to Wendy. I just got off the phone with her."

"Is Marie going to have her rally?" Rick said.

"I haven't heard otherwise, but I haven't reached out yet. I figure they must be frantically figuring out what to do and don't need a call from me. Whether she does or she doesn't, we'll still go over there. I want to see these vandalized offices for myself." We'd also booked a flight home from Missoula. I let out a cynical laugh. "I just called it vandalism, like someone spray-painted graffiti on a few windows."

"Right. It takes a firearm to shoot out windows, Matt. Not exactly vandalism."

"Toomey got it this time." I nodded toward the TV screen. "There's Jeff Hoover now."

Hoover adopted the tone I'd have expected. Serious, concerned, relieved no one was injured or worse. He supports the investigation. It's a federal crime. Everything that came out of Hoover's mouth was predictable. Way too predictable.

"Why do I think I have to hang on every word?" I said. "The guy is saying nothing original."

Rick laughed. "If I knew I'd tell you. I can't keep myself away from all this political stuff."

My secret was that I was into this more than I let on. Even with the uncertainty and, of all things, shots fired into campaign headquarters. It didn't matter. I wanted to be part of it. And like a detective, figure out what was going on.

***

Rick and I were about to part ways with Montana. I can't say we were sorry. As stunning as it was, it struck me as just another political crime scene. Sure, I was happy that no one was hurt in this latest attack on campaign headquarters. Marie spent a good part of her rally talking about fighting the criminals who would inflict violence and threats. She didn't launch into the usual lecture about bringing the country together, but spoke of these perpetrators as outliers. Good for her. The solution to shattered windows wasn't to bring ordinary people together, but to root out those who would commit crimes of any sort.

Good enough. Almost good enough for Rick. He was hoping for a promise to investigate what he was sure were right wing groups trying to disrupt the election.

The way he looked at it, if the Russians managed to get involved in the past elections, what would prevent our own homegrown hate groups from creating chaos? He persisted in returning to the point that so far, no one in the Toomey campaign had ever been harmed or even put in danger.

Pierson went through the same kind of event in Salt Lake City earlier in the primary cycle, and now he saw it happen again. So far, Pierson's campaign was relatively quiet and the manager, David Scheffler, made most of the statements. I wouldn't have noticed before, but now that the name Lori Hochberg had surfaced, I couldn't stop looking for anything that would bear her name.

Rick and I didn't see Percy or Steve again before we took off for the airport, after a swing past the now boarded up windows. We were both lost in our thoughts and our books on the flight and spoke little when we landed and headed to my truck in the parking lot. I dropped Rick off with the promise to compare notes in the morning.

But before Rick closed the passenger door, I said, "I'm not sorry we took this on. Are you? Be honest…"

Rick surprised me by not answering right away. Instead he stared off into space and twisted his mouth in thought.

I waited. My gut gave me a bumpy ride for a few seconds.

"I'm not sorry," Rick finally said, "but I'm in a different place than I was when we started. Know what I mean?"

"Tell me more," I said, extending my hand toward him as an invitation to talk.

"It's not just that Marie and the others are running into this harassment. I get that. I expected it." Rick grimaced. "But now we've got full blown terrorism going on here."

I nodded, but sensed he had more to say. "And…"

"I think it's bigger than what we're seeing. Bigger

than what we already know." Rick flashed one of the grimmest expressions I'd ever seen on his face.

"Whoa. Your face is sending a message and I'm not sure I like it."

"What's to like? Not much." Rick didn't allow much emotion to come through. He was giving me just the facts. He wasn't wrong. "Even with that, I'm okay with being part of this. In a way I got you into it. If we're in deep, it's my fault."

I shifted in the seat, tense and yet curious to hear all Rick's thoughts on this undertaking that was so different from what we thought it would be. "We could argue that point, by the way, but that can wait for another day. But what else, Rick? I can see you've got more on your mind."

"I pay a lot more attention to the crazies than you do," Rick said. "I visit the conspiracy sites, the hate pages, whatever. I look at what people are saying. The internet is lit up with crazy theories and accusations. But why isn't this violence a bigger story. We get breaking news—everyone gets upset, and then what? A few journalists stay on it, especially here in Chicago, mostly because of JoJo, but also because the Dems are having the convention here."

I'd wondered about that, too. "It's almost like people are used to this nowadays. It's a big story, but we are seeing a lot of analysis of trends. Do we really expect political campaigns to be like this?"

"That's the question," Rick said. "I don't know. Even my parents aren't that shocked by all this. At one time, it would have been almost unthinkable to even threaten this kind of shit."

"It sure seems bigger—and denser—than a couple of nut jobs breaking windows." With a shrug, I added. "I don't think you and I are in danger right now. But I think we're only a little way through all the layers. There's that Tabakin guy. Now his ex is working for Pierson. Who knows what we'll find when we dig deeper there?"

"I guess we have our work cut out for this coming week, huh?" Along with more advice to Marie's campaign, which they may or may not use.

"More dots to connect," Rick pointed out, "and when I say I think this might be bigger, I mean we might have walked ourselves into a conspiracy like a couple of innocents." He paused. "What I really think is, this goes way beyond any one election."

"You sure know how to make a guy feel good," I said cynically, but that's exactly what I thought he'd say.

"Looks like that's my job." Rick grunted with frustration. He closed the car door and walked to his building.

I drove off. He'd confirmed what I'd concluded.

***

"Ho hum," Wendy said. "Another breaking news banner is flashing across the screen. Should we bother to pay attention?"

"Nah, let's ignore it this time," I teased, knowing that wouldn't happen. But Wendy and I had the TV muted and my back was to it, so it wasn't too hard to keep my mind on the summaries Wendy provided from the large survey we completed for Marie.

"These results have shifted a little from the first survey," I observed. "Looks like she's picked up more minority support, mostly among women."

"She dropped a few points among Millennial men and the Gen Xer males, too," Wendy pointed out. "Why would young men prefer a dull old guy like Arnold Pierson, over a dynamic younger-than-her-years woman?"

I thought about that characterization for a minute. "Is that how you'd describe Marie? As someone who seems younger than she is?"

"Exactly. She's… What? Matt, there's a break in the case?" She grabbed the remote and unmuted the TV.

I swiveled in my chair. A guy in an FBI jacket stood next to the Chief of Police in Missoula Police. At least that's what the banner told me.

"It's a preliminary discovery—early in the process, the youngish FBI agent said, "but we think it's significant."

The banner below changed: LINK FOUND BETWEEN SC MALL MASSACRE AND SUSPECTS IN CAMPAIGN VANDALISM

Man, now that's breaking news. Specifically, the campaign office shooters—plural—had literature from the same organization. It turned up in a late night search of what they called the suspects' apartment in a town outside of Missoula. An international organization, according to the FBI agent. "We've been tracking many of these white nationalist and white supremacy groups that operate in many countries," the agent said. "They have a presence in most European countries, the U.S., Canada, Australia, and wherever this kind of racist philosophy takes root."

The agent admitted, however, they didn't know a great deal about White Nations First, mostly known as WNF. "This group has come to our attention in our intelligence reports relatively recently. We think it operates as a coalition, not as a single group with central headquarters. We don't know yet if they coordinate their actions…uh, crimes, I should say. But that's all I can say at the present time."

Curious. WNF, not TLTA, like JoJo's office. One of the reporters traveling with the Kent campaign shouted an obvious question about the link between the South Carolina shooter and the person—or persons—they had in custody for firing shots at the campaign office windows. "Do you have proof they were in contact with each other? Is the WNF operating mostly online?"

"At this point, I can't say. We're at the beginning stages of this investigation and piecing together what we have," the agent said. "This is our first briefing on the matter, but we'll pass on what we learn."

"Do you believe any of the campaigns are in danger right now in any other location?" a political reporter from the Washington Post shouted.

The FBI agent paused, clearly unsure how to answer. Finally, he said, "We have not changed our guidelines for campaigns. We believe all campaigns should be tightening their security plans. This is an evolving situation."

My phone was busy notifying me to texts coming in and new alerts. Rick was probably on the bus coming to the office and scrolling through his phone now.

"It doesn't tell us much," Wendy said.

"It's more than we knew before, and they're talking about suspects, so that means at least two," I said, feeling philosophical about it. This news was giving me hope that little cracks might be coming in this group of cases. "Maybe it's only a step away from getting a lead on who killed all those people at JoJo Campanella's office."

"Bo and I were talking about all this last night," Wendy said. "I haven't told him about our project, for obvious reasons, and he's not quite the political junky we are, but he still hears things. Funny, he said his gut told him these weren't copycat crimes, but maybe more like a network of people—even loosely connected."

I nodded but kept quiet.

"He hates this stuff," Wendy blurted. "He's not a Toomey fan. I think he views Arnold Pierson as safe and someone who can beat Toomey in the fall." She pushed her hair off her face, a nervous gesture I'd become familiar with over the years. "He's not that black and white about politics. I mean, he kind of liked both the Bushes. Bo calls himself an independent, although he admits that's getting tougher these days."

Wendy left it at that, which reinforced the impression I'd already had of Bo. Lots of people were exactly like him. They weren't wed to parties, or even to specific policies. And for these folks, character mattered.

When the next breaking news banner came up below a reporter doing a location shot, Wendy almost shouted, "A married couple? They arrested a couple—not young kids, either."

Sure enough, some mugshots filled the screen. A middle-aged—to be kind—man and woman weren't smiling for the camera. It was almost disheartening to look at these two ordinary people, who, even if they turned out not to be completely innocent had a kind of odd broken look to them.

I was staring at the TV when two texts came in back to back. One from Rick that was short and sweet. WTF?

The other was from Cooper. Not as short and not too sweet, either. Much to discuss. Bring Rick to Springfield for IL primary meeting.

***

Cooper Julian was a political animal as well as a law and justice analyst. That's why his show was one of the long-running legal programs on cable. I'd enjoyed appearing on his show many years back, but after I left criminal law and disappeared into my own head for a while, I no longer accepted Coop's invitations. The Marchand case changed that, and I'd occasionally appear as his guest expert on jury issues.

It didn't surprise me that Coop was following our current spate of domestic terrorism. Strange as it sounded, it was right up his alley. But his cryptic text about bringing Rick amused me in ways hard to explain. I mean, really, I was beginning to wonder if Coop was harboring old-fashioned British detective fantasies for real.

In any case, though, in the spirit of considering himself on call, my man Rick was okay with a trip to Springfield, which is how we ended up checking into rooms in the same hotel. This time, Wendy and Bo were with us. "Just in case," I'd said.

"In case of what?" Wendy asked, when I'd suggested she and Bo come along—if he was free to come with the three of us.

"Hey, who can resist a trip to Springfield in the raw days of Midwest spring?" I joked.

"Right. Bo mentioned Costa Rica the other day," Wendy said, "but I don't recall Springfield being on his bucket list."

"Hey, you guys," Rick said in a somber tone, "Springfield is an historic place. Remember that guy Lincoln, had a beard? Besides, this is the Illinois primary. Who knows? It could be when Marie tips the scales. Who knows?"

Seeing that Rick was being serious, I conceded our Chicago snobbery. "Okay, okay, you're right. I expect Coop will make that very point."

With the news of a Missoula couple arrested for shooting out campaign windows, and the FBI linking incidents to a so-called coalition of old worn out racist groups, Coop wanted in. Into what? Into what Rick and I had found. It was my idea to broaden out our confidential circle and bring in Bo, swearing him to secrecy, of course.

Before Rick and I met with Coop, the four of us ordered pizza delivered to my suite and as we sat around the table, I took charge of bringing Bo into the loop. It didn't take long for him to react to the threads we pulled together, including Percy's furtive visit to a Republican candidate's campaign rally. The frontrunner, no less.

"He's your cousin?" Bo asked, pushing his glasses up into place.

Bo had a habit of adjusting his glasses—often—and especially when something threw him. Somehow, it added to his cerebral computer genius image, as opposed to computer nerd. A long time ago, Rick set me straight about turning techies into nerds. Even in jest.

"He is, although I hadn't seen him for years,"

Rick said. "But then, the more we learned about some of the people around him, the worse it got. Meanwhile, we've got real terrorism going on."

"So, you're trying to find links between all these incidents, starting with South Carolina threats and the mall shooter, plus a really deadly bombing in Chicago, and what look like random bomb threats elsewhere. Plus, now two lowlifes shot out campaign offices in Montana."

"We think it's not as bipartisan as some claim," Wendy added. She pointed to me. "They keep coming up with shadowy players."

"These shadowy guys are in the campaigns?" Bo asked.

"Ha! One of the guys that should be in the shadows is the frontrunner himself." I took a long pull on a bottle of cold beer. "Give me a break."

"We don't get it." Rick said. "I mean, this guy is a fucking sleaze. His white supremacy rap sheet is long."

"Can you show me?" Bo asked Rick. "Send me links."

"We don't send links," Rick said. "We're cryptic on the phone, and we watch our texts."

"Bottom line? What are you afraid of?"

"Escalation," I said at the same time Rick blurted, "More violence."

"Let's not forget we work for Marie Kent. My obligation on every level is to her," I said. "We're providing data she needs in order to run her campaign effectively. I don't want this other angle we're pursuing to get mixed up with the business we're doing with Marie." I reconsidered what I'd just said. "Well, at least as much as possible. It's hard when we don't know who's being targeted next."

"She can't seem to close the delegate gap, can she?" Bo said, pushing away the stained paper plate which minutes ago was heaped with pepperoni pizza. "I've been following this from the beginning. I was hoping for new and different, rather than ending up with another white guy who's spent his life in politics."

"You and a lot of us, especially young people," I said, thinking back on the rally in Iowa. It seemed like I stood in the cold on the edge of the crowd ages ago. "And the rest of us here, too, when it comes right down to it."

"Why am I here?" Bo asked, sending a smirk Wendy's way. "Other than having a little getaway with you and two of your closest friends." He grinned. "Not that I'm complaining."

I gestured to Rick. "Why don't you answer that?"

"It's about connecting the dots."

"Isn't it always?" Bo quipped. "Gotta see the big picture. Can't do that without seeing how the dots play out."

"Yep, it is. But we don't like the picture that's filling. The dots are leading us places we'd rather not go."

Rick moved his chair toward Bo while Wendy and I cleared away the remains of dinner. We still had half an hour before we were due to meet with Coop. Then, he'd do his show, and we'd see him again in the morning. Coop wanted us in his room, not mine. It seemed safer that way. He always had a reason to meet with me, considered me his old buddy and frequent guest. He was used to having a lot of eyes on him, especially when he was on the verge of exposing information, usually through someone else. Coop had information others preferred was buried and never saw the light. It could happen again, and I was feeling paranoid all around.

"Remember, Bo, I'm skirting a line here," I said. "Normally, I'd reveal nothing about what we're doing for Marie. I'm still going to hold back a lot of that, because it's not relevant. But Rick has used what is essentially public information about the other campaigns and we've drawn some conclusions and did background research. It's plunked us into the midst of a bunch of shadowy characters."

Bo's gaze was fixed on me as I spoke, his frown deepening with concern. "Now, even the FBI is talking about white nationalists—even using the name WNF. We need you to help us make sense of it. Only if you want to dive into the deep end where the water is murky. And if you can agree not to talk with anyone about anything you hear."

Wendy glanced at Bo and spoke up. "I told him about the secrecy around this, Matt. Bo knows this has got to be kept confidential information."

"I've got the same situation in the corporate work I do," Bo said. "Under normal circumstances, I'm not sure I'd want to know what characters are lurking about causing trouble. But these aren't normal times. Not with bombs going off and shooters mowing down minorities in a mall and a crazed couple shooting out windows." He stopped to take a breath. "If you're on to something, and I can help, I'll do it. Wendy trusts you." He gave her an appreciative smile. "That's good enough for me."

So, Wendy really had struck gold. Bo trusted me and I trusted him, largely because when it came to things having to do with my firm, Wendy had never let me down.

Rick didn't waste a second walking Bo through the events, starting with his first conversation with his cousin, which led to him suggesting Percy call me. It was like I relived South Carolina and all that came next right up to uncovering these characters in Toomey's past and meeting Marie herself. I could have closed my eyes and still had a good picture of what Rick was showing him on the computer.

"So, you're seeing patterns," Bo said, "with certain candidates bunching up in the same locations and threats and the campaign office shootings occurred in clusters, except for a few outliers, like Salt Lake City." Bo spoke in an even, rational tone as if running it through his mind to make sure it made sense. "The field is basically three people now. Toomey emerged as the winner in his party, and now it's Pierson and Kent fighting it out. But that doesn't seem to matter in the pattern."

"Right, Bo, but the initial incidents are still important," Rick said. "Not to mention my cousin's visit to the Toomey rally—his chumminess with Jeff Hoover, and now maybe this Scotty character."

"And this odd couple out in Montana. I still don't get why Toomey's past, practically throwing white sheets over his head and adding a pointy hat, didn't bite him in the ass," I said.

"I don't think it's all that complicated. It's because his followers don't care," Bo said, looking up at the ceiling and shaking his head. "Fucking idiots."

Sometimes I wished I'd never heard of Percy or Jeff Hoover or any of them. Here we were looking into things no one else seemed interested in. I cleared my throat. "To be honest, none of this would leap out at us if not for the violence. JoJo and the mall shooter— so many casualties. With JoJo, the FBI identified the possibility of a connection with TLTA—the League of True Americans, but no one knows who they really are. Now WNF is coming up."

"That seems unlikely," Bo said. "Nowadays, it's hard to stay in the shadows."

"Which is why the FBI and a slew of reporters have connected the couple in Montana with WNF, White Nations First. That's the same group the mall shooter was a part of. Or, so connecting the dots tells us," Rick said.

"So how did it happen that this Scotty guy, a known racist, was hanging out with the major candidate?" I asked to anyone and everyone. "How is it the likely Republican candidate for president of our country used to work for people like him? Why does Jeff Hoover allow Tabakin within five miles of Toomey?"

Bo appeared to ignore me, but he jumped out his chair and grabbed a second tablet out his backpack. "I don't want to clutter up my other tablet or computer.

They've got work data on it." He held up the tablet. "Not hack proof, of course, but since I'm not doing anything illegal, I'm not so worried. I carry them both."

The room fell into silence, which I broke with my amused scoff. "I can't believe I'm saying this, but Rick, what if we put Bo on WNF? Why don't you look at the gun-totin' couple? Why don't I keep digging around into Scotty's sorry life? And Wendy, see what comes up on various sites about Lori Hochberg. I thought she would have come up before."

Wendy shook her head. "You know, I did a quick search a while back, but she's hardly mentioned at all. She's an assistant communications director, too, so I was surprised. And Pierson has a big communications shop. She's lost in the shuffle."

I dismissed all that and flapped my hand to wave it off. "But what about her past? She was married to Tabakin, wife number three."

"From what I read, when she left the marriage she left right wing politics behind."

"It smells bad." Rick didn't elaborate, and we all chuckled.

"Hey, Matt, somebody has to keep in touch with the Kent campaign," Wendy said. "I'll do that." She nodded to me. "So far, no one is bringing up Bentley's very short first marriage."

Rick immediately spoke in his driest voice. "Who gives a rat's ass?"

I laughed. "That's been Rick's position all along. We don't know why Coop thought there was something there. Maybe he was warning us that a doctor—a surgeon—is vulnerable."

"We needed to check it out, though." Rick conceded. "Matt's friend Cooper Julian is a serious dude. Not to be ignored."

"I think he went down a blind alley on Marie's family," Wendy said.

Bo, who had fallen deep in thought, suddenly

brushed his longish sandy hair out of his eyes. "Damn, we're in a world of effing hurt."

"That bad, Bo?" Wendy asked.

"I need to jump into a swimming pool filled with hand sanitizer just to look at what this WNF crowd makes public. If they do this in public, imagine what they do in secret."

"Precisely," Rick said. "The FBI agent talked about that yesterday. It sounded like he was issuing a warning."

Bo ran his hand over the screen. "What they make public has a patina of intellectual argument. You know, Professor Dickhead says the races weaken their genes when they mix. Lowered immunity, reduced IQs, the usual bullshit."

"I saw where they're trying to claim the whiter the gene pool the lower the incidence of Covid-19," Rick said. "Worldwide, according to them. Not just death rates, but actual vulnerability. Apparently, WNF claims mixed race people are the most vulnerable of all. Something about DNA mutations. They have some kind of bogus study based on made up numbers. No one can look at hospital admissions and claim to accurately assign mixed race status, anyway."

"We're all a mix of something," Wendy said, so reasonably, we couldn't help but laugh.

"Right. I don't think we need DNA analysis to agree on that." I scoffed. "Come to think of it, I don't want anyone taking too close a look at my ancestors. I'm sure my gene pool has more muck and algae than water lilies."

Rick snorted a laugh. "Water lilies? Good one, Matt."

Bo didn't react. But, as if just coming up from a deep dive, he said, "You know I think the trick is to search the names that aren't the bigwigs. The guy on the website is proud of his name, Cesar Adams, not a common name, but a waspy one. I'll look for him later." Bo jabbed the air toward the tablet screen. "For now, I want to know who Elly Roscoe is."

Puzzled, I asked Bo why.

"She comes up in the name in the list of references for this good-for-nothing study. A minor player? Is she American? Where does she live? What's her deal?" Bo said.

"Would that be her real name?" Rick asked.

"Dunno. But I'm searching her name and variations…and OMG, here she is." Bo's eyes opened wider as he scanned. "It's not her name, but close enough. So fucking obvious."

"Close enough to what?"

"To place her as a conservative professor at an obscure right wing religious school in Mississippi. If I'm right, her real name is Eleanor Rose, and she's on the faculty of the sociology department. Whoa."

We were all sitting forward in our chairs now listening to Bo tell us this professor taught a signature class on race in society and was considered a darling of the white superiority philosophy. Philosophy? Is that what they called it? Libertarianism was a philosophy, like socialism and democracy. I refused to give a nod of respect toward racism by calling it a philosophy. All in all, I had a feeling Dr. Rose wasn't calling in bomb threats.

I checked the time on my phone. "Holy shit. We've got to go. Remember the professor with the two names, Rick. We can mention her to Coop, but it probably won't go anywhere now."

"Not so fast. Who knows? Maybe she knows Scotty and his ex," Wendy offered. "That would actually bring us closer to the two campaigns."

"And this Elly can't be too important in anybody's campaign. It was way too easy to find her and see what she's about," Bo said. "This Elly Roscoe is all over WNF website. I can't be the first to figure it out she's really an academic."

"In the loosest sense of the word," I said. "Besides, the hate-watch groups probably know all about her."

"Seems impossible they don't," Rick said as the two of us headed to the door. "We have dozens of anti-hate groups in this country to follow every word these idiots write and every step they take."

"Except when they miss something." I didn't like that train of thought.

"While you guys are gone," Bo said, "I'm going to follow another trail."

"Which one?" I asked Bo.

"What do you really know about Jeff Hoover, other than he's some kind of buddy of Percy's?"

I looked at Rick and shrugged. "Go ahead, fill in the blanks."

Chapter Sixteen

We took the stairs up two flights to Coop's room, where he answered the door while talking on his phone. He waved us to the table off an alcove that was home to the bar sink and fridge. Unlike the messy remains of our pizza dinner, Coop had a table with room service china and linen. The remains of his dinner looked a lot classier.

"Okay," Coop said into the phone, about the time Rick's phone chimed. "Scratch the guests. It's strictly breaking news." He nodded and repeated "Okay" several more times before cutting the call. Without a word, he turned the channel on the TV. "It seems we have another shooting. This time at a casino in Ohio."

"The day before the Ohio primary," Rick said, barely above a whisper. "Another item in the pattern."

"I'm not jumping to any conclusions. We have shootings like this every day, just not massive enough to make the news," Coop said. "Those casinos are mostly filled with middle-aged and older white people."

I brushed that aside. We didn't know enough to even talk about victims.

"So, we meet for real," Coop said to Rick, extending his hand.

I could see from Rick's eager expression he was impressed to be in Coop's presence. But more important things jumped to the head of the line. "What happens to your program now?"

"The news is breaking as we speak," Coop said. He pointed over his shoulder at the TV. "The producers are cancelling our guests, and scratched the segments, but as always, the show must go on. I'll be on set with network anchors. No scripts tonight, obviously."

Suddenly, everything was muddled again. "You know, Marie is running out of chances," I pointed out. "If she can't pull out a win tonight here in Illinois and Ohio, and a couple of other states, she has *almost* no path to the nomination. It's moving toward May, so there'll be a lot of pressure for her to drop out."

"Last I looked, she's up by six points over Pierson in Ohio—and Illinois polls have her favored here."

Rick hurried to confirm that. "That Ohio poll just came out—the night before the primary. I don't trust it. Looks like an outlier to me. I doubt the Kent campaign will trust it either."

"We don't have much time now," Coop said, pulling out a chair at the table and inviting us to join him. "I'm not focused on the primary anymore. It's the country that's threatened. I don't care if Kent or Pierson win. Whoever it is, the job ahead is huge. We can't have Toomey."

Coop spoke more bluntly, maybe less theatrically than usual. I liked this Coop. The old world affectations could be a little tedious at times. "It's the mix of overt political violence and shootings that won't let *me* go. If there's a connection between the mall shooter, now dead, unfortunately, and the couple in Montana, and maybe all the dead and injured in JoJo's office, an election can't fix it. But, I'm with you. Kent or Pierson. All the same to me." I quickly added, "Of course, we're doing good work for Marie."

Rick gave Coop a rundown of what we'd learned online about WNF and people connected to it. "As far as we can tell, there's a coalition's public face, White Nations First. "They go by WNF. They've tried to put an academic façade on their racist research." Rick explained the one Eleanor as Elly.

As he spoke, this struck me as meaningless, because as many connections as we made, the important one were missing. If we'd looked at patterns, would we have been able to predict the Ohio shooting? By rights this is what we were after. "It isn't good enough to look into all this after it happens. That's what we've been doing for decades and look where we are." My frustration bled through, but neither Rick nor Coop looked surprised.

Coop's furrowed brow told me we'd hit a vein he'd like to explore. "Would you be willing to send me notes on that academic side? Might not mean anything, but you never know when information like that could come in handy." Coop pulled a business card out of his pocket and handed it to Rick.

"Everything is out there for the public to see." Rick pulled out his business card, too. "By the way, Matt and I don't like to share links."

"That doesn't protect you from creating a history," Coop said, reasonably.

"No, but we try to be careful about our phones. Too easy to have a phone grabbed and checked." Rick glanced at me. "Ooh, I sound paranoid."

"I don't give a damn. We're involved in politics this cycle, so we have to be paranoid." Some footage flashing on the TV caught my eye. Cell phone video of people rushing for cover in the casino. So far, 12 dead, nine wounded. I nodded to the TV. "Mass shooting sounds way too benign these days. It's another massacre." The fact that my mind translated 12 dead people into *only 12 dead* brought me up short on my own callousness.

Coop needed to be on his way, so we never did talk about whatever had concerned him regarding Marie and Bentley. No matter, I had a feeling that had been contrived. I think rather than learning what Coop was up to, he was interested in what we were coming across. Still, it felt like a trip with no progress to report. Rick and I had no choice but to leave and go back to my suite where Bo and Wendy sat at the table watching TV and drinking cheap red wine.

"We can go to our room, Matt, if you'd rather work here alone."

I shook my head and flopped on the couch. Anger rose in my chest as I waved frantically at the TV. "I suppose this is work. The sad part is, even if I weren't sitting here in Springfield and wondering how Marie is going to do tonight here and in Ohio, I'd be watching this horror show with a couple of dogs curled up next to me."

I looked up just in time to see Wendy exchange a pointed look with Bo.

"What? What's with the look?" I demanded.

"Nothing, Matt. Don't get upset with me. I told Bo this violence is like a trigger for you. It's unsettling." Wendy glanced at Rick. "But as for me, I was telling Rick I was worried about not feeling it anymore."

"Hell, I worry about becoming desensitized all the time," I said. "A shooting here, a shooting there, and suddenly the numbers don't seem so bad." I decided to admit my fear. "I listened to the early Ohio body count now and was kind of relieved the numbers weren't even worse, as if a dozen people gone in an instant isn't a huge deal."

"We're way too used to this," Rick said. "That's the only explanation for being a sick and damned man, but not taking to the streets."

"Right. You and most everyone else," Bo said. "What the hell would we demand with our picket signs and banners? Please, please, you armed haters, don't kill any more people? That's like asking a dog not to bark. Besides, who's even shocked?"

I laughed cynically. "If effing bombings and shot out windows don't shock us, then we're steeped in our new normal. Like we've done with the shootings? Another day, another nut with a gun." I glanced at the TV screen. "Update on our stats. Thirteen dead in Ohio."

Rick pointed with his chin to the TV screen. "I think the violence up to this point is noise and diversion. It's causing upheaval and intimidating people. Another form of voter suppression. Scare people to death to keep them away from the polls."

"Diverting us from what? It feels like this is all just random trickling in." I looked at the screen. "I'm obviously upset, like you all are, but as much as we see small patterns, are we missing the bigger picture?"

Bo shifted his gaze to include the three of us. "Yes, that's exactly what we're missing. At least, that's my opinion."

"Mine, too," Rick added.

"Go on," I said.

"I think someone, and I'm not sure who, is planning something big. Yeah, yeah, we've got these weird bomb threats and all that. But we had WNF shooters before this. I think we're chasing around, even looking at international journals with bullshit research by Eleanor somebody," Bo said. "Meanwhile, how many followers could the WNF have?"

"A scary number," Rick said. "And they don't need numbers. Terrorists never do. Look what happened to your Congressman JoJo."

I was listening with only one ear. Bo stopped me with "planning something big." Hadn't that been the fear all along.

"How big?" I blurted.

Rick looked at Bo before he spoke. "Awful as all this is, something's missing. Tell me, Matt, why is it we don't use the A word."

Bo grimaced and turned to Rick. "*A* word? Is that what we're calling assassinations now?"

"Assassinations?" Wendy said, throwing her hands in the air.

I stared at Rick. "Plural. That means more than one."

Bo and Rick stared at each other and shrugged.

***

It was after midnight when Rick knocked on my door. I opened the door to let him in but before he stepped inside, he looked both ways, as if making sure no one saw him.

"I'm spooked, but that's me. There's no reason for it." He gave me a sidelong glance. "Were you sleeping?"

"Dozing." I pointed to the couch. "In addition to all my other crappy habits, I've become a couch sleeper. I swore I'd never…" I let my voice trail off. I'd sworn off a lot of things. "My mind won't shut down."

I went to the fridge and got us each a beer. The TV was already muted, but the cable news station was still running footage about the shooting. B-roll from other shootings filled a quarter of the screen. Below that was earlier footage from the casino, the anchor took up the other half of the screen.

"I was bouncing off the walls in my room. I suppose you saw that Marie won in Illinois, but not by much. It will shake out to be by only a point or two here. Pierson pulled out a win in Ohio." Rick took a long pull on the bottle. "Okay, man, enough. You're the lawyer, so you tell me. If we're wandering into assassination territory, or attempts to blow up an election through constant threats of violence, aren't we coming close to finding treason when we weren't even looking for it?"

"We are if people are supporting the overthrow of the government and are taking up arms to do it. Or doing things like spilling state secrets, like a traitor would." I answered in a matter-of-fact way. "Those White Nationalist groups that Scotty and Lori were involved with skirted that. And this Elly-Eleanor Roscoe-Rose. This stuff could add up to treason… depending." I shrugged. "Treason depends on any number of things, including motivation."

I mentally ran through cases that came up in constitutional law seminars in school. "Overall, treason is a word people carelessly toss around. Like traitor. So, maybe I don't like some military action you want, so you call me a traitor if I vote against it. Accuse me of giving aid and comfort to the enemy because I have a different idea. Or, I uncover your plot to fudge budget numbers and you accuse me of treasonous behavior. Now that's bullshit."

"But if we uncover an assassination plot, we'll hear the word plenty."

Rick and I fell silent. I stared at the ceiling and the dark blue drapes and the gray carpet and the array of furniture that looked like it could be in a chain hotel anywhere in the country. For just a second, I was so deep in thought I forgot what city we were in. I really was letting this wear me down.

I noticed Rick staring at the TV screen where docs in scrubs stood on the sidewalk in front of the hospital to update the press. "We don't have any proof that this shooting is anything other than typical mass shootings. I mean, we can't say if it's politically motivated." I slapped the cushion between us. "I can't believe how cynical I've become. Typical shootings? What the *fuck* are we coming to in this country?"

"Yeah, I know, but what worries me has nothing to do with what's on that screen right now." Rick let his head drop back on the cushion. He closed his eyes.

"What? What do you mean?"

He kept his eyes closed when elaborated. "I keep thinking that whatever this is, wherever the intrigue leads us, my cousin is in the middle of it." Rick suddenly started rubbing his eyes so hard I winced just looking at him. "If he knows what's going on, then he gets what he deserves. But if he doesn't, if he's being tricked, then…"

"He'd still be in trouble, Rick." I shook my head. "But you talked about a big picture, and Bo also made the leap to assassination and you'd been thinking about it. Now the only question left in my mind is how many go down with whoever the target is."

Rick still looked troubled, which prompted me to ask why he was thinking about Percy at all. "We're looking at stuff like the WNF and shady characters like Scotty and Lori. You've gone backwards and ended up where we started, with Percy visiting Toomey's campaign."

"Right. Because my cousin is a sneak," Rick blurted.

I couldn't argue with him. "We don't know for sure that he's done anything underhanded or illegal, much less treasonous."

"At the very least, I suspect he's not really who he says he is in Marie's campaign," Rick said.

"Once you open that can of worms, then we're obligated to ask who he is. And what about Steve? We haven't talked about him for a while," I pointed out. "I haven't changed my mind about him. I think he's exactly who he says he is. A not very personable campaign manager with a really lousy disposition and a temper. But whip smart. He lands these jobs because he can deliver."

Rick and I both took a couple of gulps of beer in the silence that hung around us. It was like another person in the room. But maybe his train of thought was similar to mine, because suddenly he stood and started pacing.

"However we look at it, Scotty is connected to Toomey, and Lori is a convert to Pierson." Rick's raised voice revealed his extreme frustration and startled me back into the room. "And these people we'd never heard of mere weeks ago, Scotty and Lori, hung out with the worst kind of white supremacists."

"Toomey has deep connections in that world. He lived it. Then he turned respectable," I said. "Sort of."

"If voting to eliminate public radio and food stamps is respectable then he's Mr. Citizen. And he also happens to be against the new voting rights bill," Rick said. "Toomey is a snake. Worse. A viper." He scoffed. "What's the difference? I don't know. But if there's something worse than a viper, he's it."

I waved him off. "We can't go down that road again. We have to do something."

"What if we went to the FBI?" Rick asked, suddenly serious.

"With what? Our hunches?" We didn't have anything solid to offer the real investigators. If we'd had evidence, that would be one thing, but all we had was a hodge-podge. We didn't know if anyone else was connecting any of these dots.

"I'll tell you one thing. I'm curious about this Lori and her change of heart," Rick said. "And how did that get by the press, just like Toomey's past seems to have aroused so little interest."

I thought a minute and came up with one word: diversion. "In a normal campaign these things would matter, right? If you have bomb threats and shootings and people killed in explosions, then who cares about an ex-husband who trafficked in so-called southern culture?"

Rick had a point and I said as much, but my capacity to reason was gone. I was too tired to think, except in wispy thoughts that might make sense—or not— when the sun came up. With our bottles emptied, Rick mumbled something about seeing me in a few hours and went on his way. I avoided the couch and stumbled to the bed.

I closed my eyes and the next sound I heard was a text notification. A text from Coop. It was simple enough. A 1 pt win...is it enough?

Coop was referring to what almost missed the news altogether, Marie's one percentage point victory over Arnold in Illinois and his tiny margin of victory in Ohio. The night was essentially another wash.

Meanwhile, I knew it was time to take advantage of whatever chips I had with Lourdes Ponce. She was on my contact list. While I used the last pod left in the puny coffee service in my room, I thought about how we could use Lourdes to do some of our work for us.

Keeping it simple, I typed a text. What do u know abt Lori Hochburg Tabakin?

I was halfway through the pot of coffee before

Lourdes came back with: Why?

Lourdes didn't fool me with her one word response, which is what I expected. As sure as if I was peering over her shoulder, she had the full name typed in and the search was underway. I also kept my response brief. Curious

I almost laughed out loud at our coy exchange. Lourdes knew very well I wouldn't text her randomly—or even contact her to say hello. We were friendly without being friends. If we showed up at the same gathering, it was because we were both on the periphery of lots of overlapping circles of people from media and politics. More importantly, she knew a tip when she saw one. She liked to be right, so if the tip panned out, she'd claim credit for whatever came from it.

A couple of hours later, I ordered room service breakfast for four in my suite and texted Wendy. By the time we were finished, we'd agreed that even with Marie keeping it close, Arnold was heavily favored in the remaining couple of states. Marie was a true long shot now. I expected within a matter of days she'd be coaxed to drop out for the so-called good of the party. But maybe not.

As the three ate French toast and I ate pancakes, I told them to keep tabs on Lourdes' Twitter feed. "In the next few hours or a day, maybe two, Lourdes is likely to bring up Lori, which means she'll gossip about the Tabakin divorce."

Wendy smacked her palms together in a show of enthusiasm. "She'll pose all those questions to pique curiosity, too, won't she, Matt? And people retweet Lourdes. I can hardly wait."

Bo frowned at Wendy, but her enthusiasm over what Lourdes would do couldn't have come as a big surprise. Wendy was a celebrity watcher, which went along with gossip. If it had to do with politics or anything in the news, she'd claim she was staying informed, not soaking up idle chit chat.

Rick, although he wouldn't admit it, liked a juicy story as well as the next person.

And who was I talk? I followed Lourdes religiously!

"I see you sitting on the edge of your chair waiting for word from Lourdes," Rick teased. "You can't fool us."

"I'm not trying to." Wendy, who had no guile, got laughs all around with that claim.

Rick suddenly turned serious. "I had a middle of the night thing...you know, the lightbulb went on."

"Don't hold back. Tell us about it," I said.

"We've been paying attention to Toomey and his past, and I'll admit I've been wondering about what Percy is really up to," Rick pointed out, "but we haven't dug deep on Jeff Hoover. I mean who the hell is that guy? Are we missing something?"

"Isn't he a Washington pro—started young, kind of like Percy? Does a really great job getting mediocre people elected?" Bo looked smug over nailing that one.

His observations matched mine. "Sometimes it *does* seem like politicians' typical advisors and staff are smarter and more competent than the office holder." I paused to gather my thoughts. "I used to think they might be all around better people than the politicians. Given what we're seeing, I'm not so sure."

Rick, who'd been scrolling through his phone, looked up long enough to say, "Did you know the casino shooter is alive? He's recovering in the hospital. The police shot him before he could shoot himself."

"Maybe he'll talk," Wendy said.

"Let's hope so," I said. "Too much coincidence for me in all this violence, especially another shooting, not just in Ohio, but the night before the primary."

"What does a guy like that have to gain? Why should he talk?"

"His lawyer might convince him to tradeoff the death penalty for info," I offered. "Depends on how much of a true believer the guy is. Or who leans on him to come clean. On the other hand, some guys get scared and spill everything. It's easy to say you're willing to die for a cause until you're actually staring death in the face. Or, spending your whole life in prison."

That answer was the best I could do, especially under the circumstances, so we moved on. By the time Bo and Wendy left, we had worked out some angles we would pursue. Wendy would continue doing the lion's share of work for Marie. Rick and Bo would work together to dig for background on Jeff Hoover and the non-couple Scotty and Lori. Meanwhile, I would monitor Lourdes, but more important, I'd keep track of the Pierson campaign's response to the outpouring of publicity sure to come. With any luck, Lori would make a statement denouncing her past, which might give us—and every media outlet in the world—some insight about where to look next.

Lourdes was sharp. I could easily imagine her wheels turning to take the kernels of data and decide what to release. Fortunately, she'd started out a journalist and knew what I was up to. And she'd never tell.

I doubted even Lourdes had any notion that for Rick and me, we'd added *assassination* to our list of worries.

***

It was mid-afternoon the next day when I dropped Rick off at his apartment, I texted Wendy and told her I was bypassing the office and going home. I missed Maude and Quigs and went straight to Samantha's apartment to give them sweet talk and hugs. A little socializing with Samantha to exchange our serious opinions about the weather and dog food lifted my mood. But underlying my pleasant facade, I was tired in that world-weary sort of way that comes from being caught up in the realities. Now I was ready to retreat from other people, even Wendy, Rick, and Bo. Even if I had no direct involvement in this primary season,

I'd have still found the state of the country dreary. It was almost as bad as that year-of-Covid-19 we'd all endured.

I took the dogs out and picked up dinner and was reading the Tribune, the actual paper version, when Lourdes dropped the first tweet. Battle of the exes. Anyone wonder why Lori Hochberg...walked away from more than a husband. Scotty T sighted on the road with Toomey. Lori T working communication shop for Pierson. Rd. to Damascus conversion?

I chuckled to myself. She'd used references to popular songs, movies, and even TV series to make her point. She certainly wasn't above using a reference to Saint Paul to embellish a point. Moses coming down the mountain with the tablets might be next.

A hot minute later, she had 21 retweets—she was off to a fast start.

By the time the second tweet came in, she had more than 200 retweets of the first. I knew ordinary Twitter followers weren't likely to be sending her tweet around, but interested voters who were following the election would jump on it. Plus, some of the retweets were most certainly initiated by people like Lourdes, pundit types, or those who followed bloggers and freelance journalists.

The second tweet said: Appearing on Cooper Julian's show tonight. Topic...social media & candidate data.

An appearance on Coop's show seemed a little premature. More than a little. I was kind of shocked. But Coop had his sources, so maybe he was on to something.

I turned on the TV to see what I was missing. BREAKING NEWS. Ho hum. But wait. The banner clarified it, and sure enough, Lori Hochberg made the news. But so far, Lori had no comment.

***

None of the work we did for Marie could have done what that one tweet from Lourdes Ponce did to shake up Arnold Pierson's campaign. The statements had gone from none, as in "no comment," all the way to the last one about "redemption." Lori was achieving sainthood. It was a conversion of the highest order. It all but billed itself as a great American story.

Yep, we love to watch mighty fall, but we're suckers when they pick themselves up again and confess their transgressions.

When my phone rang, I casually glanced at the screen, thinking it could be Coop. I almost laughed out loud when I saw it was Lourdes.

"Well, well," I said, "you've joined the Cooper Julian fan club."

"Hmm…I prefer to think he joined the Lourdes Ponce fan club."

I groaned.

"Just kidding, Matt. This *is* a big deal for me. Thank you very much."

"Don't thank me. I never told him about you. He saw that tweet all on his own." I had no doubt Coop's producers and researchers were gathering everything they could manage on both Lori and Lourdes.

"I know Coop is going to ask why I went down this particular alley," Lourdes said. "So, what can you tell me about Lori?"

"Probably no more than you found out on your own." I was vague on purpose to buy a little time to consider how much I wanted to reveal. But, in a way, I was counting on Lourdes to do some of the dirty work for me.

"You must have sent me in her direction for a reason, Matt. You know what kind of following I court."

"Anyone, not just me or you, would wonder why the popular, if dull-as-toast, Arnold Pierson would hire Lori Hochberg. The campaign had to know who she was married to, and what beliefs she spouted."

"Used to spout." Lourdes paused. "Or, are you

implying this isn't all in the past?"

"I imply nothing," I declared, almost laughing out loud. "I passed this on to you to see what you learn."

"Well, the Pierson campaign isn't returning my phone calls, I can tell you that," she said with a chuckle.

The image of Lourdes with her little baby girl Maddie in a pouch came into my mind and got stuck there. Lourdes was sharp, but I'd never live with myself if… "Off the record, Lourdes. Okay?"

"O…kay, if you insist."

I got off the couch and went to the window. The sky was darkening now and ending another day of what was shaping up to be such an odd time. I hadn't thought a little information gathering for a candidate would take over my days so completely. Now I was considering how to word a message to Lourdes.

"Here's the thing. I don't know anything for certain that isn't more or less public record. But the reason we came across this information about Hochberg is because of her ex's link to the Toomey campaign."

"I discovered that, too, and without much effort," Lourdes said. "It does make Lori's new life as a progressive Dem even more curious. Not unique, just a novelty."

I told Lourdes about my early sense that the violence and threats of it in all its forms were connected, but I left out the part about Percy and Jeff Hoover. Too vague. "After what happened to JoJo, we got deeper into nosing around. I didn't expect we'd find such close links between Scotty Tabakin and Toomey."

"When you say 'we', Matt, who are you talking about?"

I could have begged off the question. Instead, I said, "Oh, you know I have some people helping out with projects."

"Got it. Need to know."

"That's not my point." I took a deep breath and started walking around the room to calm my nerves. I wandered into the kitchen and grabbed the sponge and wiped down the sink rim and counter just to keep my free hand busy. "We don't know how deep into the campaign this goes. Some of the bomb threats and damage is a little coincidental, too convenient. I dropped that hint about Lori to start raising questions, ones I can't without being obvious. But you sure can."

"Right. I got that. I'm asking why you think any of this is important enough to pursue," Lourdes said. "I get that Lori is a real piece of breaking news, but a part of me wanted to leave it alone. Why help Toomey?"

"Or expose him," I suggested. "Remember, Tabakin's connected to Toomey. The reason I'm talking about these links is the amount of violence we've seen. I don't know who's perpetrating it, but you exposed Lori and now you're going on TV. Be careful, that's all I'm saying."

Lourdes took her time to answer. "Well, that sounds ominous."

"I don't know anything for sure, Lourdes." I paused. "Except that Tabakin and Toomey have always been low-lifes. I want you to know up front what you'll find out for yourself when you start looking. Are you going down to the studio or are doing the interview from home?"

"I'm going to the studio. In fact, I need to get going." Lourdes chuckled. "By the way, I got a call from the producer. I think they've booked Lori. I'm the opening guest, seven minutes."

I wished Lourdes luck. Then I flopped back on my couch, my new headquarters, and closed my eyes. I dozed off and woke with a start. I didn't know what my subconscious mind was doing while I dozed, but I picked up my phone, alerted my three staff and Bo about Lourdes' upcoming appearance. Then I texted Rick privately. J hoover...speed up search.

Chapter Seventeen

"Let me clarify," Lourdes said. "I posted the information about Lori Hochberg because it was an interesting side story to this already highly contested election, which sadly has been marred by violence from the start."

Good summary, Lourdes. She appeared relaxed and competent against the live shot of the Chicago River bridges lit up behind her. She looked chic in a red jacket and modest jewelry, and as always, very attractive with her long dark hair flowing loose. Lourdes had a distinctive look and with her calm, confident voice she could have easily taken her journalism career to TV.

"And what—or who—led you to look in Lori Hochberg's direction?" Coop asked, all innocence.

Lourdes smiled coyly. "A couple of sources expressed interest."

"Ah, but am I correct in assuming it would be a waste of airtime to ask you to name these mysterious sources?"

Lourdes scoffed. "You know I wouldn't reveal my sources for any story."

"But is Ms. Tabakin's past relevant, Ms. Ponce?" Coop asked in his formal interviewer voice.

Lourdes didn't hesitate a second. "That's for the voters to decide."

"I see. But are you saying you believe in Ms. Tabakin's political change of heart?"

"I'm like you, Mr. Julian, I'm waiting for more information about Lori's past ties with White Supremacist groups through her former husband, Scotty Tabakin, now a supporter of Senator Toomey." Lourdes smiled at Cooper. "Let's get the facts on the table."

Ha! Coop wouldn't need a teaser for his next segment. Lourdes just handed him one.

"Does it strike you as odd that the Pierson campaign has said little about the former Mrs. Tabakin's past?"

"If their silence continues," Lourdes said, "I would find it odd."

"Well, well, perhaps that wall of silence will soon crumble."

Coop thanked Lourdes and went to break with a teaser about his next guest, Lori Hochberg herself.

"What do you think?" I asked Rick, who was on speaker. He'd listened at home along with me."

Rick didn't hesitate to say, "She teed up Lori. Plain and simple. No one's going to change the channel."

"She's good. You know, I haven't always been in Lourdes' fan club, but right now she's triggering a lot of reporting," I said. "Everyone covering the campaigns will want the next scoop on this, especially with Pierson so close to the nomination."

Rick and I talked through one commercial after another. Auto insurance, drugs for diseases we'd never heard of, and food deliveries, and on and on. Finally, Coop came back and didn't waste time doing a long introduction. Instead, he invited Lori Hochberg to explain to the audience why she accepted the invitation.

Rick's voice came through the speaker. "I like how he did that."

I didn't agree or disagree. I was trying not to evaluate until I saw it play out. "Hmm…I'm waiting to see what will happen next."

Lori's smile was a little tight, a bit nervous, but not bad under the circumstances. She smoothed her short, straight blondish bangs off her forehead. She was fair skinned in contrast to Lourdes' olive complexion. It wasn't right to judge, but she looked tired, a little washed out. Lori was older than Lourdes, too, so my comparison of the two women was grossly unfair. But Lori looked overly made up for TV and while whatever lines were expertly removed, filled in, or otherwise camouflaged, she couldn't hide her age.

"I'm aware this isn't exactly what people expect me to say, but I want to be clear. I'm not resigning my position as Assistant Director of Communications for Arnold Pierson's campaign. I have the full support of Senator Pierson and his campaign. I'm here tonight, Cooper, because I believe in Senator Pierson and intend to help him win the party's nomination for president of the United States."

"Your statement may come as a surprise to many, Mrs. Tabakin. But even more I'm certain my viewers want to hear you describe the twists and turns in your political path that brought you to this point." Coop's voice was nothing if not cool. But that couldn't last.

Lori's smile never changed as she spoke. "I believe it's a common path, Cooper. I would bet many of the men and women watching your program tonight have experienced a change of their political heart. They've left behind old, pitifully outdated beliefs and are focused on a bright future for our country based on the strength of its diversity."

"Quite true. However, you have to admit it's quite a radical shift. Wouldn't you agree?"

I braced myself for what was coming. "He's focusing now, isn't he?"

"Right. And her facade is beginning to crack a little," Rick said. "Already."

Maybe, maybe not. I wasn't so sure that was happening.

"Cooper, let me be clear, I'm not proud of everything in my past. That's why I renounced my old beliefs," Lori explained in a quiet voice. "I've been public in my statements and have opened the book of my past."

"I'm told you're writing a book about your years in the White Nationalist Movement in Mississippi."

"Yes, I am writing a book about that time in my life. But I was never a proponent of white nationalism." She shook her head, just a subtle move. "It was, in fact, those attitudes that drove me away."

"Are you referring to the years you were married to Scott Tabakin, a well-known proponent of separatist politics?"

Coop was a master at letting words speak for themselves. His true genius was his ability to state painful facts without seeming to judge them.

Lori was getting a little more comfortable now. She'd expected this line of questioning and was prepared for it. "Yes, my book delves into this in detail, but for now, I want people to understand that I understand hate from living *inside* a movement that operates *outside* of the mainstream. It doesn't make the evening news unless an event triggers the coverage."

Coop jumped in with the next question. "Are you aware of connections between some of the, shall we say, *virulent* groups such as the WNF, White Nations First, with those who aim to reach their goals peacefully?"

"*Virulent*?" Rick said. "Can't he use words a simpleton like me understands?"

I laughed, but kept my eye on Lori's body language. I had the strangest feeling she was going to skirt the truth. In other words, lie. Sure enough.

"WNF is an extreme organization, Cooper." Her gaze shifted. "I certainly was unaware of connections between anyone in my network and with those advocating violence."

"Yep, she lied," I said, as Coop went to another break. "She lowered her eyes, looked to the side. She'd been looking straight into the camera before."

"Why would she bother lying? It will come out," Rick said. "Hell, Bo and I could probably unearth a photo or two at a fundraiser or some kind of white heritage conference. She should have owned it."

"We'll probably do just that. On our own time," I said, "although it seems to happen to every politician. Some are unlucky enough to be caught shaking hands with a serial killer."

Rick let out a hearty laugh. "We should be so lucky with Toomey."

When the commercials were over and Coop came back he asked all the right questions that led Lori into the heart of her political marriage. Nothing wrong with marriages based on politics, and I'd usually cringe at probing around in private lives. In this case, getting into personal territory was a big part of the ballgame. I had to give Lori credit for knowing where to begin.

"When I married Scott Tabakin, we shared the belief that race relations were a community and state matter. We believed that interference in the form of federal legislation made matters worse. Scott in particular, believed that the south, or the old Confederacy, was never given credit for its pride in its role in building this country. He resisted attacks on the white southern heritage by celebrating it and bringing it to prominence."

Coop broke in before she could continue. "Is it not true that Scott Tabakin has talked openly about his belief that the best solution to the tragedy of racial strife involved setting up separate regions or even whole states for the African-American population? Do you share that belief?"

Lori paused and took a deep breath. "That, Cooper, things like forced segregation and going backwards was one of the issues that, well, you might say, it awakened me. I came to understand this movement was not about Scott's pride in his heritage but was rooted in a belief in racial superiority. That realization is where our paths diverged. I understood the conservative principles, but not the racial bias."

"And you reexamined your beliefs?" Coop asked, his voice still measured.

223

"I reevaluated everything I'd been taught as a child." Lori leaned forward a little—a sign of earnestness. I read her as eager to be understood. "I want your viewers to know that I went about the process of educating myself. Maybe they, too, are uneasy with the bias that's still alive and well in our country. I would advise them to speak to historians and ask for advice. By doing that I was able to separate the fiction I was raised with from the facts."

"Sounds like a quest of sorts," Coop said.

Maybe, maybe not. For some reason I wasn't buying this.

"That's the perfect word for this new journey I took. But I also saw what was going on around me. Lack of equality showing up everywhere in education and in the economy. It was humbling, Cooper, so humbling."

"Are you buying this?" Rick asked.

"Can't say one way or the other."

Rick and I listened to Coop ask a few more questions. Only one exchange stood out.

"How did your journey lead to your prominent position on Arnold Pierson's communication team?" Coop asked in a tone that suggested he didn't understand that element of the story.

"I'm glad you asked that question," Lori said with a bright smile.

"No she's not," I blurted. "She's lying."

Lori kept the smile on her face when she said, "The word conversion has been used to describe what happened to me. And I don't reject that. In fact, I own it. The best way to affirm my new beliefs is not to run away and hide from the public light, but to work for good and do it without fear or shame."

"Oh, brother," I muttered. "She's good."

Rick scoffed. "She practiced that line in front of a mirror until she could nail it."

I tended to agree. But why? I absently patted first Quig's head and then Maude's, and thought about Lori's words while Cooper closed out his show.

"Is this fair?" I asked Rick when the show was over. "Why am I having trouble buying it?"

"I don't know. Seems awfully convenient," Rick said slowly, as if his mental wheels were still turning. "Pierson apparently bought it." "I guess. But let's keep an eye on this," I scoffed in my best cynical tone. "We're in so deep. No turning back now."

Chapter Eighteen

"I believe the best way to contribute is to throw my support to Arnold Pierson, a colleague and a man I'm proud to call a friend," Marie Kent said to a cheering crowd. "I will be proud to be his campaigner-in-chief."

"Must these pols use every cliché in the book every time?" I asked. Rhetorical question for sure.

A few weeks had passed since Marie and Arnold faced off in Ohio and Illinois. Arkansas and New Mexico, and Maine followed and the next week Alaska and Wyoming straggled in. Marie kept it close, but just days before this announcement, it was obvious the campaign was over. Marie was a close second, but in politics there is no silver medal. Although she conceded, this rally in Philadelphia was the biggest joint event so far.

"Who gives a rat's ass?" Rick said in response to my rhetorical question from his place across the table. This had become his signature challenge. It was almost embarrassing how many times the answer was some variation on "zero to none."

"Okay, okay, enough. My poor feelings can take only so much teasing." I let out a guffaw. "Due respect, please. You're still on the payroll, my payroll." The firm's official connection with the Kent campaign had officially ended the day before.

Rick looked up and I thought he was going to say something about the work we did, but instead he pointed to the screen. "There must be twenty-five thousand people on the streets. I have to give both campaigns credit. In the midst of the chaos of the primaries, they've managed to stay above the fray, haven't they?"

"Makes me wonder if they're going to break with tradition and team up now. Marie is as qualified to be president as Toomey is," I said. "Why not save a lot of speculation and name her as his VP pick now?"

"I'm all for that." Wendy pumped both hands above her head. "It's about time."

"She speaks," I said. Wendy had her nose buried in case files on small class action suits and had commented very little on the non-traditional rollout of the presumed nominee's campaign. I think she mostly wanted to avoid talking about her disappointment in Marie coming up short.

"Don't they usually do a long vet and keep the suspense going?" Rick asked.

"These aren't usual times," I said.

"I'll say," Wendy added. "I don't recall any election like it."

"And we're told every one of them is the most important election of our lifetimes," I said, "and each time it seems more and more true."

We sat in silence while they ended the rally with their families around, but not holding up clasped hands in unity and victory. That went the way of the pre-Covid-19 days and so far wasn't coming back. Instead, all the family and operatives and elected officials clapped to the beat of the music.

"I like my idea," I said. "I'd like to see it settled."

"Do you really think that will stop the threats on Pierson's campaign?" Wendy asked. "They had to clear out their headquarters in two different cities just last week."

"Hmm…Charlotte and Santa Fe." This time no one took credit, and once again Toomey played dumb. Fortunately, they were threats with no action. But it wore on everyone, even voters across the country to see one more alert about offices being cleared. No wonder Pierson could do little of the traditional campaigning. "Given everything that's gone on, I think those thousands of people in Philadelphia are pretty gutsy. They're showing some of that 'you can't scare us' American energy."

"Good thing Janet and I still have work to do," Wendy teased. "What with a new client coming on board to keep this establishment afloat."

"I told you the Ann Sather's pancake platter would be my ace in the hole," I teased back.

When it came down to it, Rick wouldn't be off my payroll for long. A couple of weeks tops. The three of us were being low key about what we were up to in the office. Janet was aware we hadn't dropped our concerns about the violence in the elections, but privately I told her I'd just as soon not share too much. I didn't want her implicated, just in case our snooping unknowingly crossed a legal line. Or spooked an agency or even Toomey's campaign.

In her usual amusing way, she agreed she liked being kept in the dark just fine.

We got to work on behalf of our new client, a formidable legal team defending a hospital system accused of systemic negligence in the emergency department. It was a class action suit I predicted would settle in the end, the way most of these kinds of cases did. Plaintiffs in a relatively small class action suit get impatient for results and the hospital system would just as soon not have the publicity. Rick could help us with the prep work that would take several months but come to a halt at any point as settlement talks continued.

Meanwhile, the days ticked by and Marie and Arnold did a series of rallies and town halls in swing states that solidified not just her support for him, but started the road to unity before the convention. Rather than easing the tensions around the country, the end of the primaries triggered more violence—or threats of it.

I had my eye on one of their events streaming on my tablet while I waited for Bo and Rick to show up in Lincoln Park. This was no walk in the park, as Janet would say, so I'd left Maude and Quigs at home. We were all business, but Bo was clear about wanting to be extra discreet. Since spring had finally made an appearance in Chicago, the park was one place we could meet up and find some privacy in the middle of the day. As it turned out, Jeff Hoover was a lot like his boss—only worse.

Rick arrived first, but we barely had a chance to say hello before Bo approached from the other direction. He looked grim as he pointed to a spot on the edge of the lagoon where a picnic table was empty. "It's far enough away from the walking path we can be isolated from…" he glanced around "…anyone."

Rick and I exchanged glances.

Bo, as it turned out, was as serious about the information he was pursuing as either of us. It had started when Bo quietly picked up information on Hoover's pastimes, which turned out to be hanging out at shooting ranges. Nothing wrong with that, Bo had said repeatedly, except for the company he kept there.

"Bo, before you start, will you tell me how dangerous this is getting?" I asked, serious now. We joked a lot, but this wasn't the time. "Have you made any direct connection between Hoover and any of the bomb threats or violence?"

"Direct? No. Indirect? The jury's still out." Bo closed his eyes and shook his head. "I can't believe I said that."

Rick slapped Bo on the back. "Don't worry, bro. We say that all the time."

"Right," I added. "I preach to my crew about not being judge and jury. A little jury consultant humor can't hurt."

Bo knew we were bullshitting him, but he shook it off and got serious again. "Jeff Hoover is one helluva political operative. And he's got all the creds. I mean, Toomey might not be an intellectual powerhouse, but Hoover is. Like I told you before. New England prep schools. Princeton. Two degrees."

Bo had heard rumors about Hoover creating the immigration policy that wasn't yet going public. According to Bo, they'd kept it quiet because it was so easily attacked as racially biased. Hell, yes. But, lucky for us, Hoover had written a column about his dream immigration plan for a fairly prominent right wing magazine two decades ago. Toomey had voiced similar views, even before being anti-immigration was trendy.

For his part, Bo found it pointedly odd that Toomey's policy papers on the campaign website were sparse and full of vagaries and meaningless talk about immigration law with teeth. Rick called them fangs. But, in one of the failed immigration reform attempts in the senate Toomey had pushed the resurgence of the long-gone, ugly quota system. The proponents, and Toomey found a handful of allies, including Jeff Hoover, wanted immigration to more or less shut out countries south of the Rio Grande in our hemisphere and Italy's boot across the pond.

This peculiar bias was one reason Bo thought Hoover deserved a closer look. We'd decided I should mention immigration to Raphie Michaels, our *Chicago Tribune* guy, who covered Midwest campaign events, tag teaming with the national political correspondent. Now, a couple of days later, Bo teed up the video on his tablet. "Courtesy of C-Span streaming, by the way. They don't miss much on their Road to the White House coverage."

Bo provided the context for what was coming, not that there was anything unusual about any of it. Toomey had agreed to take some questions from a gaggle of reporters following him around. He'd just come from a roundtable with small business leaders. "None of it matters much until we get to this" Bo said tapping the play arrow.

There was Raphie in the back of the semicircle with his hand in the air. "Can you comment on the quota system included in your prior immigration plan?" he shouted.

Hoover's head snapped around to glare in Raphie's direction.

Toomey said nothing.

Ha, surprised the fucker. And upset him.

Jeff—and Toomey—jutted their jaws and narrowed their eyes. Jeff, a quiet guy, not especially affable, but not icy cold, either, was suddenly breathing fire.

Bo froze the frame. "So, earlier in the day, Toomey made noise about future rollouts of his immigration reform proposal. He stumbled and fumbled and now Raphie brought it up again. They thought that was below the radar, but this reporter, a guy they don't know so well, caught them off guard."

"They don't like that so much," I said as Bo restarted the clip.

Hoover took a couple of steps forward and shouted to the press. "We're only taking questions about the economy and supporting small businesses today. Limit yourself to those topics."

I was proud watching Raphie refuse to take no for an answer. Like all reporters he could be annoying as hell, but he was doing his job in this exchange. "Senator Toomey, explain how an immigration quota system would have a positive impact on the small business sector of the economy." Bo froze the frame.

Bingo. What a millisecond.

"You can see the apprehension in his face," Bo said, pointing to Toomey's grim mouth.

"Ha! That little question scared the shit out of 'em."

Both Toomey and Hoover were displeased, and Hoover had his mouth hanging open. They were staring at Raphie wide-eyed, and didn't have time to catch themselves in the act to hide it. For some reason, Toomey was afraid of Raphie now.

Hoover was furious. So, he struck using the only arrow he had left in the quiver. Jeff pointed at Raphie and shouted, "What outlet are you with?"

"*Chicago Tribune,* Sir." Super polite, my favorite reporter looked as calm as he sounded. Not good enough for Hoover, though.

Based on the next frames, Jeff decided a scuffle with Raphie was better than taking on the challenging question, his piece of shit immigration plan. "You know what, man? You are out of this press conference. Get moving." Jeff yelled as if he had the authority to pull Raphie away from a bank of microphones set up for a gaggle exactly like what we were seeing on the screen.

"This isn't a formal press conference, Sir," Raphie pointed out.

"I'm asking you to leave." Jeff's hands gripped his hips so hard, his knuckles probably turned white.

Raphie stood his ground.

Then Jeff nodded to a couple of private security guys, clearly not Secret Service detail, but more like bar bouncers. They approached Raphie in a low-key kind of way.

Raphie took a couple of steps back and waved off the two men. Then he pointed to Toomey. "You'll be hearing about this, dude."

The video ended with Hoover calling an end to the gaggle and more or less dragging Toomey off.

"I wonder how they could have been so blindsided. Especially Hoover." I let out an evil snicker. "Good for Raphie. Given their reaction to his question, he'll stay on it."

"But what's the punchline?" Rick asked. "I mean, so what if Hoover doesn't like Raphie's question?"

Rick had been uncharacteristically quiet through Bo's narration through the clips. Now he was back to asking logical questions, like who gives a rat's ass about Raphie being asked to leave a gaggle.

"I knew you'd ask. It's not a smoking gun, but

here's what I've got so far." Bo pulled up a photo and enlarged it so we could make out the grainy figures in the background. "This is a photo I got off the internet. That's Scott Tabakin at the speakers' table. And here's Jeff Hoover leaning against the back wall."

I had a "so what" reaction, and I expected a dismissive shrug from Rick, but he grilled Bo. Who, what, when, where, and why.

Over the next few minutes, Bo explained the picture had appeared in a publication that called itself a journal in order to polish its image. It was a cover for what was supposed to pass for respectable white supremacy. "It was only two years ago. And what a farce." The meeting had specifically been on a twenty-five year plan to all but eliminate immigration. Madly in love with their own white skin, their goal to deport millions and stop immigration altogether from most countries was a natural outgrowth. They devised a complicated scheme to try to limit citizenship to individuals making over a certain amount of money. One way to discourage lower earners from applying. Keep the voter rolls down.

"They're stealthy," Bo said, "but they meet under the guise of being the movement's big brains, the intellectuals. Phony science, phony social science. Even wild genetic theories."

It was bad. Lots of deportations, moratoriums, and bans. Ugly stuff.

"These folks are patient," Bo said. "They look ahead—years out. But all the while they look for openings to see what they can do incrementally starting with a Toomey administration."

Rick frowned. "Still, Hoover and Tabakin were in the photo, not Toomey."

"Or Lori," I added.

Rick shrugged that off. "Lori had already renounced everything, so that explains why she's not there. I've been reading a lot of background on the wish list of the right wing. Kinda scary how much of it they've managed to put in place already. They wanted to weaken unions and take over state houses. They're damn good at accomplishing their bullshit goals."

I was itching with impatience now. "So, here we are in the park, looking over our shoulders. And are we any closer to finding out if there's a connection between all these shady characters and the violence going on?" I paused, checking the accuracy of my own observation. "Of all the campaign reactions to the political terrorism, Toomey is first out of the gate with the big condemnations, but he's also the first to move on. His answer to every challenge is to tout the Second Amendment. Period."

"Wait. I'm not done," Bo said, holding up his hands to stop the direction of the conversation. "I did the obvious background scan of the website for this so-called heritage group. The usual Civil War ancestry stuff, harkening back to the golden days of segregated education, blah, blah, blah. But Scott Tabakin is prominent. No secrets or attempts to hide. He used to write a regular column. So did Lori."

Bo pulled up more photographs, all of which featured Tabakin. A few included Hochberg. "See? She was active in this group. It's based in Mississippi, but has followers all over the country. I went into their advertising site and pretended to be a business looking at advertising rates. I sorted by zip codes. They actually have almost 100,000 subscribers."

"Mostly in the South?" Rick asked.

"Uh huh, but they've got a big following in Montana, where that couple shot out the campaign office windows. Let's just say that wherever we saw political violence, there were subscribers in the zip code." Bo quickly added he knew that proved nothing. It was barely a clue.

"Look up the case in Montana," I said, realizing too late it sounded as if I was issuing an order. I'd almost forgotten about that Montana incident. "Let's find out who's representing them."

I skimmed beads of sweat off my forehead. We weren't under direct sun, but the breeze had died down and the lake was still as glass on the unusually warm June day.

"Can we buy the list of subscribers?" Rick asked.

"Nope. I checked," Bo said, still typing and tapping. "They commit not to sell subscriber info. Makes sense, considering who they are. All I could get were zip codes."

Rick raised his hands and wiggled his fingers. His signature "I'm prepared to hack if necessary" sign.

"What do you think, Bo?"

Bo shook his head. "Might not be necessary to get in that way. Let's see if we can get connections another way."

Rick nervously patted his hand on the concrete surface of the table. "Do you have other photos? Any of these people have a notorious college student past? You know, demonstrations and things like that where they'd show up in clips and photos?"

"You've searched every nook and cranny of the internet to find shit on Percy," I said. "You came up empty. Do you think he's a younger version of Lori Hochberg?"

"No, Matt, I'm worried he's only an older version of himself and hasn't changed at all," Rick said. "I worried that working for Marie is a piece that's part of a bigger agenda."

Before I could respond, Bo broke in. "Kathy Travis," he said. "An attorney out of Missoula. She owns a small firm—has two associates. Ever hear of her?"

"No, but that doesn't mean anything," I said. "I would expect them to start with a local attorney, for expediency, but they'll bring in a bigger gun later for the trial—if there is one. If they'd broken the windows of a candidate for city council, it would be local. The dopes targeted a U.S. senator, so now it's a federal case. See what else you can find out about her."

My mind was racing around two tracks. Rick's

worries over Percy, for one, but the links between the Missoula couple and Jeff Hoover and Tabakin. "My gut tells me the couple was set up. Kind of a dirty thing to do to them. One or both ending up in court, firearms violations at the very least, and who knows, maybe some treason going on at the worst."

"You don't think it was their idea?" Bo asked, obviously surprised.

"True believers know the law and skirt it. The two could have strutted around the headquarters sporting their AR-15s legally," I said. "That sends most people running for cover." I struggled to find something close to sympathy for this misguided—a polite word—couple, who I now believed were duped. "A little fire power parade would have achieved the same effect and kept their asses out of jail. Whip people up, scare folks."

Bo plunked his elbow on the table and rested his chin in his palm. "I smell a conspiracy." He looked from Rick to me. "I'm *not* kidding. I don't trust any of this. I'm sorry to say this, but I'm not sure we can trust Percy."

Rick almost shouted, "Don't apologize. It's been gnawing at me. I've never come up with a good explanation for Percy's stealthy visit to the Toomey rally. I think his near disguise was the part that got to me. He was in such deep conversation with Jeff. Now we know Tabakin was there."

"But that's all we have," I pointed out to Bo. "We've never been able to link these people in ways that bring out more than suspicion. It's not against the law to be a white nationalist, even if it should be."

"You do have Jeff and Tabakin," Bo said, waving at the tablet. "There are many more photos of them together at these right wing so-called conferences."

"With Lori Hochberg present at some," Rick pointed out.

Bo led us through what he found out about her. She'd dropped out of sight after leaving Scotty Tabakin, presumably to write a book. By that time, she'd moved from Mississippi to Arlington, Virginia, where she consulted on communications strategies for lobbyists working for not-for-profits. She was mostly quiet for a year or so, and then she ended up on Pierson's payroll, first on the advance team, and then communications.

I thought back to Rick's graphs about the campaigns crossing paths and asked Rick to pull them up on his screen. I had a couple of seconds of regret when Bo and Rick both seemed to case the area around us. In the middle of the day, the picnic tables were mostly empty.

"You know I hate this," I said. "I never thought taking on this job would mean looking over our shoulders, like we were being followed."

"I never imagined my cousin doing this work at all," Rick said. "I never would have guessed being afraid of what he was up to."

Bo stared at his screen. "When was the last time you saw him, Rick?"

Rick looked at me and frowned. "Montana, right? When we met Marie and her family."

"I had a conversation with Steve Novak after Marie dropped out and our involvement with the campaign was done," I added. "He told me Percy was signing on with Pierson's campaign as an advisor."

"I sent him a text just to touch base," Rick said. "He mentioned Marie in a way that made me think he might be involved at a low level in the mountain of paperwork that has to be done to vet VP candidates. And Pierson would be a fool not to look at Marie. I know they convene a special task force for that, but they probably take input from the campaign."

Bo studied his screen. "Toomey is in Michigan now, and in Wisconsin tomorrow in a town with an unpronounceable name outside of Milwaukee, at least according to the map. Let's see where Arnold's campaign is right now?"

"Iowa," Rick said. "But according to the schedule,

they'll be holding a town hall in Milwaukee tomorrow. Then both campaigns are moving north in the state, Toomey to Green Bay, Pierson to Eau Claire."

"Okay, let's be clear that just like the primaries, ending up in the same place isn't unusual," I said. "Wisconsin is a critical state."

"Why don't you go spy on them?" Bo said.

I let out a loud guffaw. "You said that in the same tone you'd suggest a heading out for a burger."

Bo frowned. "Yeah, I did. But here's a tidbit. Milwaukee police and the FBI are investigating a bomb threat at the campus theater at Marquette University where the town hall is taking place." He looked up at the two of us with a pained look on his face. "You know, I'm only involved in this mess because you guys pulled me in."

Rick scoffed. "What's your point?"

"You guys both have hunches that nothing is quite as it seems. Why don't you call your cousin and tell him you want to go to the town hall, grab dinner or a drink." Bo shrugged. "Then you can also get a ticket to Toomey's event. See who's there."

"At the very least," Rick said, "chances are good Tabakin and his ex will be in the same city—or nearby. Percy and his old pal Jeff, too."

"Text Percy now," I said. "Time is running out."

"What do you mean?" Bo asked, frowning.

"The convention is coming in July. A few weeks away," I said. "Thousands of people are convening right here in Chicago at the United Center. So far, the history of bomb threats and mass shootings isn't boding too well. I wish they'd put the effing convention in some other city. We've got enough problems."

I got quiet while I tried to talk myself out of something that wouldn't let me go. "Okay, let's drive. Rick, you check the locations and make hotel reservations. Why don't you come with us, Bo?"

"Can't. Right now, my Minneapolis teammates think I'm at the dentist. I can't take all my work on the road. But I'll keep track of you."

There was an elephant in the room and her name was Wendy.

Bo looked at me with a puzzled expression.

"Wendy is up to her ears collecting data on medically-related class action suits right now over the last decade," I said. "That means we don't need to involve her. At least, not directly."

"She knows we're deep in some kind of shit," Rick pointed out.

"I don't know what you should do," Bo said, "and I have to keep my mouth shut about every damn project I work on. I don't have a problem staying quiet. My only concern is safety. Is she one hundred percent safe?"

"That's the point, Bo. It's easy for me to say we're all safe, more or less. No one is on to us, at least not that we know of, and I don't like keeping this from her. We have talked and shared a lot of it, but we're getting closer to these white supremacist types hiding in plain sight in the campaign." I'd about made up my mind to keep quiet, but changed it again. "Then again, I've never kept her in the dark on anything this long. It's going to look odd since this trip isn't on the company dime. From here on out, we're on our own." I glanced at Rick. "On my tab, but Wendy will still know something's up."

"If that's the case, you can tell her I'm involved behind the scenes," Bo said. "Then, she'll know we can't communicate about it over the phone or through email. Whatever."

"I have a feeling about this trip," Rick said. "It isn't a good feeling, but I believe we should go."

We got up and walked toward the lot, with Bo offering to give Rick a lift.

I was left alone with my thoughts about politics and leaving Maude and Quigs again. I walked into my building and reluctantly knocked on Samantha's door.

Chapter Nineteen

In our casual clothes, it was easy to blend in around Marquette University, not a hive of activity in the summer. The threats of violence that started in South Carolina and kept up during the primary season had left its mark. Crowds were even smaller this year than at any other time in recent memory. It was disheartening in a way, but the big rally approach to politics had never come roaring back after the campaign season when the virus meant almost no public events of any kind. No one drew in tens of thousands anymore. Both Toomey and Pierson were doing more town hall style events than the big rallies. That said, it seemed almost gutsy to hold big events in Wisconsin. Arnold's town hall in the city drew more people than Toomey's suburban event.

In order to be sure we weren't noticed, Rick and I had to be careful to stay on the edge of the large public park. That could be why I was stunned to see Lori Hochberg standing outside the campaign tent engaged in animated conversation with Jeff Hoover. Neither saw us, but they were looking at a computer screen.

"Are you sure it's her?" Rick asked, taking the small field glasses from my hand. It was his idea to bring them along and it had paid off.

"This is too blatant," I said. "I'm not buying it."

"Let's put Raphie on it," Rick suggested. "Or some other members of the press. Really. Lori had to make a special trip here. She's in their territory."

Assume Treason

I looked around at the press corralled behind a rope barrier. I didn't see Raphie. "I have a better idea. I'm texting Lourdes." I got out my phone and sent a text saying simply: Trust me...a scoop.

Then I sent her a second text. Pierson's L hochberg spotted in deep conversation with Toomey's J hoover... what's it about?

"Do you trust her that much?" Rick asked.

"I do. Let's go. We don't want to be spotted." We walked to the edge of the park and nodded at the Secret Service detail watching the exit. "Raphie will pick up on Lourdes' tweet. So will other journalists. If there's a benign reason for it, we'll soon find out."

We got in the car and headed up the interstate to Green Bay. By the time we stopped for gas in Sheboygan, a little more than an hour later, Lourdes' tweet, almost word for word what I'd written, had gone out.

"Okay, the campaigns' rapid response teams are on it," Rick said, scrolling his phone as I filled up my truck. "This is going to be hard to argue with."

"What?"

"Well, they're saying Jeff and Lori conferred over the issue of logistics when the campaigns ended up in the same region," Rick said. "According to the Toomey people, they're trying to minimize traffic slowdowns and strain on law enforcement."

I had to admit that made sense, and I said so. "They're being responsible. Campaigns can be inconvenient for locals and at least temporarily, they loathe the candidates whose presence means the roads are blocked or the traffic comes to a halt. There's so much security. It annoys the hell out of voters. All the candidates look bad."

"Wait, wait. They met in person, Matt. They could have handled it over the phone. By text, even." Rick swatted the air. "Besides, what can any of them do about the traffic?"

"I don't know," I snapped. "Maybe stagger the time

241

the campaign bus and caravan use the same highways."
It was the only thing I could think of offhand. "Maybe
they didn't want to use phones for the same reasons we
don't. Security." Other than that, I wasn't sure what
they were up to.

"Okay, but I still think it stinks." Rick offered his
opinion as we drove down the street to a roadside
restaurant that opened at 3:00. It was 3:10 and we had
the place to ourselves and put our order in without a
wait.

"Another one of these places," I said, looking around
at football and baseball memorabilia on the walls of
the cave-like restaurant. "We could be in Montana."
I rested my head on the back of the tall booth. I knew
why we'd made the other trips during the primary
season. For a minute sitting with my eyes closed, I lost
track of what this was all about.

"You look beat," Rick said.

"Not so much tired, really, as busy questioning
my judgment. Bo thought we should make this trip,"
I pointed out. "Now we saw what we saw. I'm glad I
tweeted Lourdes, but we don't want to hurt Pierson in
the process."

"Here we go," Rick said when his phone and mine
beeped and buzzed simultaneously. "Twenty years
ago, hell, ten years ago, no one would have known
about the meetup in the park between the current and
former racists. Now we can't eat a BLT without our
phones giving us headaches."

"It's not our job to protect the Pierson campaign,"
I said, looking at a tweet exchange between Lourdes
and the campaign, "but it's Lori's job not to embarrass
them. She's not doing a very good job."

Lourdes had put out another tweet questioning the
optics of Lori and Jeff meeting, even over campaign
logistics. Then Lori responded by talking about a
couple of minutes visit with someone she'd known for
years.

"I doubt that's the end of it," I said.

"Do you ever think the bomb threats and even the actual bombings are background, but don't have anything to do with the election at all?" Rick asked.

From across the booth I observed Rick was beginning to look like I felt, at a low point, but not knowing why. Something about Hochberg and Hoover was suspicious, and that was depressing. Yet, we weren't close to tying up loose ends. If this wasn't really about the election, then this would go on long after Inauguration Day.

"Do you think it's possible WNF and those other losers, TLTA, are playing us?" I asked. "Maybe they're putting us on a trail that means nothing, but we end up missing the big picture."

Rick nodded. "Yeah, that thought has gone through my head. Like all the time. They've succeeded in frustrating us."

Neither of us asked the question about who the "we" was. It all came back to Percy, even though hard facts were scarce. We ate quickly and didn't hang around. For the first time in this whole election escapade I questioned myself about continuing this chase—and it wasn't just the money. But with the income stream from the campaign dried up, retreating would be the logical choice.

Too late. Despite my doubts, I was hooked. Even the top law enforcement agencies in the world hadn't made significant arrests that would point to a conspiracy or coordinated efforts. It was obvious to everybody they weren't random acts. I didn't consider myself a sleuth, but somehow, Rick and I had managed to make all kinds of connections. We'd figured out the Marchand case on our own, and that's what kept luring me to keep going with this one. So far, not one official FBI press conference convinced me we were wasting our time. Call me crazy, I'd muttered to myself many times.

Once we were on the road, traffic was light. Suddenly, the brake lights on the cars ahead came on.

I slowed way down until I was at ten miles an hour and after a mile or two, the sea of cars came to a complete stop.

I couldn't see a thing ahead of me. We were stuck at zero with cars and SUVs and semis all idling. I put the truck in park and waited. Rick silently looked for news.

"Oh, fuck," he said.

"What? A big pileup? Campaign delays?"

Rick waved me off. "We're not going anywhere. This is for real. More windows shot out in Pierson's headquarters in Eau Claire. Two injured. A fucking bomb threat at Toomey's rally site. The place has been cleared, but the rally is cancelled. The bomb squad is doing a search."

"We're over fifty miles south of Green Bay. I wonder why we've stopped."

Rick went back to studying his phone.

I turned on the radio and tracked through stations until we heard the automated emergency voice of highway patrol talking about roadblocks and urging people not to drive into Green Bay, to avoid Appleton and Oshkosh, too.

"I'll bet they set up roadblocks all over the state," Rick said. "Once we get moving, we'll probably be directed off the highway at the next exit."

"I suppose. The last time this kind of thing happened to me it was a hostage situation in my neighborhood. I couldn't go to my apartment for a couple of hours." I was resigned to a long slowdown. "At least when we get off the highway, we can turn around and be headed back home."

"I suppose, but we'll have to stay tuned. I'm glad we ate lunch," Rick said. "We've got water and a bag of trail mix—the kind that's heavy on chocolate and low on sunflower seeds. My kind of trail mix. It should hold us until dinner."

I laughed at the notion Rick was probably right. We'd be stopping again. Knowing we wouldn't be moving, I tracked through the radio until I came to a Milwaukee station with onsite reporting. They were in their *breaking news* mode, which meant some awkward pauses while they waited for updates.

Finally, a reporter's voice came through and said she had an important update. "The representative from Arnold Pierson's campaign has confirmed that an organization known as The League of True Americans, or TLTA, has claimed responsibility for the gunshots. We haven't yet heard from the Toomey campaign.

"Holy shit...finally someone steps up and takes credit, if you can call it that," Rick said.

We might have known that eventually someone would come forward. But on the one hand, TLTA was a much more shadowy organization. WNF, on the other hand, had names that went with faces, even if some were evil.

As if reading my thoughts, Rick said, "Did you ever wonder if TLTA is a front. Smoke and mirrors designed to cover up the real actors in WNF?"

"I was thinking about that just now," I said. "People like Scotty Tabakin and even Lori Hochberg flew close enough to TLTA to singe their wings. They might not use the same words in their celebration of white culture, but it all adds up to the same hate."

The minutes ticked by while Rick and I were at a complete standstill on the packed highway. Under other circumstances, I might have been impatient and thrumming my fingers on the steering wheel, cursing under my breath. Given what happened, I was almost happy to wait.

"You know, I'm glad we're not chasing the two campaigns today," I said. "We can leave the explosives and AR-15s to the experts. I think both parties should probably cancel the conventions. Too much risk."

Rick punched my arm. "Not on your life, buddy. Thanks to you, we've got tickets to this shindig and that chance isn't likely to come around again."

"I hear you, Rick, but this is getting more and more

dangerous. Speaking of…" I tuned into Wisconsin Public Radio and heard a reporter's voice talking from the field as they tried to keep listeners updated on the current violence and threats.

Meanwhile, we waited. Some people got out of their cars and lined up on the shoulder, some to smoke or make calls. A few apparently just wanted to get out of their cars. Others walked their dogs—or their kids. I considered getting out of the truck to stretch my legs, but inertia took over and I stayed put. The car ahead inched up a few feet, a gap hardly worth closing, but I did anyway to satisfy the drivers behind me. Soon, people were scrambling to get the kids back in their car seats and dogs settled in.

We moved forward a few feet at a time, then stopped, then started, but each time we moved little more than a few yards, or less. It was getting dark, too, not because night was falling but because the sky was turning an eerie green in the northwest while the sun was still bright overhead.

"You do realize we're going to get caught in a storm now, right?" Rick asked, with a cynical laugh in his voice.

I laughed. "Find the weather, willya? We might as well hear the bad report. We're not getting much in the way of other news, anyway."

As I followed the cars and trucks, we didn't need the weather channel to tell us what would happen next. Progress forward slowed even more. Charcoal clouds formed rapidly and hung low, blocking visibility ahead.

The wind picked up, the temperature dropped, and the sea of traffic came to a stop again. Streaks of lightning broke through the clouds and thunder rocked the truck a couple of seconds later. Rain pelted the windshield, making me wince against the deafening rat-a-tat-rat-a-tat as small hailstones battered the hood and roof.

Rick put his head against the seat and closed his

eyes. The sound of a storm seemed almost normal as I thought back to the icy roads Rick had navigated in Montana. How far had we come? Not enough to count. A sense of defeat slowly took over my mood. Coming to Wisconsin was a mistake, getting involved in the campaigns was a mistake. Involving Lourdes and Raphie was one of the stupidest things I'd done.

I drained a bottle of water and let self-recrimination eat away at me for the next twenty minutes, at which point the storm died down and remnants of rain covered every surface and glistened under the late afternoon reappearing sun.

I put the truck in drive and moved ahead with the other cars. We were in the right lane and in a few minutes, we were moving at about fifteen miles an hour. Not bad.

"So, during the storm I decided this trip was only the latest in a long string of mistakes," I said. "Once the convention is over, I'm swearing off."

"Oh, yeah?"

"Yeah." I glanced at Rick, who opened his eyes again.

"Why now, Matt, when we may be getting to the point when the mystery unravels? TLTA is taking credit for this mess." Rick paused. "And we saw Hochberg and Hoover together.

"Which could mean nothing."

Rick didn't respond and I kept driving.

Finally, I broke the silence. "On the other hand, Hochberg and Hoover could be the key to this whole fucking mess."

***

"Now, why would a jury consultant be calling me?" Kathy Travis asked when she returned my phone call, made four hours earlier. Her tone was an inch or two this side of flirtatious.

"Curiosity," I answered. "It's not like you're hard to find."

"So, that doesn't answer my question." She spoke slowly, with a certain deliberation. "If I didn't know better, I'd think you were setting up a blind date."

"Are you flirting with me?" I asked in the best voice of innocence I could fake.

"Oh, maybe a little," Kathy said. "It's my way, since I doubt very much this is a business call."

"What other reason would there be?" So far, I found this conversation very weird. I could be a reporter for all she knew.

"I don't know, but I assume you'll tell me."

"I'm calling about your clients, the Garrons, Lucy and Fernando, Ferndy, I guess he goes by."

A couple of seconds ticked by. "What about them?"

"For one thing, I'm curious if you intend to take this to trial." I paused. "Are you going for a plea deal? Or, perhaps…they'll talk. You know…"

"So, if we go to trial, I suppose you'll want to be my jury consultant—pro bono, of course. I get that. But why do you care if we go a different direction?"

Ha! Pro bono. No, this would not be one of my pro bono causes. "Because a middle-aged couple with grown up kids and a couple of grandchildren generally don't fire shots into the campaign office of a candidate they don't like," I said. "Usually, they rally around the other guy and check a box on one of those quaint things called ballots."

"Maybe so. Unless the candidate threatens their very way of life," Kathy said.

"Nope, even then, the most they do—typically— is maybe cause a ruckus or throw a punch at a street demonstrator. They don't willingly stumble their way to committing federal crimes." I paused, but then added, "Crimes that result in prison terms measured in years, not mere months.

"What's your real game here, Mr. Matthew Barlow?"

Since she was done with the small talk, I got serious, too. "I don't have a game. I have an interest in what is supposed to look like random acts of violence that started early this campaign season."

"Like my clients' *random* and *impulsive* act of shooting up a campaign headquarters? Is that what you're getting at here?"

"Precisely. Because maybe none of this is random, at all, Ms. Travis. Because The League of True Americans has claimed credit for the political violence that took place in Wisconsin yesterday." I could have gone on, but I held back.

"I saw that," Kathy said, thoughtfully. "Look… you know very well that I can't tell you a thing about this case and what's going on behind the scenes. My clients have entered a plea of not guilty and the judge set a trial date. That's public information."

"Which also means there's plenty of time for a deal. They have time to save themselves, or at least try." I wasn't done. "I saw that a defense fund has been set up for them online. An ad for it ran in the online version of one of those racist journals these violent groups love so much."

"What's your point?" Kathy challenged.

"The point is that Ferndy and Lucy, acting on sheer impulse, so you say, have allies in very low places." I kept my tone matter-of-fact, as if none of this aroused any feelings. As to reinforce how casual this whole conversation was, I leaned back in my office chair and swung my feet up on my desk and crossed my ankles. I didn't have a care in the world.

"I guess we'll all need to wait and see what happens, won't we?"

Now what did that mean? Was she talking in code? In my now churning gut I knew for sure the information that would fill the gaps in what I knew. My hunch in that moment? The Garrons were going to talk.

"I suppose you're right," I agreed amicably. "But we're a little on edge here in Chicago. As you know, we do have the Democratic convention starting in Chicago soon."

"And the Republican convention soon after," Kathy pointed out.

"Right, but I'm not worried about them." I let that hang out there.

"Oh? And why is that?"

Good. She took the bait. "Because when you look at the patterns, at least most of the time, no one gets hurt. Oh sure, Republicans get threats and lots of attention, but their windows stay intact. Along with their bodies."

"Unlike your local Congressman's tragedy? Is that what you're saying?"

"Giuseppe Campanella, yes. Needless to say, we're still reeling out here." I was being terse, even a little challenging. The games were over. I went farther out on the limb than I'd planned to when I said, "We can't help but wonder if the same crowd of white supremacists has something bigger planned."

"Seriously?" Kathy said. I detected a faint squeak in the background. I think she shifted in her chair.

"Deadly serious." I let out a sigh. "Well, I know I've kept you. I've been following the case and wondered what was happening other than fundraising, which I guess will take care of your fee. But I'm not only following your case. I have friends here who've been alarmed by what's gone on since the South Carolina primary and we're trying to keep track of the totality of the violence."

"A group of Democrats?" Kathy asked.

"Not necessarily," I said, thinking that Bo's past Republican votes made an honest man of me. "Like I said, some of us are political junkies. We see the patterns. They're as plain as can be. Anyone who even has a fleeting interest can see them. I'd think the Garrons were aware they committed that one act alone, but they weren't the only ones disrupting the politics of the hour."

One at a time, I was spitting out seeds, sowing some doubt, at least I hoped that was the effect. But I'd have been shocked if any attorney working with people facing federal charges wouldn't have looked pretty deeply into the motivation behind the crime.

"I'm something of a junkie myself," Kathy said, "so I'll be paying attention to what's up in your town."

The breezy tone didn't fool me. I expected she'd get off the phone and see the patterns for herself. If she hadn't done that already. I wondered how long Lucy and Ferndy could possibly stay quiet.

Chapter Twenty

Wendy nodded at the TV screen. "Nice house, huh?"

Janet, Rick, and I let out an identical laugh.

"What? What's so funny?" Wendy asked, looking genuinely surprised.

"We finally have something to give a rat's ass about and you're commenting on Arnold Pierson's house?" Rick observed.

"It's a VP nomination, girl," Janet said.

"A big *effing* deal," I added.

"Okay, okay. You've had your fun. But you have to admit it's a nice house."

Like other political junkies all over the country—and beyond our borders—we were waiting for the Piersons and the Kent-Bentleys to emerge from Arnold's house with his wife, Kristie. How excited must she be after a lifetime of lesser elections?

Kidding aside, Wendy was on the money. The house was something special, almost big enough to be considered a suburban estate. It was a Tudor style place with banks of leaded windows on three floors. Purple hydrangeas grew so thick they formed a wall in front of the house. The long driveway was lined with black-eyed Susans and a bunch of other flowers I couldn't identify by name. If I ever knew what they were, I'd forgotten them.

A bank of microphones was set up and when the camera panned the neighborhood, network and cable

TV trailers, and roped off corrals for reporters told the world this was indeed a big effing deal. I found my own excitement about the moment growing. Jaded as I'd become during the campaign, and worried about who was going to live through it, there was still something special about VP announcements. Earlier this morning, our phones had lit up with the announcement and now we'd see this first live look.

"I'm half expecting Will Shakespeare to come out to the lawn," Janet said. "The house has the look."

"See? Couldn't have said it better myself," Wendy declared. "And you laughed at me. Janet is exactly right."

"Good thing we didn't have an office pool for the VP pic," Rick added. "Hard to do that when it looked like Marie was about the only candidate."

We'd all bet on Marie, which didn't make us geniuses. Reporters were following every lead to see who else was being vetted and the list was short. In the end, Arnold had won by a handful of delegates and their popular vote count was so close it might as well have been a tie.

Marie, especially, looked more like the future of the party—and the country—than any other combination of candidates. Only in her fifties, she was opening doors to leadership for her generation and those coming up behind. There was a benefit to such status.

"The social media universe views this as a fair pick," I said. "We don't often get a VP choice that's about who came in second. I think people like it. We're like kids who want a prize for the runner up. It should mean party unity."

Rick, who had been scrolling through his phone, agreed. He read tweets and comments from random people that were on board. "What's surprising is the tiny number of people who are negative about her. It's like what Matt said. People see it as fairness in action or something."

Our attention was drawn to the screen when secret

service agents and campaign operatives flanked the door. A few seconds later, Arnold and Kristie stepped out of the doorway and Marie and Parker followed behind. No kids were around, but I suspected they were lurking.

Watching the two of them standing together gave me a sense of pride and just as much relief. Even after the toll the campaign had taken on the country, there was still this kind of moment. Perhaps there was comfort in this familiar ritual we went through every four years. These teams that formed on VP announcement day might go on to win or lose, but they were optimistic and happy for this rollout event.

We watched the event through all the speeches. Marie and Arnold talked and played off each other like old friends, which was true in a way, since they'd briefly worked together in the senate before Pierson had become Secretary of the Treasury. The spouses looked proud, a little awkward, maybe, but proud. Kristie had taken charge of Parker and subtly indicated where he should stand. She gave him subtle cues about when he should be slightly back and off to the side, when it was okay to squeeze Marie's shoulders, and when an affectionate husbandly hug or quick peck on the cheek was okay.

We muted the TV when all the kids came out of nowhere and gathered around. Arnold had a baseball team of grandchildren, and at least two, maybe three siblings with partners. It was hard to know who to match up. They also had kids and grandchildren, so the Piersons looked like an old-fashioned clan, whereas Marie had a sister and brother-in-law and their one child to fill out a family portrait that looked more modern, at least through my eyes. Besides, like Rick said, who would give a rat's ass about how many kids the Bentley-Kents could produce?

Eventually Janet went off to answer the phone and Wendy went to her office, but Rick stayed behind. I told him I'd spoken with Kathy Travis.

"Were you fishing for what angle she was going to take to defend them?" Rick's puzzled expression made it clear what I'd done mystified him. And he wasn't an easy guy to take by surprise.

I repeated back an abbreviated version of the conversation. "When I dropped TLTA into our banter, I could almost see her jotting notes. My guess, Ferndy and Lucy were pretty honest about the reason they shot up the campaign office and I think they're involved in WNF."

"Not TLTA?"

"What if they were one and the same?" I thought about something Bo had said about overlap, not so much in the organizations, but who law enforcement had looked at when they tried—and failed—to identify anyone associated with TLTA, even internationally. Talk about shadowy and elusive. Bo had crosschecked names, and our old buddy Scotty Tabakin came up. Lori had, too. But nothing linked them to this loosely defined group. It was a stretch to call it an organization, at least now. All the anti-hate groups and federal and state investigating agencies had poked around and found nothing. The usual suspects came up regularly and were known as part of the alphabet soup of organizations that represent a bleak picture of the country. WNF is one of the names.

"And?" Rick tried to get my attention by waving his hand at me. "Where are you? You've obviously left the building."

"Bo told us to forget TLTA and stick with WNF," I said, not totally convinced. "He seems to think we'd find our answers in the players we do know, not necessarily in the ones we don't."

"We can include the Garrons in the ones we know. Right? Did you glean anything from Kathy that would lead in any other direction?"

"Not this time, but there is information there to be had from Ferndy and Lucy. I have to figure out how to get it." I chewed on my bottom lip and tried to figure out what angle I could take with Kathy if I found an excuse to talk to her again. "Those two people didn't act alone. They didn't even try to hide themselves. They acted like they expected to be caught. The whole thing had duped written all over it."

"What does the indictment say?" Rick asked.

"Nothing about the Garrons being set up. Supposedly, they claim to have acted alone. I can't believe that's the story they're telling Kathy." I paused to take a breath. "The charges aren't nothing. The indictment covers everything from unlawfully discharging a weapon in a public space, threatening harm to public figures, conspiracy to do all that, and causing harm to private property. They're each charged with a dozen offenses—and that's just a start. They could face a charge of treason. The state gets its turn, too."

"Conspiracy?" Rick arched an eyebrow.

One of the trickier areas of law, conspiracy. Proving the reality of a conspiracy to do something didn't mean the crime had to be committed by all named parties. "In this case, bringing charges of conspiracy covers them for whatever else comes to light. Presumably, Lucy and Ferndy conspired with each other, but it does leave the door open to add more parties to the conspiracy to bring harm to another person."

Rick chuckled and then rubbed his hand across his forehead. Apparently, he'd finally reached his limit.

"What's so funny?" I asked, even as I chuckled along with him.

"The picture of Ferndy and Lucy sitting at the kitchen table cooking up a plan to shoot out Marie's campaign office windows strikes me as funny," Rick said, rubbing his eyes like he didn't know whether to laugh or cry. "Like a comedy sketch."

"Right." I put one hand out to the left, the other to the right and pretended they were Ferndy and Lucy. 'Hey, Ferndy, what are you up to today?' 'Well, Lucy, I thought I'd drag out my assault rifle and head ⌐wntown and shoot up that Kent woman's campaign office.' 'Want some company, Ferndy? I never did like that woman. And we could get some lunch after.'"

As funny as that sounded, it was also totally implausible. "More likely, they were part of a network. Was it domestic? Maybe foreign? Someone encouraged this. That someone or many people likely implied that come the election they'd be off the hook—maybe even hailed as heroes. It wasn't the first time it happened in this primary season. Maybe they called in the threats to Toomey. Maybe that's part of the conspiracy to harm."

When our phones signaled a text, we both hurried to take a look.

"Mine's from Lourdes," I said. "She retweeted something from Raphie. Wow, the Ohio shooter is still in the hospital, but he's talking."

"That's what Bo says. How do we know it's true," Rick said. "Who says he's talking?"

We looked at the TV. Once again, the Breaking News banner spun in and took over the screen. "Talk about stepping on the VP announcement," I said. "Marie and Arnold and their big day will be yesterday's news before bars offer their first happy hour two-for-one special."

"Looks like Lourdes is taking this on now." I put the phone on the desk. "I wonder how Raphie got the news."

"We don't have leads to throw their way, Matt, so what difference does it make?"

I patted myself on the back. "Not taking credit or anything, but I think we hooked Lourdes to keep following this, and Raphie has been taking on even more of the political stories."

I slapped the table—my spur of the moment way to refocus my attention. "I need to get to work." I tapped my temples. "Our work, here in the office. The lead attorney on the new case and I are talking face-to-face tomorrow morning. I have to get up to speed on Wendy's research." I snapped my fingers as if getting

Rick's attention. "Don't go too far. We'll need you."

Rick looked up and grinned. "Don't worry. I'm not going anywhere. Too much going on."

I got to my feet. "Sometimes I think I'm delusional thinking we can play any part in unraveling what's going on with this constant violence—or threats of it. Since it doesn't seem random, I guess there's nothing to do but keep tracking it."

I was almost to the conference room door when my phone rang. I didn't hide my surprise when I glanced at the screen. "Well, well, this is getting interesting." I answered the call and bypassed the niceties.

"Hey Kathy, I didn't expect to hear from you, at least not so soon." I glanced across the table at Rick, whose fingers stopped mid-air over his keyboard.

"To be perfectly honest with you, Matt, I'm not sure why I'm calling you." She paused.

I waited.

"It could have something to do with something, if you know what I mean."

"I'm not sure I do." It was a mere tiny fib, since I was jumping to conclusions already. "Is it okay if I put you on speaker? I'm on the move and my assistant Rick is with me. It's fine if he hears this talk, if it's okay with you."

"Yeah, I guess, if you're sure he'll keep this confidential with you." Her voice was shaky. "It won't take a genius to figure out I'm calling about the Garrons."

Since a clever response didn't immediately come to mind, I settled for, "I see."

"Well, okay, you probably *don't* see. How could you? But here's the deal…*they're gone*."

My stomach flipped. I glanced at Rick and he gestured with his outstretched hand to encourage me to keep going.

"I assume you don't know where they went or wouldn't be calling. Did they miss a court date? Were they released on home confinement?" I asked.

"No and no. I argued—rightly so—that they weren't a flight risk," Kathy explained, maybe a tad too defensively. "They had such deep roots in the community and they needed to work."

Kathy elaborated, and on its face, Ferndy and Lucy's window shooting spree came out of the blue. It was one thing to be survivalists, with bunkers filled with food and water—and a few weapons, although not as many as some, according to Kathy. The two owned a small campground. Ferndy had some summer mowing contracts, and Lucy also did private work as a seamstress. "The judge went with a reasonable bail and they managed it with some help from a bunch of friends."

I glanced at Rick who had his eyes on my phone, as if it were a real person telling this tale. Being released on bail made sense to me, sort of. But the crime did involve firearms, so I wouldn't have been terribly surprised if they'd been denied bail. "Uh, you obviously were persuasive. I get that, but why are you calling me?"

"Good question." A heavy sigh came through the phone. "Look, when I took the case, they were run-of-the-mill survivalist types—preparing for the coming apocalypse. I get that. I've got a couple of uncles who live the same way. They could get by for a year, maybe two, with the supplies and gadgets they've stockpiled, including generators. My uncles wouldn't have shot out campaign office windows, either, but I learned more about the Garrons. Now, I still have to maintain my silence. They're my clients, but I'd be lying if I said their disappearance doesn't worry me."

Rick scribbled a note and slid it across the desk.

Ask about white supremacy!

I'd been searching for a way to bring that up. Hint around or ask directly? I settled on a little humility and went for ignorant. "Indulge this city guy, will ya? I don't understand the nuances of these terms I hear thrown around. To be blunt, are Ferndy and Lucy, sort of survivalists *plus*, like some you hear about, sort of white supremacist types?"

"Interesting question," Kathy said in a grim tone.

From what I could tell, she wasn't especially thrown by what I asked.

"I didn't think so. Now I'm not so sure."

"What made you change your mind?" I asked innocently, knowing Kathy would have to choose to withhold or reveal information.

"They may be into something way over their heads, I can tell you that. Or, it's possible they've fooled us all, including their family and this community." Kathy sighed again. "They were smart about some things. They said nothing, admitted to nothing when they were first arrested. You know, usually people are panicky and deny everything—or spill all the beans. Their first call was to me. Unbeknownst to me, Fernando had my business card in his pocket—literally. So, even though I didn't know them, I was there from the start. Other than giving their names and address, they offered nothing. Now I'm wondering if they were coached."

"So, you went into this with some important facts missing." I had a feeling the missing information might have turned up on their property when it was searched.

Rick frowned, as if he wasn't sure what the mystery was. "Is what you discovered part of the case? Are you going to attempt to keep it out of evidence?"

"Exactly. I might have gotten lucky, too. But that's out the window now that they're on the lam."

"How do you know they're really gone, as in not coming back?"

"A neighbor called the chief of police. The van was gone, and Fernando didn't show up to mow his client's six acres across the road. He got suspicious, and when he stopped by, he found one of the grown kids running the campground." Kathy stopped and took a breath, a little more stress seeping into her voice with every word. "The Chief went out there himself and got the story from the son."

Rick and I listened to this small town story of Ferndy and Lucy telling their kids they needed to spend some time in a favorite spot deep in the mountains, but not so far as to alarm anyone or make them unreachable. At least, that's what the adult kids claimed to the authorities and to Kathy. Their parents needed this getaway before their trial—or their plea deal. But the trial was many months off. The neighbor investigated when Ferndy, an otherwise reliable guy, didn't show up. First the local police were on it, but almost immediately the feds got involved.

Kathy had done her part. Exactly the right thing. When Ferndy had called from the police station, she'd told the Garrons to stay quiet, and she continued that advice, even when more damaging facts came out.

"Info that linked the Garrons to white supremacy groups," I stated as a fact. "Tell me I'm wrong."

"I can't," Kathy said. "The fact is, much of this will soon be going public because of the manhunt underway. The Garrons were a lot more than people who stockpiled canned chili." She laughed cynically. "Oddly enough, though, they didn't have many weapons in the house. Now I wonder if they stashed weapons somewhere else."

"Why is that odd?" I asked.

"Because around here, having all kinds of firearms isn't unusual. In some circles, it's the norm," Kathy said. "My granddad had a couple of dozen guns. He was a collector and mostly bought antique guns that were worth something"

"You're saying the Garrons weren't collectors as such?"

"Not at all," Kathy said. "They had some hunting rifles, two handguns, and a semi-automatic."

"That sounds like a mini-arsenal to me, but what do I know?"

"Well, here's a comparison. Around *here*, we have gun confiscation stories break a couple of times a year.

In one case a couple of months ago, *two dozen* weapons were found, many not registered," Kathy explained. "The guy carried one of his semi-automatics to his ex-girlfriend's house and threatened her. Then, he shot off some rounds inside her house."

"So, the Garrons' handful of weapons was insignificant. Is that what you're saying?"

"Exactly, and it's why I suspect they have guns stashed somewhere else. Legal or not. Maybe they're hidden on property one of their kid's owns. Typically, the deeper these types get into white supremacy, the more guns they stockpile."

"Do you have *any* idea where they went?" I asked. "Were they part of a network of like-minded folks? Maybe their kids don't even know what you've learned about them. Could they be hiding out with other people they already know?"

"If you'd asked me when we spoke the first time, I'd have said no. But now, it's plausible to me. Maybe the most logical conclusion," Kathy said. "In my last conversation with Ferndy, he admitted he'd begun posting on a couple of private social media sites. Here's the thing. Apparently, the mass shooter in South Carolina posted on the same site, too."

Bingo.

Rick's eyebrows shot up.

We finally had the direct connection we'd been looking for. "They offered that tidbit on their own?" I asked.

"Ferndy told me. They took their computers with them, of course. He thought eventually other places he posted would come to light. But, he told me no one used their real names. He only put two and two together that the guy in the group was the shooter after the guy acted and was killed."

"I happened to be in South Carolina right after that guy went to a crowded mall and hunted African-American shoppers—and other people of color—for sport." I let out a low guttural growl. "That shooting is a good part of the reason I've paid such close attention to what's been going on these last few months."

"Yeah, I know. I believe Ferndy. This dark, stealthy group, my description, obviously, not his, communicated in a kind of code." Another cynical laugh. "So, I surrender, Matt, when these two turn up, either on their own or in cuffs, I'm going to need a jury consultant after all. Are you available?"

"It's a little early for that, Kathy." She couldn't know she was talking to someone who'd been in the state and worked for the candidate whose campaign office her client had targeted. Conflict of interest flashed like a neon sign. I could never work with her on the Garron case. But that was a bridge I didn't have to worry about crossing now.

"The feds don't like trials nearly as much as bargaining," I said, "but you already know that. Firearms, politically motivated attacks during an election year and with spotlights on them, they can go for a charge of treason before this is all over. This might be just the time to get the best deal you can for them. How far can pleading not guilty possibly take them? They ran, they didn't even deny the crime."

"Yeah, maybe so, but it's not how far they go, it's for how long. Their sentence, I mean. As it is, their kids and grandchildren are going to be visiting them in prison for years."

"You're assuming they'll be found," I said. "They've apparently covered their tracks and maybe they'll disappear. But that doesn't explain why the two never even tried to hide who they were when they did the shooting. Hell, they were blatant." Either she knew more or she didn't, but Rick and I had more to go on now.

"So, how about telling me the real reason you called the other day?" Kathy asked. "You might as well at this point."

I calculated how much I needed to dangle out in front of her, a few facts here or there that would prompt her to spill more information. "Let's say I got hooked on this ugly primary season. I have a passing acquaintance with a couple of journalists covering this story. I've also followed what happened to Representative Campanella, the congressman who lost some staff and volunteers in a bombing that also killed restaurant workers next door."

"Yes, yes, I know all about that. Do you think there's a connection?"

I told her about the false arrest and the witness who described seeing a guy who looked like a survivalist near the scene. "So, they picked up a kid thinking they had the right guy. The real culprit had time to get away. We don't know if he—or they—were local or traveled a long way to this neighborhood shopping street. The accused kid, accused for a little while, anyway, was spotted ambling around in camouflage and a vest with a dozen pockets. That's exactly the nut job type you are looking for, right? Good thing the guy had an alibi that could hold up."

"No other suspects?" Kathy asked.

"Not that any of us regular people know about. I don't have anyone inside to pass on tips." I laughed. "Even if I did, I wouldn't know what to do with them."

"Look. I've been in private practice for a while, but this is the first time I've dealt with a federal fugitive," Kathy said. "I reached out to you because this shook me up a little. And you reached out to me the other day for a reason."

I was glad I had. Kathy and I ended our call with the promise we'd stay in touch. When the call disconnected, I made a fist and whacked the table. "Finally, connections."

Rick raised his index finger in the air, which let me know to keep my mouth shut until he'd finished with whatever had grabbed his focus.

I'd find out soon enough.

Chapter Twenty-one

Even during normal times, Wendy and Janet wouldn't have been surprised that I had lunch delivered from one of our prized Chinese takeout places. We all unloaded the bags and set up the food at the end of the conference table.

"My gut tells me this is a working lunch," Janet said. "I hope I'm going to hear you tell me you solved some crimes."

"That's not our job," I teased.

"Appearances to the contrary," Rick said, digging into his favorite spicy beef dish.

I told them about Kathy and brought them up to date on my conversations with her, then explained why I'd called her in the first place.

Rick filled in details about what Bo had told him. "He thinks if we focus on White Nation's First, we're more likely to see patterns. Maybe see more connections."

"Then, if Rich Foresman, that Ohio shooter, starts talking, we might be able to read between the lines and see if we can find other links," Wendy said.

"Nothing seems to get anyone closer to solving JoJo's case," Janet said. "It didn't even match the other incidents."

Rick was busy on his phone but looked up long enough to say he hadn't seen anything about the Garrons in the news. "Why don't you tip off Lourdes or Raphie?"

"It would look pretty obvious—they're both local. The fact they're gone isn't confidential," I said, "but other things she intimated about the searches and their lifestyle are."

"That leaves Cooper," Wendy said. "Why not feed him information?"

"It's too easy to trace back to me," I mused, but I looked at the others as I mulled it over.

Janet spoke up without hesitating. "It's public information. Anyone can find out they're fugitives. What difference does it make if Coop does a segment on it? Seems to me they're dangerous people."

"All true," I said. "I'm trying to make sure that anything I tell Coop doesn't breach *her* attorney-client privilege."

"So, what are they up to, our Ferndy and Lucy, now that they're on the run?" Rick asked.

"How do you know they aren't planning to come to Chicago, Matt? We already know the convention is going to turn the city into an even more complicated place." Wendy's eyes reflected worry, maybe even fear.

"We don't know," I said. "Kathy didn't contradict me when I speculated about Ferndy and Lucy being white supremacists and may be involved in the movement." Something jabbed at me, prodding me to take a stronger stance, even though I was skirting privilege—or, Kathy had. "Ferndy admitted to Kathy he had contact with the South Carolina shooter. He assumed the posts on the shooter's computer would eventually trace back to him."

"So, he owned up to it with his lawyer," Janet said.

I nodded and glanced at Rick, who was paying attention only to his screen.

"If you know this, why wouldn't law enforcement already be on it?" Janet asked. "The federal marshals and local police must be all over this in Montana and looking for these two."

"It's one of the easiest places in the world to hide in,"

Rick said, still not taking his focus off his computer. "Remember the Unabomber?"

"Exactly who came to my mind," Wendy said.

I shook my head. "No, I'm not buying it. The Unabomber had no associations with anyone. Ferndy and Lucy have kids and grandkids. They wouldn't have done this kind of action, or gone on the lam, for that matter, to spend their lives in hiding."

"They're in it for something bigger, Matt? A cause?" Janet sat with her arms crossed over her chest. "Once you put names on these people, they seem real. And dangerous."

"Hold on for a second," Rick said. "Don't go anywhere."

"We're captive in our home away from home." I glanced at Janet and smirked. "Come to think of it, except when I've been on wild goose chases, this is pretty much where I've been for months."

"While we've been holding down the fort," Janet said, smirking back.

"Come on, Rick. What are you up to?" Wendy asked in a plaintive tone. "Tell us you know where the gun-toting racists are."

"If I made a few connections and we take Bo's concerns seriously, I would say they might be right here." Rick turned the computer monitor so we could all get a glimpse of what filled the screen. It was a shot of the United Center on the near west side. The statue of Michael Jordan set it apart from every other basketball venue in the world.

I closed my eyes to block out what Rick was implying. I didn't stay silent for long. "I assume some connections are coming next."

"Exactly. As it turns out, almost everyone we've been observing for months is going to end up in the United Center," Rick said, pointing to the screen. "Starting with the Piersons and the Kent-Bentleys."

"C'mon, this is going to end up looking like flimsy evidence of anything, Rick. You know that's true."

I was frustrated that so many individual events had loose connections, but in total, added up to nothing."

"Give me a second, Matt." Rick wasn't smiling, and he wasn't kidding.

I lifted my hands in surrender.

"Do I have all the answers here?" he asked. "No, but neither do you."

"I'm sorry, Rick." Again, I raised my hands, hoping to make peace. "I'm tired of the dead ends, and I know all this frustration points back to me.

Rick changed the page. "Percy is with the Pierson campaign now. He signed on the day after Marie dropped out. They're using him on the advance team. That gives him information about logistics and where the candidate is going to be way ahead of time. Steve Novak agreed to serve on the convention program, working on the party platform, and later, the transition. I looked it up."

"I suppose Lori Hochberg will be there," Wendy said.

"But not Scotty, I would bet," I said.

"Jeff Hoover will be there—or at least he'll be in Chicago."

"How do you know?" I asked, leaning forward. I owed Rick my attention, even if I didn't quite believe in what I was seeing. "Isn't Jeff continuing as Toomey's campaign manager?"

"Nope, he'll be a senior advisor for the general election," Rick said. "I got that right off the website and checked it with the campaign's twitter feed. And it's on their Facebook pages. But for the convention, he's going to be a commentator, safe in a Chicago TV studio, mind you."

"A little color commentary?" Janet asked.

I nodded. "It would seem so."

"So far, that's quite a group," Wendy said. "We can't forget that JoJo Campanella will be there. He's still raising money for the families of those killed or wounded in the bombing. Bo thinks he'll be a powerful primetime speaker on one of the nights."

It did seem cozy in a way that Marie's top people ended up with Arnold's campaign. All logically so. No one could question any of it. Scotty Tabakin was the wildcard.

I puffed out my cheeks and then blew out the air. I couldn't ignore my heart beating hard in my chest. If I were prone to panic attacks, I'd be having one right now. "Is it such a stretch to think that all these threats, all these seemingly unrelated incidents could be working up to something here during the convention?"

"There isn't too much you can do, is there, Matt?" Janet asked. "All these people have legitimate reasons to be at the convention. No one can deny that."

"That's the dilemma. No one is uncovering much about TLTA or WNF."

I absently picked up my phone and started scrolling through it. "Wait a second. Here's something." I switched the channel to another cable news station and saw Raphie doing a live spot standing in front of the cyclone fence. A corner of a brick building was visible behind him.

Standing with the hood of his rain jacket pulled over his head, Raphie said, "I stand by my reporting. Now, it's true Foresman's legal team has denied that their client has 'cracked the case', language some have used to describe Foresman's willingness to talk." He glanced behind him. "Of course, the hospital is not allowing members of the press corps inside and no reporter has talked to him directly."

"Foresman's legal team has brought out the old cliché and called your reporting fake news," the studio reporter said. "They say this is just another example of the danger of social media."

"All I can say is that I trust my sources," Raphie said. "I stand by both the tweets I posted and the full story in this morning's *Chicago Tribune*." A gust of wind blew Raphie's hood off and that brought a laugh from the anchors and Raphie.

"Too bad Raphie's story didn't have more details."
I frowned. "He owes me one." I sent a quick text to
him. "I'm going to see if he'll talk to me."

"He's in Ohio. That means the phone…" Rick gave
me a warning look.

"Maybe he's coming back," I said, hoping it was
true. "For now, I want to know two things. Does the
guy know the Garrons, and in all this information he
supposedly dumped, did he mention WNF?" I could
ask Raphie. That wouldn't be violating anything I got
from Kathy, my source. If he knew, then maybe he'd
tell me. If not, then it was a dead end.

I sent a second text to Raphie. Did RH mention
Garrons or WNF?

"Done," I said.

***

Later, when Bo stopped by the office to pick up Wendy
for dinner, he ended up in the conference room looking
at Rick's convention notes, namely lists of the familiar
names. Like Rick and me, we agreed everyone had
legitimate business there, more or less, unless they
weren't who they said they were in the first place.

Now that we were face-to-face, I filled Bo in on the
Garrons. "Who knew they'd take up so much space in
my head at this point in the election?" I snorted. "It's
about the only thing in my head."

"Mine, too, as a matter of fact, but then it's on
Wendy's mind, too." Bo rapped his knuckles on the
table. "We're running out of time, you know."

I looked at Bo, expecting him to fill in the blanks.

Across the table, Rick stopped fooling with his
tablet.

"Uh, you mean with the convention starting?"

"Damn right. I haven't stopped thinking about what
could happen," Bo said. "I mean it. TLTA or WNF, any
of them. We don't know all that much about them, but
what about the groups we never heard of. The Garrons

aren't going to go on TV and announce the hate group they're involved with."

Bo had been the first to mention assassination out loud. That had been months before when we were in Springfield. He wasn't dropping it.

"Wendy tells me you have passes for the five of us," Bo said.

I nodded. "We're all taking that time off. We might as well, because we all have a bad feeling about it." I pointed to Bo. "I suppose you do, too."

Bo grimaced. "Not so bad I'd stay away altogether. I've been keeping track of wild tweets and conspiracies. If we believed half of them, we'd have to call off the convention."

The internet had been lighting up with tweets disavowed and taken down or retweeted thousands of times. Arnold Pierson, a moderate liberal-type, was called everything from a secret communist dating back to his college days to a secret follower of Islamic law. This mainline Protestant, a Methodist, was regularly accused of coddling terrorists. Good old Arnold was now apparently the Pied Piper of shadowy figures who, if we believed the social media nonsense, had an evil plan to take over private education. This exposed the unbelievable gullibility of the jerks who rely on social media for their news and ultimately their beliefs.

"To gullible people, or perhaps we can call them what they are, idiots, Arnold seems like Satan," Bo said, groaning.

"We've seen this movie before," Rick said, "but this time it's reached new lows."

I glanced at my phone, picked it up, then put it down. Waiting.

Bo cast a quizzical look my way.

"I wish Raphie would get back to me, damn it." Bo understood my conflict about tipping anyone off about even what little I knew. "If this Rich Foresman, the casino shooter, knows anything about South Carolina or Lucy and Ferndy, at least some of this might unravel."

271

More than the rest of us, Bo never believed in Lori Hochberg's so-called transformation. It had all seemed too neat, too planned. He repeated that again as we sat in the conference room waiting and not knowing what to do other than keep trying to put the pieces together.

"I'd feel a lot better about this if I had a sense other people were making the same connections we are," Rick said, not for the first or tenth or twentieth time. It had been frustrating from the start, made even worse when we'd seen no arrests in the bombing of JoJo's office.

When Wendy finished up her work, she came into the conference room.

I encouraged everyone to leave, including Rick. "I'm going to take the dogs out and then I'll finish up a couple of things and go home myself."

Everyone looked reluctant to leave me on my own, including Janet.

"Hey, I'm fine here. Go, go." I shooed them out the door, not taking no for an answer. "In a couple of days, we'll be spending hours and hours together at the convention. I'll get my fill of you there, believe me. For now, go away."

After the others left, I was relieved to be alone with Maude and Quigs, but admittedly at loose ends, too. It was a hot night in Chicago, and I didn't stay out with the dogs for long. With a sense of dread I didn't like but had almost learned to live with, I started to turn out the lights and get ready to lock up.

Raphie's text caused a change of plans.

***

"I came straight from the airport," Raphie said when I opened the door to let him in. "I think you need to hear what Rich Foresman had to say. The guy is trying to save his own ass. I believe my source, who has heard every word he's said, but so far, no one else seems to. Or they won't come out on the record."

"Come into the conference room," I said. "Don't mind the dogs. They're friendly." I looked at the two of them stretched out on the carpet in the corner. "It's past their bedtime."

Raphie grinned and made a couple of remarks about how obviously wonderful my two companions were. That Raphie knew his way around dogs and their owners showed he was a dog lover himself. He nodded to the muted TV. A clip of Cooper's interview with Mike Toomey was being replayed. "Cooper's been busy this election season."

"He hates the violence. He knows something is going on—like we do."

"I'm a straight up reporter," Raphie said, nodding to the screen, "with my Northwestern journalism degree to prove it, but I don't give a damn now. I'm convinced Toomey has plans for this country and they aren't good."

"You won't find any argument around here," I said. "We've put together a lot of information about all this, but we still don't know what to make of it."

For the first time since he arrived, or maybe the first time ever, Raphie eyed me with suspicion. "Weelllll, who's we?"

I waved off his fears. It wouldn't pay to have him afraid of me. "We, as in people who work for me." I pointed to the chair at the head of the table. "Sit, I'll give you the bare bones. Off the record. Every word. Are we clear?"

Raphie sat, putting his tape recorder and spiral reporter's notebook out of reach. "You have my word."

I started from the first encounter with Percy in Millennial Park and took him with me on that South Carolina trip, the bomb threats, and actual bombings. "So far, we've uncovered nothing of any note about JoJo's office." I looked into Raphie's face and noted the slightest flicker in his eye. If I hadn't been looking for it, I'd have missed it. I quickly ran down everything that had happened, including my contacts with Kathy.

"Foresman heard the two escaped," Raphie said. "He didn't know them personally, but he knew them through what he called the network. He believes that Montana husband and wife are true believers in the worst sense. They're like him. Ready to die for this cause."

"Did he mention WNF or TLTA?"

Raphie mumbled about needing to check something and got his tablet out of his carryon bag. "According to the source, WNF is operating in what are almost cells. Only a few people know what the next move is. Foresman thinks the JoJo bombing could be the work of the Garrons themselves. It's all leading up to something, and he thinks Chicago is the target."

My heart beat a little faster. "You mean Pierson himself?"

"My source wasn't certain," Raphie said, closing his eyes as if not wanting to see the facts. "But he did say, there were others involved, some foreign involvement, too. He hinted that some of the players had gotten themselves high up into the campaign structure."

That put me in *cold sweat* territory. Percy came to mind, but Lori Hochberg didn't escape my notice, either. Or Scotty Tabakin for that matter. I groaned inside. The whole bunch of them made me nervous.

Raphie studied my face. "You don't seem surprised."

"I'm not." I patted the table. "Do you know when any of this information is going to be made public?"

Raphie shook his head. "There's a problem with that. Naturally, his lawyers don't want him talking right now. Publicly, they're going for insanity, mentally unbalanced, maybe impaired—many things, and all of those words that cover up ideology."

"So, the guy's a true believer?"

"My source thinks so. Foresman has made a couple of statements that made their way into the public, and according to him, he planned to shoot himself but got gunned down first." Raphie checked his notes. "Seems the guy is lamenting this as his biggest failure, but he's saying he's willing to talk."

"I guess what he's dropping are teasers," I said. "I doubt they'll reach an agreement with the lawyers before the convention. Not enough time."

I fell silent thinking about the Garrons traveling from Montana and putting an explosive device in JoJo's office. It didn't make sense. "I wonder if the Garrons made the device and gave it to someone else who planted it in JoJo's office."

"Could be, I suppose."

"Let me try something," I said, punching a number on my contact list. "I'm calling the Garrons' lawyer. It's not so late out that way."

"*What?*"

That got Raphie's attention. I snickered. "Took you by surprise, huh?"

The slightly sultry voice on the phone said a surprised hello. I got right to the point. "I need to put you on speaker, Kathy. I need you to help me."

"I don't have any idea where the Garrons are, if that's what you're about to ask me, Matt."

"As far as I know, they haven't been sighted. That's *not* why I'm calling. I've got a journalist here in my office with me," I said, "and he's got a source into Rich Foresman, the Ohio shooter. He's still in the hospital, but he's spilling some beans."

"Real McCoy beans, or made up beans?" Kathy asked.

"Maybe you can help me figure that out. I won't compromise you here, but you can maybe confirm or deny," I said.

Kathy let out a deep breath that created a staticky sound as it came through the phone. "I'll try to help."

"Will the Garrons sacrifice themselves for whatever cause this is they've committed to?" I asked.

"You mean die, I assume, and that's no secret. Their kids believe that. Or, one does for sure." Kathy paused for a couple of seconds. "I think they're in this together. Their son believes they're great patriots, not the traitors they probably are. That's why they didn't hide what they did."

Somehow, covering their tracks on a faraway bombing in Chicago, but blatantly shooting out campaign windows didn't make sense.

"Do you think it's possible they're heading to Chicago, maybe meeting other people here?" I asked. "I'm specifically thinking about the convention."

"If they show up there, I believe it would be part of a plan. They wouldn't go there alone, unless they were planning to be observers. And I doubt that."

"Can you think of anything else that could be helpful? I asked. "They surrendered their passports, right?"

"They did. They didn't travel much, but they'd gone to visit family in Minnesota. Lucy's sister. That was in February."

Raphie's head jerked up. We both shook our heads. I was glad Kathy couldn't see us. "There would be proof of that, I assume?"

"I didn't fact check that," Kathy said, "but it came up when I argued they weren't a flight risk. They turned in passports that had never been used."

"Is there anything else you can tell us? We're only trying to protect people here, and so far, the journalist—a top notch guy—is not uncovering specific threats Homeland Security is looking into." I heard a groveling desperation seep into my voice. "They get hundreds of reports of threats, but nothing is standing out. At least not now."

Kathy had no more info to offer, so we ended the call.

Raphie was already typing on the tablet.

I stood and took a turn around the long conference table.

Raphie got to his feet, but he made no move toward the door. "This never happens," he said. "This lack of clues or specific plans. If this is true, then these cells, or whatever they call these small groups, are better than anyone knows."

"We have a strong hunch that at least two people involved don't care about their lives."

Raphie didn't agree or disagree, but headed to the door. "I'm staying on this, Matt. I don't know where it will go, but I'm sticking with it."

I followed Raphie to the door. Almost as if I momentarily forgot what this was all about, I said, "I'll look for you at the convention."

Raphie scoffed. "Right."

He hurried down the stairs. Before he got to door to the street, I hollered, "Hey, Raphie—be careful."

We *all* had to be careful.

Chapter Twenty-two

Over the noise of the roll call, Bo called out my name from his seat, two down from mine. "This has been going on for what seems like days," Bo said, "and they just finished Illinois."

Rick laughed. "He's bored already. It's only night one."

"How can you be bored?" I asked, gesturing around the United Center, a spectacular arena for far more than Bulls' basketball. "The nominating roll call is a great slice of classic Americana. And it's a lot cooler in here, even with thousands of companions than it is from our living rooms." I pointed down to the main level where the Illinois delegation was still waving their signs. "Charles Marchand is down there, right in the thick of it."

"Sit tight, Bo," Wendy said getting to her feet and clapping along with the crowd.

"And look alive," I said.

Everyone got that message. That night we were on our first watch. We got the convention passes because of the work the firm did for Marie, but fear would keep us planted in our seats on time every night.

The next convention evening passed in a blur—lots of speakers, but few spectators paid attention until President Andersen ran down all the accomplishments of his administration that were threatened if Toomey won. It was a sea of signs bobbing on sticks and or being waved side to side. Every night's events provided a good enough reason for delegates to boogie in the aisles.

By the third night, I was ready for Marie, who was a much better speaker than our nominee. She was warm and funny and very persuasive, even making jokes about her second place finish in the primaries but being prepared to be part of a team claiming the win in November. Wendy and Janet, completely enchanted by this new ticket, were on their feet for what Janet called the hootin' and hollerin'.

On the fourth night, I was about ready to concede that my suspicions were way off base. Not that we were out of danger, but that whatever the newest domestic terrorist scheme was, I doubted it would play out now. But Wendy and Rick told me "not so fast." They convinced me it was too early to drop our guard and we showed up as vigilant—and nervous—as we had on night one of the convention. We watched the aisles and scanned the crowd, and were a little on edge.

The part of me that wasn't involved in the violence this election cycle brought us could enjoy the spectacle of the final night, the nominee's send off, the celebration of uniquely American traditions. Too bad the general election was already filled with accusations and recriminations.

When Arnold Pierson came to the stage, confetti came down like snow. Some of the streamers had come loose, but the balloons were all set to descend as soon as the speech was over. This was a first for me, being in the live audience for a presidential nomination. For the sake of the TV audience, I hoped Arnold could manage a decent speech. Electrifying he was not. He was much more like a stereotypical former Secretary of the Treasury, but that wasn't so bad I concluded when the mood of the country was so serious.

We had practiced how we'd surreptitiously watch what was going on. We didn't want to be noticed, and we weren't even sure what we were looking for. Bo and Kathy Travis were convinced the Garrons would show up ready to take themselves and as many people as possible out in a fiery blaze of glory. Martyrs for the cause of white supremacy. Oh, joy.

Nancy Smith was chosen to introduce Pierson. It was a sentimental choice, and no one who followed the Dean Andersen administration didn't claim a soft spot for Nancy Smith. Eight years earlier, she was considered a shoe-in when her turn came. Despite early onset Alzheimer's, she still functioned well, but also had been keeping a low profile for the last year or so.

Her introduction was as heartfelt as it was short, and Pierson gave her a big hug when he stepped to the podium. He held her hand in the air to keep her by his side and then stepped back and let the crowd show their appreciation for her before she retreated backstage. Good move. It set up the emotional atmosphere for his speech.

"This is going to be over soon," I said over the applause for the VP. "I haven't seen anything out of the ordinary." I looked to my right at Bo and Wendy, and to my left at Janet and Rick.

"Nothing…*yet*," Bo said.

Out of the blue, Janet did what she did best and tried to lighten the mood with one of her clichés. "Are we sitting ducks or lambs to the slaughter?"

We were a little too tense to tease her.

Pierson droned on for about five minutes too long. I knew that was true because I couldn't stop muttering, "Good enough, Arnold…quit while you're ahead… time to finish while the energy is high."

Arnold didn't listen. Plus, he skipped over all the horror of the last months of election season violence. That was his prerogative, but I was disappointed in a speech only filled with happy talk. Finally, the families came on stage, the balloons dropped, and all was right with the world.

It was now or never. With all eyes on the stage and balloons floating everywhere, it was a good time to do another scan of the crowd with my field glasses. Bo had his binoculars out, too.

With Springsteen's voice reverberating in the background, all five of us scanned the crowd.

Suddenly, a face appeared. Not any face, *the face,* one of them.

Lucy Garron didn't look like herself, but it was her. Faced with the reality I nearly froze but managed to yell for Rick to look where I was pointing, trying not to be obvious about it.

Rick turned ghostly white. Before he had time to speak, Wendy elbowed me in the side. "I see him. He's in a uniform. Look."

I used the glasses to follow her line of vision. My heart pounded in my chest. I could barely speak. Sure enough. The Garrons had come to Chicago.

"Damn it! They're dressed like fucking security guards," Rick hollered in alarm.

"Okay, it's time to scatter," I said, "like we planned. Find real security, the Secret Service." I shouted about what we had to do to grab attention. Basically, anything necessary to stop this without causing a panic.

"Got it," Wendy said, pushing Bo to the end of the row.

He finally caught on that what he'd feared was coming true.

With the crowd preoccupied with the big show, all five of us rushed to the exit doors. We'd talked about spreading out and Wendy and Janet took off together, Rick and Bo went the opposite way. I headed straight back.

I ran to the uniformed guard and shouted, "Block the stairwell from the upper level. Two people are disguised as guards. They're fugitives."

That got their attention. Two female secret service agents ran toward me, but I kept shouting and pointing above me.

I glanced behind me. Janet and Wendy were following behind a male agent, who was coming our way. Farther down the arena's second level lobby, more agents and guards surrounded Rick and Bo, who were already being handcuffed.

"I'm unarmed," I said. "The two men up ahead are with me. They're unarmed, too. And we're with two women. Don't hurt anyone."

With an agent holding me by the arm, we headed toward Rick and Bo. "You've got to empty the arena! Look, it's possible there are two shooters up there." I pointed to the section above us. "They look like guards, but they're not! They're federal fugitives. Their name is Garron. You've got to take them down, now!"

No immediate rush into action, but at least I had their attention.

"Those two men are with me," I said, pointing with my chin to Bo and Rick. Like that would matter. Who the hell was I? "Listen to me."

Miraculously, the two women let me lead them closer to Bo and Rick and got out a coherent version of who the Garrons were. It was easy enough to check, and one agent took off to transmit the name.

"For all I know, they have convention credentials," I said. "The two look like any other guards here." I introduced myself as they kept leading me toward Bo and Rick. "You need to listen to me."

Finally, they did.

The crowd was still roaring and cheering, and the music was deafening. Even with the noise, though, I heard agents' voices transmitting about the ruckus. From what I could hear, agents were on the level above and other agents blocked off the elevators and stairs. By this time, most had guns drawn.

"We can point them out. Let me follow. I can help," I shouted.

No luck with that.

Bo shouted a question about Wendy's whereabouts, but I yanked my head backwards, hoping Wendy and Janet were still with the agent handling them and weren't far behind me.

I shouldn't have been surprised by the piercing explosion coming from above me. It could have been the balloons popping, but of course it wasn't. I was almost resigned when the second shot rang out.

The five of us weren't going anywhere.

More shots rang out.

People screamed.

Surrounded by the armed security guards protecting us, I stood with my crew. We lined up against the back wall and listened to the shots above and then below. All I could think of was how colossally I'd failed. We'd chased around campaign violence for months, putting little puzzle pieces together and yet here we were surrounded by people with guns while other people were firing shots in a rapidly emptying building.

Finally, I looked at the grim faces of my friends and woke up. I patted a guard on the arm. "What about Pierson and Kent? Are they okay? And their families? Can you tell me?"

"They're okay," a Secret Service agent called back. "One dead shooter, one injured, and two other people apprehended on their way to a van. That's all we know."

"Four shooters?" Wendy said. "I wonder who…"

"We'll find out soon enough," Janet said, shaking her head. "Were others shot?"

"We believe so, but one fatality. One of the shooters. A female." The agent shook her head. "Look, I can't talk about any of this right now."

"When can we leave?" Bo asked.

My cynical laugh even surprised me. We weren't going anywhere. It was going to be a very long night. "Don't get antsy yet, Bo. They'll want witness statements. We've got facts to put on the record."

Over the next couple of hours, the United Center was transformed. First, it was an instant crime scene, and then we were shuffled off to rooms to wait for the

FBI agents to make our statements.

"I'll be the attorney of record for everyone," I said. "They only want to make sure it's okay to let us go. We didn't break any laws."

We were sitting outside of a makeshift area set up for taking statements when something—or someone— caught my eye.

Percy. In handcuffs, being led down the lobby and heading our way.

"Rick, Rick, there's Percy," I said.

Ricky groaned. "That little fuck. He's in this up to his neck. You know he is."

"No, Rick, I don't." I gestured for Rick to follow me and I took some tentative steps toward Percy. I wanted to see what he'd do when he saw me—or Rick. "We can't ignore him."

"What are you going to do?" Rick asked tersely.

"I'm going to wait to see what he says."

I stood my ground, and Rick grudgingly stayed with me.

Percy looked disheveled now, but I could imagine what he must have looked like at the start of the night. Flanked by two officers, Percy was coming toward us, his face a study in misery and defeat. He glanced up and saw Rick first, but a split second later, he saw me, too. "Rick! Matt!"

The guards looked our way.

I stepped forward to see if I could get them to stop. "I'm Matt Barlow. I'm a lawyer."

"This isn't what it looks like, Matt," Percy said, his eyes dark and frantic. "I didn't shoot anyone. I'd never do that." He looked at Rick. "You know that, man."

I intuitively put my hand on Rick's arm to signal that he shouldn't respond. "Where are you taking him?" I asked.

The officers nodded to an area sectioned off with chairs. "Someone will be taking his statement."

"They think I had something to do with the shooting. Hoover, too. It's not true. I was…"

I looked Percy in the eye and held up my hand. "Don't say another word. You need a lawyer. Do you have someone to call?"

"I need *you*," Percy said. "Please, Matt."

"I need to make a statement. I…we…were witnesses, sort of. You go with these officers." I let out a long sigh. "But don't say one word until I get there. You tell them you're waiting for your lawyer."

Percy nodded and I stepped out of the way.

"Not one word," Rick called out to Percy, almost spitting the words.

"You have to believe me," Percy was pleading with the officers now.

At that moment, I was too tired to care what he did or didn't do. But he needed a lawyer.

"I'll be there as soon as I can." I turned away and went back to my group.

Rick spoke fast. "You don't have to do this, Matt. Really."

"No, Rick, I really do." I extended my hands, palms up. "If he's in deep, he needs a lawyer right this second. If he's done absolutely nothing illegal, he still needs a lawyer. If he's done something less than ethical, I can't do anything but I can be sure they give him his rights."

I watched Percy walk away.

A few minutes later, a woman's voice called out from a nearby doorway. "Matt Barlow, we're ready for you now."

I hoped they had time. This story was going to take a while.

Epilogue

Six months later

"Party time." Wendy wrapped a towel around the neck of a bottle of champagne and filled all our glasses.

"The whole day has been party time," Bo teased.

"True," Wendy said, "but I bet they'll have champagne with the inauguration lunch, so we might as well have a toast before our lunch arrives, too."

I smiled to myself. A catered lunch, thanks to Bo. We were the five musketeers once again for the day. With the firm's class action suit underway, I was back on solid ground, which matched the improved mood of the country. Arnold Pierson was safely sworn in, as was Marie Kent, at noon on that snowy January 20 in Washington. It happened like clockwork, just as the Constitution requires.

The weather didn't stop the record crowds. And we five could have been standing in the snow and watching the whole thing live. The Pierson-Kent inaugural committee offered us tickets, and wanting to be fair, I put the trek to D.C. to a vote. No takers.

I was glad. After all that had happened, we opted to watch the festivities from the comfort of the conference room.

Despite the champagne toast Wendy instigated, it wasn't a completely happy day. There had been months of death and destruction. Not that many people were shedding tears for Lucy Garron, who'd been shot and killed when she aimed a service revolver at a secret service agent approaching her on the upper level of the United Center. Sensing the plan for a mass shooting had been blown, she'd shot randomly down to the lower level, pretending to the end that she was a security guard.

She wounded three people, although the victims had fortunately fully recovered. Fernando Garron had been taken down quickly, but survived, if you call losing a leg and having a paralyzing spinal cord injury the measure of survival.

In the press, it was reported Ferndy Garron confessed to bombing Giuseppe Campanella's campaign office, but the masterminds were the Tabakins, Scotty and Lori, lovers—bonded by hate—to the end. The Garrons had been funded by the Tabakins, the money and the energy behind WNF—and TLTA. No one shed tears over the end of their lives as free people. Journalists couldn't get enough of the story of the couple who had *almost* pulled off a brilliant act of political terrorism years in the making.

Many talked about what happened as an act of treason, an attempt to interfere with the peaceful transition of power and stability of American democracy. In fact, the term treason was frequently applied in newspapers and on television, even though the reporters likely knew this was not exactly the legal if not dictionary definition of that term.

"Hey, Matt," Janet said, "you're a million miles away."

Rick grimaced. "Or maybe he's a little too close to home. Like me."

"I'm sorry, Rick," Wendy said.

"No need to apologize." Rick took another sip of champagne. "You know, what Percy did has *nothing* to do with me."

"How is Percy?" Wendy asked.

Rick shrugged. "Okay, I suppose. I'm not in touch with him right now or anything. He's working the night shift in a convenience store. His parents are not pleased with their kid these days."

"I imagine not," I said.

As it turned out, Percy was a spy and secretly working for Toomey, with the right wing nut, Jeff Hoover as his contact, just as we'd thought. The two were political novices, little babies when it came to treachery. Lucky them.

The night of the shooting, which was recorded on hundreds of cell phones, Lori Hochberg and Scotty Tabakin were taken into custody trying to escape. They hadn't ever done anything to get their own hands dirty, but Fernando Garron wasn't taking the fall for anyone, especially since Lucy had been killed and Scotty and Lori almost got away. They were defiant in their interviews about standing up for white culture.

Lori coldly explained her deception and how patiently she and Scotty had planned to create havoc to call attention to our declining country. It was sickening but made a little easier because Coop scored the interview.

"Percy walked away as a traitor to Marie, but he and Hoover never committed a crime," I said. I was his lawyer, and he was never charged with anything. He was a weasel and harbored hateful attitudes, but there was hope for him.

"Sometimes, I wonder what would have happened if we'd not been involved at all," Rick said, leaning back in the chair. "I wonder if the Tabakins might have pulled it off."

"We helped expose it. We failed to stop the event from starting, but most everyone involved agreed we likely helped bring it to an end before massive carnage took place," I insisted. "Maybe it wasn't enough, but it's not nothing."

Bo initiated the next toast, and Janet opened another bottle of champagne as we toasted again.

"So, what's next, Matt?" Rick asked.

I started to answer, but Bo's phone signaled a text. "No more serious talk. Lunch has arrived."

I smiled to myself, glad the question would be left to hang in the air. What's next? Other than winning the class action suit, I had absolutely no idea. But no matter what came my way, Maude and Quigs would be in the thick of it.

Acknowledgements

Books are the result of the efforts of many people who are part of an author's life and sphere, and successful writing requires a support network related to both the work itself and needed emotional support. I've written many nonfiction books but writing fiction, and this second novel at that, is a more interesting challenge for me. But it was fun to bring back my cast of characters that readers have told me they enjoy spending time with.

I wouldn't be where I am or have accomplished what I have in my life without the lifelong love and support of my parents, Seymour and Sandy Lisnek. My mom left this earth on June 16, 2018 after a valiant battle with Alzheimer's disease, a horrendous challenge that science must work to conquer. Dad left us on January 7, 2020, a loss I continue to feel on a daily basis. I am filled with a pride knowing they did their job so very well here on Earth and pray they are watching over me and mine every day in every way. My memories and their spirit continue to guide and inspire me every day of my life.

I wouldn't want to live without the support of my children, Alexandra and Zachary, their mom, Janet, and my brother Rick and sister Judy (legally sister-in-law, but that is a mere technicality because we couldn't be closer!), along with my nieces and nephews. These are the people who provide the emotional support and love I need to see this and every project through to the end. They sustain me.

The pet lovers will appreciate that I derive spirit from my wonderful four-legged kids, Matthew and Myles, and their departed predecessors Mertz and Maude, all of whom lead me to admit that sometimes I think I enjoy pets more than many humans.

As close as family, I couldn't make anything happen without the full support of Diana Briggs, who has worked with me for over 35 years, allowing me to attend to business and life. And to Raphael Sangel, you understand when I say: *salamat sa lahat ng iyong suporta. Napaka espesyal mong tao sa buhay ko.*

My thanks also to Samantha Salzinski (and Briscoe) for caring for my dogs so I could get some down time. Thanks, too, to Marc Matlin, Denise, Marco, and the team at Chicago Dog Walkers for their flexibility and assistance always. Thanks to Oscar Usky Fabian for insuring I'm always relaxed, and to Adel Madi and Toshia Lee for keeping me looking my best above the neck.

My colleagues both in front of and behind the cameras at WGN-TV are always supportive of my efforts and inspire me to keep exceeding expectations.

Similarly, my Comcast TV family is so unendingly supportive of all the projects I pursue. I do extend personal thanks and warmth to Rebecca Cianci, my producer and friend, for always going beyond any expectations to be sure I'm well and in a good place.

I appreciate my partner and friend, Richard Kleban Gabriel, jury consultant extraordinaire and the entire team at Decision Analysis, Inc.

Big thanks to my agents at National Speakers Bureau, Brian Palmer and Don Jenkins, for sending me around the nation and world to inspire others through my seminars and speeches.

And to Rick Duffy and the National Student Leadership Conference and Foundation for giving student leaders the tools they need for a lifetime of success and making the world a better place.

The support of friends is always inspiring and

while too many to name here, they will see that I pay homage to many of them throughout the book, often in the form of a character name or description and the occasional inside joke. I hope they enjoy the tribute when they come across it. My thanks to you all!

And to Virginia McCullough with whom I have worked for over 25 years, I've lost track of the number of projects we've worked on together through these years. You know my voice well and often express a point far better than can I. Your talent for writing and editing knows no bounds. Without your effort and inspiration and careful editing, the vision would never come to fruition. You always keep me going when I want to call it a day and I thank you, Virginia. You are a writer's writer and no words of thanks do justice to honor the extent of your contribution to this book.

And finally, thank you to Brittiany Koren and the team at Written Dreams Publishing who have believed in my ability to create a work of fiction that readers will enjoy and for encouraging my keeping these characters alive and well through new adventures.

Paul M. Lisnek

January 2021

About the Author

Paul Lisnek's world includes television, radio, jury consulting, and politics. These worlds converge in *Assume Treason*, a political thriller. This book follows *Assume Guilt*, which introduced Matt Barlow to the world. Prior to his novels, Paul authored 13 works of nonfiction. A political analyst for WGN-TV, Paul appears on all of its #1 rated newscasts seen throughout the greater Chicago area. He also anchors "WGN-TV Political Report," a weekly look at national and local politics. From 2010 to 2020, he anchored, "Politics Tonight," a live nightly TV talk show seen on CLTV in Chicago. Paul hosts *Broadway in Chicago Backstage* and *Newsmakers* for the Comcast Network. He anchors a podcast for WGN Radio called *Behind the Curtain*, which can be heard at WGNPlus.com.

Paul holds a law degree and Ph.D. in communication from the University of Illinois at Urbana. He is a jury and trial consultant with Decision Analysis, Inc. based in Los Angeles. His firm has worked in notable cases including O.J. Simpson, Whitewater, People vs. Phil Spector, Heidi Fleiss (Hollywood Madame), Casey Anthony (Tot Mom case), and People vs. Kwame Kilpatrick (Mayor of Detroit).

Paul has taught at the University of Illinois, Loyola University Chicago, DePaul University in Chicago, and Pepperdine University's Institute for Dispute Resolution. He is a national lecturer on Constitutional Law and Ethics for BarBri Bar Review and speaks at conferences, corporate meetings, and for government entities around the world. The Museum of Broadcast Communication in Chicago hosts the Paul M. Lisnek Gallery, a permanent exhibit honoring Paul's life and career. Learn more about Paul's books or contact him at www.paullisnek.tv; you can also follow him on social media.

CPSIA information can be obtained
at www.ICGtesting.com
Printed in the USA
LVHW090055160121
676619LV00002B/235